Seven Days in May

Jennifer Luitwieler

© Jennifer Luitwieler, 2014

All Rights Reserved. No part of this book may be reproduced or transmitted in any form or by any means, electronic or mechanical, including photocopying, recording, or by any information storage retrieval system, without permission in writing from the copyright holders.

Cover design by Chad Thomas Johnson
Author photo credit: Marleny Marsh

This is a work of fiction.

For Mom and Dad

Table of Contents

Preface	7
Chapter One	11
Chapter Two	21
Chapter Three	25
Chapter Four	31
Chapter Five	35
Chapter Six	47
Chapter Seven	65
Chapter Eight	81
Chapter Nine	89
Chapter Ten	99
Chapter Eleven	105
Chapter Twelve	119
Chapter Thirteen	127
Chapter Fourteen	139
Chapter Fifteen	153
Chapter Sixteen	165
Chapter Seventeen	173

Chapter Eighteen	177
Chapter Nineteen	183
Chapter Twenty	189
Chapter Twenty-One	197
Chapter Twenty-Two	203
Chapter Twenty-Three	207
Chapter Twenty-Four	211
Chapter Twenty-Five	217
Chapter Twenty-Six	227
Chapter Twenty-Seven	233
Acknowledgements	243

Preface

The headline on June 1, 1921, read "9 Whites, 68 Negroes Killed," but these day-old estimates were far below the final count. In eighteen hours, 35 city blocks in Tulsa burned to the ground, mostly the property of African Americans who had built a city within a city. Some reports say it took Tulsa ten years to recover from the destruction, but there are some who insist the riot of 1921 still affects this town.

Black Wall Street, also known as Greenwood, is an area near downtown Tulsa that was built and owned by African Americans. Some were slaves who traveled west on the Trail of Tears as property of Native Americans. Others traveled west after Emancipation. Still more came when the oil boom offered jobs and prosperity to anyone willing to work. As a result, Greenwood became a sort of blacks-only town within the perimeter of the larger city. Doctors, lawyers, businessmen built offices and owned homes. Women owned and ran confectionaries and hotels. This was not uncommon; there are still black-only towns in Oklahoma.

The actual starting point of the riot was some kind of dustup between a white woman and a black man on an elevator. Stories vary about exactly what happened, but the young man—a boy really—was arrested and taken to the courthouse. Whites converged demanding justice. Blacks, many of whom served during World War I, also converged, offering to help the sheriff protect the prisoner and the peace. A white man approached a black man with a gun. They scuffled and a gunshot rang out. Within hours, Tulsa was under siege.

For eighteen hours, whites fired on Greenwood, guerrilla-style. Blacks tried to protect their property, but in the early morning hours, machine guns were firing into the burning district, and witnesses reported seeing airplanes strafing the city with bullets. When the fighting stopped, African Americans were escorted by armed guards to fairgrounds, baseball fields and schools for "protection."

All told, 35 city blocks burned to the ground, including a brand new Baptist church. Over 800 people were treated for injuries, and the death toll of African Americans climbed to 300. This number is still debated as witnesses claim to have seen mass graves being dug for uncounted bodies. If they stayed, African Americans lived in tents during the winter of 1921-22, with no water, facilities or walls. If they left—as many did—they never returned.

Tulsa remains a largely segregated city, but we can't focus the blame solely on racism. Money, property and politics all played a part in the growing discord of the city. Lynchings of Industrial Workers of the World (IWW) activists—known as wobblies—who disagreed with democratic politics created a violent culture. African Americans held property that gave them access to trains, roads and downtown. In the year after the riot, politicians deftly changed zoning laws so that rebuilding was untenable for African Americans. Additionally, white community leaders worked to stall or prevent the payment of insurance claims. Greenwood has seen bursts of renewal, but the wounds of the riot have cut deep gashes through the community. Some people who grew up in Tulsa have said, anecdotally, that they were never taught anything about the riots. There are new movements to rename certain parts of downtown; currently, the names are tied to prominent whites who were also active in inciting the riot and in bringing the Ku Klux Klan to Tulsa.

Tulsa was the Magic City that erupted from the soil just like the oil that could make anyone, regardless of color or creed, a millionaire. With rapid prosperity come major growing pains. With so many people spilling into this boomtown, we may guess that the riot was inevitable. It is against this setting that our story begins.

Thursday

Grace

"Leading Men Lost Lives in Tulsa."
The Afro American newspaper, June 16, 1921.

1

That day, in the kitchen, Grace didn't know it would be the last peaceful time they'd all have there. She didn't know that in a few days' time, one of the white linen napkins they pressed and folded would become a shroud.

Her mama sweated over the ironing board, a silk scarf that Miss Willie had given her one Christmas tied up around her head, her shoes squished on the floor as she reached from the pile of clean linens, plucking up the next napkin for pressing. Then she bent back to the board, making a tidy game of aligning the square of cotton, as though straightening the corners of a terribly wrinkled swatch could make the ironing unnecessary. Her fingers pulled the corners away from each other on the diagonal, opposed to each other, as if that could make it whole.

Mama made it clear that hard work was no magic; she knew it was hard and necessary, so she found ways to make it more bearable. She spritzed the cloth with the fine, clear, lemon-scented water, then held the hot iron to the cotton in vast sweeps, pressing firmly, moving quickly, maintaining pressure over the trouble spots. Grace watched Mama as her eyes closed with delight, smelling the lemon as it rose to her face in steam. Sure, it was work, but Mama enjoyed the measured process of the task, the quiet hum of the kitchen, a peaceful Thursday with all *her girls*, she called them, which included Miss Willie. There was something fulfilling about accomplishing set tasks and leaving the house in domestic order, with a handful of cash on Fridays.

Grace had asked Mama once, at a picnic, how they were different from her grandmother. Mam, Grace's great-grandmother, had been the cook in the Big House back in Alabama. When she had asked her, Mama had fixed her eyes on her daughter's face for a full minute, swept them over her like a hot sheet on a sticky night, and Grace squirmed under her silence and her intensity.

"Grace." The name in her mouth could be any number of things, depending on how she spoke it.

"Grace." Now it was a steel beam, lowered down, something to watch. "For a long time, Mam did not have a choice. You hear me? She was not paid. She could not quit, and she was no more than that ignorant man's property, nothing more than one more farm tool."

Grace had fidgeted under her gaze and the slap of her words. She knew about slavery and all that. Not from Mama, though. Mama rarely talked about Alabama. What little Grace knew about when Mama met her daddy and their big move to Tulsa she had learned by eavesdropping when Daddy sat outside the confectionary on Sunday nights, talking to the boys.

Grace and Mama had been sitting on the grass across from First Mt. Zion, when she had asked Mama this question about Mam. A breeze lifted the edge of their picnic blanket, its soft edges melting into the green grass. Spring in Oklahoma meant summer in Oklahoma. Already the ladies of the congregation picked at the hems of their skirts, wishing cool breezes onto their legs, loosening the laces on their church shoes, unbuttoning one more button than would be proper just inside the building.

"You like your job, Mama?" Grace had asked, taking a bite of crusty bread, flipping crumbs from her skirt.

She sighed. "It's just fine, honey. I like it just fine."

That was hardly satisfying. Grace had pressed. "You don't like it?"

"Grace." Her name again, softer but still like a load groaning into place. "I am thankful I have a job. I am thankful that you can come with me, and I'm thankful that Miss Willie, shoot, even Mr. Dub, are not mean old ogres. I could work there forever just fine. I consider it a great blessing that they're smartly educated to boot."

Grace had weighed this, still not satisfied. "Well . . . " She had given her daughter that sidelong look only a mama can give when she's trying to decide if she wants to laugh or pinch an arm. Grace scooted out of arm's reach and finished. "Do you like having the same job your mama had? Sort of like a family job."

That was when Mama lit Grace's face with the fury of her serious eyes and told Grace what she had never known, or had known but not recognized. As she talked, about her grandma working all day, every day, on duty at the whim of the lady of the house, Grace looked over the lawn, watching her friends talk and play. Mama unfolded like a square of cloth the story of how Mam had got the fat pink, rippled stripes across her back. She unpacked like a basket the truth about the serpentine coils that snaked up Pap's arms. About being awakened in the night to fix a snack for the white sons who came home drunk and hungry at three in the morning.

Grace's brothers ran around the church lot, playing baseball with their friends, and she listened to the crack of the bat over the drone of Mama's lecture, praying her voice would grow no louder.

"We might both have cooked and cleaned for other people, white people," her mother was drawing her lesson to a close.

Grace was bothered by the story, and ashamed at the same time, because all she really wanted was to get the picnic over with and meet Mercy down by the river. The girls had promised to meet at four.

"But don't you ever think, Gracie....Honey. Grace?"

"Yes, ma'am?"

"You listening?"

"Yes, ma'am."

"What did I just say?"

Grace sighed. Again. "Mama. You said," She made an exaggerated exhalation her mama could not miss, "That I 'was not to ever think'...and then you griped at me."

She pursed her lips. Gave Grace a softened glance. "I'm sorry, baby. My grandma had a very different life. She did not have a job. She had no choices. Okay?"

"Yes, Mama. I understand." She did understand. She just didn't want to think about it. Being friends with Mercy was hard enough.

"Now get. I know where you're going. I'll see you at nine." She had winked and shooed Grace off like a pest.

Grace did not want to think about it that day in the kitchen either. Their last Thursday. Of course, she didn't know that as she pushed her mind away from the scars and focused instead on the fine scent of lemon thrown around the room by the heavy fan humming in the corner, rotating its ugly head like an overseer managing the plantation. The sharp tang of citrus mixing warmly with freshly trimmed grass heightened Grace's anticipation for the summer stretching before them, wide open, this one lovely season before high school. Mercy and Grace sat at the table, dutifully folding the crisp, white, freshly pressed napkins, their knees bouncing up and down, just itching to get outside and run down the street, willing their mamas to work faster so they could be free.

Mama had draped a cherry pie with a perfect lattice crust that morning. It sat cooling on the counter next to the Dutch apple pie. She had refused to make the pecan pie, so Miss Willie had done that, managing to create a gooey mass of nuts and syrup that was, Mama had said, just simple beauty; a job well done. Even if it was pecan, the nut she promised never to touch again. She had spent too much of her other life, in Alabama, crunching over the hard shells, picking them up for countless pies. Mama hated pecans.

The iron hissed, she looked back to her work and deftly moved the flat face of the iron to the corners of the napkin, edging the pointed tip into the precisely mitered corners, stopping to spritz and press, and angle and push and coax the four points into submission. Some things really could be that easy. She sighed, placed the upright iron on the board and, using her thumbs and forefingers, carried the napkin to the girls as if each newly starched square were a wet finger-painting by one of Grace's brothers.

Mercy sat across from Grace, and they bumped legs under the table. They tapped out a language all their own, fingertips sliding along the knife-edged hems. Grace fidgeted watching Mercy. The hurried carelessness that girl gave the job was going to keep them in that hot kitchen all day. Grace glared at her, flicking her fingers toward Mercy's lazy pile of mostly unfolded napkins. Mercy sighed, ignored her friend, knocked her knee against Grace's again.

Across the kitchen, Miss Willie rested her arms on the counter by the sink, letting the water from the tap rush over her hands covered in pie crust and pecan bits, taking the remnants of her chore away, away, away from her. Grace listened to the water splashing in the sink; something about the way Miss Willie stood there. Whatever it was she could see, or not see, through the window out into the backyard, must have been interesting. She was frozen.

Miss Willie. Oh, how Grace loved that woman. The day they met, Miss Willie was still pulling on her shoes when she met Grace and

Mama at the door. She drew Grace near her, rested a long pink arm on her shoulder as she reached down and slipped a tiny shoe onto her bare foot. She smelled like pink, she looked like pink. She was pink. She wore a wide orange ribbon around her short hair, and red lips smiled wide, showing her neat gums, the curved arches of her bow-shaped lips. She had laughed and pulled Grace into the kitchen, urging Mama behind her, her words tumbled out of her mouth in such a fountain, Grace couldn't understand a thing she had said. Grace had stared at her. Gaped. Miss Willie was used to people gaping at her, especially in this town. Rachel and Grace had learned that her words were a shield, and behind them ebbed the quiet. They learned how to settle around her silence, when it arrived.

Suddenly the entire kitchen seemed to focus in on her stillness and the coursing water. The hum of the fan, the hiss of the iron, the creaking of the ironing board, even Mama's squishing shoes stopped. They were all aware that Miss Willie had been standing there longer than a normal hand-washing would take. The room held its breath.

Then, the sound of her laughter bubbled over the room as she twisted the twin faucets off and turned to face six eyes peering at her with a mix of curiosity and concern. The balloon had not burst yet, though. While Miss Willie laughed, three other women tried to find a purchase on what it meant.

"You all!" she whirled around. "This room went so still I thought you'd fallen asleep."

Mama moved toward her, just a step. "Miss Willie, you all right?"

"Rachel. Of course I'm fine." She dried her hands on the tea towel and patted it back into place over the lip of the sink. The heavy look she gave Mama didn't register with Grace until later, but Mama nodded, like she understood. She waved a pink hand in the air as if to wave away the thoughts that had made her so still.

"I drifted away." Her eyes went soft for a moment, just a small dilation of her pupils, then she was back, again with a laugh. Another moment passed where Miss Willie was quiet, silently messaging Mama.

Mama filled a glass with water and handed it to Miss Willie, who swallowed and swallowed, her throat bobbing with relief. Then Mama resumed her chore.

"I drifted away; then," Miss Willie found the thread of the story. "I felt the stillness of the room like the train coming through town. I knew you all were watching me. I was struck by the silliness of it." She picked up the towel and flicked it at Mercy. "Honey. You can do a better job than that." She bustled her starched skirt over to the table, hovering around the girls like a bee, more of her hand waving, more of her fussing.

"Look, Mercy. Look at your friend." Mercy's eyes met Grace's, and Grace clamped her teeth down hard on her lip. Behind the house later, the girls busted up mimicking Miss Willie calling Grace her "friend." The way she said some words, it was like she thought they were still in diapers. Really. Miss Willie had a way of saying words like they carried extra meaning, each letter its own sentence in a paragraph of implications. Then again, she was from "back east," and so she had that flat way of saying her vowels, like her mouth was always open, busy, forming the sounds. "Do you see how she's matching the corners before pressing the crease?"

Mercy was eyeing Grace, daring her to laugh. Grace kept her head low and worked at her perfect pile of napkins. No way was she going to get swatted for Mercy's sake.

"I know how to fold a napkin, Mother dear."

"Now, Mercy," Mama spoke from the ironing board, a low warning, swimming on the current of a quiet laugh, trying to defuse the flare with a smile.

Miss Willie cut her off. "Then why, Amelia, do you insist on assembling a mess like this?" The last syllables nearly broke the boundaries into shrillness. When Miss Willie called Mercy by her Christian name, the show was about to begin.

The room was hot enough, but when those two went at it, the temperature was like to rise, and that day, Grace wanted outside more than she wanted to have something to talk about over the dinner table later. She reached over and pulled Mercy's pile toward her. She shot her friend the archest eyebrow she could manage and kicked her hard under the table. If she kept her eyes on the job, Miss Willie would relent. She would let it slide, just this one time, but she'd be sure to mention it to Mercy. Later. Mercy. Mercy was not as predictable.

It must have been the heat, or that Grace had left the knot of a bruise forming on her shin. Whatever it was, Mercy grabbed onto the wisp of an argument like a dog with a bone. Grace shook her head. They were in for it. Grace saw it in her eyes before she heard Mercy's words.

"Well, Mother," making special emphasis of the maternal. "Just 'cause I know how doesn't mean I will."

Now, instead of flicking the towel in jest, Miss Willie attempted to crack Mercy's hand with the fine pointed corner of it, making it her weapon. Mercy was too fast. Her hand was out of range before the towel could twist into a lashing rope.

Miss Willie was caught in the center of the kitchen, one hand ready to strike. She hesitated. Mercy was a statue, a tower of willfulness, with not a speck of fear. It was in this way that knowing Mercy helped Grace to cultivate a towering vocabulary. When Grace read books with her daddy, he asked her to guess what the characters were thinking and feeling by how they were described. Grace read Mercy the way she read books. Mercy was both the content and the form. Grace read the literal meaning of Mercy's words and then scanned her body for the context. Grace translated Mercy, which is how Grace learned what it meant when the books talked about flashing eyes. The lightning in Mercy's pinprick pupils struck the kitchen.

Mama had finished the ironing, but stood behind the board, making an account of the situation. Grace made hers. Without a word, while the two white women squared off, Grace pressed the creases from Mercy's pile, fuming at her. Her temper was keeping Grace stuck inside, but she was stung, too, by what Mercy didn't say, what she somehow continued to forget. Mercy was the one between the two who had a choice in the matter, at least in this house, in this part of town. Which is when Grace understood a little bit about what Mama had said about Mam.

Grace took up one stiff white square and married one corner to another. Then she slid Pointer between the two white skins, keeping the linen taut between Thumb and Tall Man, along the length of the fabric until she could marry the next corners. A trickle of sweat slid from her neck down the center of her spine. Laying the napkin flat on the table, she matched more corners, pressing the folded edge into the oak table, the whiteness of her fingertip the only sign to Mercy that if her mother didn't lash her with the towel, Grace would be sure to wag her tongue later.

That was the thing about Mercy. That girl could pick a fight with those pacifists who had protested the war down at the courthouse. She could make a monk disavow silence to dress him down for insolence, and then, not five minutes later, all you'd want to do was hold her hand, run down the street, laughing harder with each step, unaware of the way your blood still boiled in your veins.

"My stars, Amelia. Sitting there while your friend does all the work. A thousand times better, I don't need to say."

"My stars, Mother! Then why say it? We all know Grace's better at that. Grace is better at everything," choosing to overlook the fact that the reason Grace was more adept at napkin folding was because it was her job. Sort of her job, at least: helping Mama when school was out.

Mama caught her daughter's eye from the corner where she stood. Her message, so complicated that to speak it would probably confuse everyone, was channeled to Grace through motherly Morse code. She chose this moment to fold up the ironing board, making a big to-do about it. The board clattered and groaned and heaved as she lifted the bar to release the leg holds. Mama grunted with it, making more noise than strictly necessary. The movement distracted Miss Willie long enough to take some steam out of her. Grace mouthed a silent warning to Mercy. "Stop. It."

Mercy shook her off. Grace kicked her again. "I'm leaving," Mercy mouthed and pushed her pile back toward Grace. It was one thing for Mercy to mouth off to her mother, it was quite another for her to ignore Grace. Grace tried to stay off the minefield between that mother and daughter. She had her own to worry about. Mercy shook her head again. "I'm serious." More unspoken words, Grace made her face hard. Then, Mercy's shoulders softened. She pulled her pile back and looked at Miss Willie.

"Okay, Mom. Fine. I'm doing it. Okay? Happy now?"

That girl. Even her apologies were willful. Miss Willie did snap her with the towel, as soon as Mercy had applied herself to proper folding. Snap. Cracked her, right across the hand. She deserved it, too.

Grace smiled at her across the table. She stuck out her tongue. Grace's admiration for Miss Willie grew.

Grace wondered in the days and weeks after how she could have changed the day. If she had known it was the last time she'd touch her skin, or see her smile or hear her laugh, would Grace have taken the measure of Mercy's voice, memorizing the tone she used to question or to tease one of them? Would she have gauged Mercy's sturdy, resolute presence with fingers, touching her arm to make sure it was she who stood there, rather than the ghost that lived in her memory? The ghost who called every day to Grace like a looping newsreel, flickering onto her mind the things that happened, the things that took Mercy from them. From her. Would she have peered into Mercy's fierce blue eyes, trying to own the whispered secrets she already knew like she knew the sound of her own heartbeat? Would she hold onto those secrets, so that one day she could whisper them aloud, to someone else?

Grace wanted to believe she would have done these things, but she knew it wasn't true. That's what death gives: a final, agonizing bullet in the heart; death makes us wish we'd done the things, said the words we thought we'd eventually mutter. If Grace had known, they would have spent their day the way they always had. In other words, they'd have done exactly what they did.

2

Later, behind the house, Grace did as she vowed. "Coulda been out here an hour ago, Mercy."

They sat in the late afternoon sun, propped against the back wall of the garage, a miniature replica of the main house that nestled behind it under a burst of trees. The sun had sunk just enough to give the perfect ratio of cool spring shade to glimmers of hot summer sun. After they had finally finished folding the napkins, Mercy poured them each a glass of lemonade, grabbed the blanket off the back porch and they walked out, letting the screen door slam behind them.

Those girls had been letting that screen door slam behind them for years. Mama's voice used to make a duet with it. Slam went the door, and right on its heels, "Don't slam that door!" She had given up; she couldn't always stop them or be near enough to scold, so they thumbed their noses at the rule. Really, it wasn't rebellion. It was the undeniable exuberance of youth. Maybe with a dash of rebellion. As the door slammed behind them, year after year, the memory of Mama's voice continued to ring in Grace's head. She always felt the sting of this. Knowing she was letting the door slam, unwilling to grasp the thin wood and slow its arcing back toward the jamb. Grace was stuck, urged by her silent mother to stop the noise and urged equally by her silent friend to let it go, let it slam.

Before Grace had learned to read, Daddy used to pull her onto the sofa with him, wrapping a giant arm around her and smoothing a hand across the flat cover of a book. Every night he did this. After dinner, and after they had cleaned up the kitchen. After rolling in the grass with her brothers and chatting with the neighbors, when the sun dipped into the trees, he clicked on a lamp, picked up a book and settled down, letting the furniture become his spine. With a final exhale, he swooped her up saying, "All right! Let's get to business."

Daddy read to Grace like she was doing him the favor, but Grace got to sit next to him, feeling his chest rise and fall with the rhythm of the words, smelling his sunny skin and clean cotton. He read every book like it was a brand new idea, even those they wore thin, dragging their fingers under the words, pointing to different shades in the illustrations or noticing new parts of the stories. Grace felt the bass of his vocal cords striking out the words, his voice like a swath of velvet unfurled, the characters leaping to life at his call. Daddy stayed on a page longer than most parents; he picked apart each idea, saying, "I like this word. Listen to how it sounds." The two said the word together, *rabbit* or *plunging* or *mesmerize*, then stared back at the page, examining the pictures, linking sounds to ideas to words.

Daddy read every book Grace was assigned to read for school. They read them together, he making pencil notations in the margins that she could neither read nor understand if she could decipher them. He circled compound words, or deconstructed sentences. Grace liked rereading the words after he had removed the supportive phrases, condensing them down to the one main thing: *I ran, she laughed, they died*. Then, putting the phrases back into place, tumbling each piece of the code, unlocking the mystery.

Nearly every day, Daddy ended their reading with the same lesson. "If you can read, you can do anything." Seems like the kid who can't read has an easier time embracing this idea than the pubescent who can. For the kid who can't read, the dancing shapes on the page are a secret, a grown up knowledge that once acquired, loses its patina. A better way to put it might be that teenagers will resist anything if their parents think it's worthy. This is another one of those adult secrets. Grace was caught, hovering between these different places and people. Like Mercy.

Mercy held a dandelion between them, its fluffy, white head bowing to a mild wind. She rounded her mouth and blew the tiny seeds into the space between them. "Give it a rest, Grace. We're here now, okay?"

Grace shook her head. "You are impossible."

She tried to take Grace's hand, but Grace pushed her away. "Mercy. I'm serious."

Mercy stopped.

"You're always pushing things. You ever think what you do might affect someone else?"

There it was again; the flicker of heat in Mercy's eyes. Grace allowed Mercy to read the anger plain on her own face. She tried to surround herself with the same kind of fire Mercy stoked, knowing it would come close. Just close. She gave up as Mercy's eyes came to almost instant understanding. That's why they were friends. Rather, it was why they were still friends. They were friends because when the girls were babies they were their own world. They were still friends because their shorthand solved nearly everything.

"You're right, Grace. I'm sorry."

Grace grumbled.

"Really. I am."

Grace wanted to make her understand, to make her uncomfortable. Grace enjoyed the power to make Mercy dance; she knew she'd get there eventually. "You're really what?" Grace asked, prodding.

She rolled her eyes. "I'm really sorry. I know what I did was wrong, and I apologize. Forgive me?" She blurted the words like a Sunday School prayer, all sound and no substance.

"What did you do that was wrong, Mercy? What?"

"I picked a fight with my mother. I kept us inside longer than necessary. And . . ."

"Go on."

"And I didn't do my chores well."

"Which means?"

"I disrespected you and your mother." This came in a rush, on top of which she added, "Grace, you know I didn't mean it. I'm your truest friend. I'd never hurt you on purpose."

Oh, Mercy. "Do you even hear yourself?" Grace pushed away from the wall and stood over her. "Do you understand anything?" Grace's voice rose. "You don't do anything on purpose. You don't think. You only do."

Again, Mercy's bright blue eyes rolled in her alabaster head, her freckles reflecting the sun. "OK. Now you sound like my daddy. I get it, Grace. What do you want?"

As quickly as she flared out against her, Grace shrank, folding down again next to her. Mercy grabbed her hand, and Grace let her pick it up, but holding it limp, making her work. She did. She pinched each of Grace's fingertips, then slipped a dandelion stem she'd twisted into a circle around Grace's wrist. Grace pushed her arm. Mercy laughed.

"I hate you," Grace said.

"Good. I hate you, too." Then: "Let's get to the river."

3

They weren't stupid. "See you in a bit?"

Grace nodded and Mercy dashed off. Mercy's route took her to the corner, where she hopped on a trolley, made a circuit of downtown, then to the river, where she'd jump off and walk to where Grace had promised to be waiting. Because Grace didn't have to, or get to, use the trolley, she walked through her neighborhood as if on an errand for Miss Willie. It was like a hall pass, a delicate bubble around her, tolerated in the shops in this part of town.

The friends had tried to sit together, on the trolley, once. Just a few summers before, Grace was bringing the twins home from a baseball game. Mercy hopped on and spied her. She made her way towards the three, sitting near the back, Jacob on Grace's lap and Samuel falling asleep on her shoulder. His lips puffed out as he began to snore. When one of them laughed, or sweated rivers while resting, they were nearly irresistible. Her brothers, Grace liked to think, would be inseparable even if they weren't twins. She called them JacobandSam or SamandJacob. Everyone did. They were of a piece. Sometimes, being in charge of those two during the summer was worse than being stuck in Mercy Williams' kitchen.

When Grace saw Mercy edging toward the back of the trolley, knocking into elbows and knees on her way through the crowded trolley, she tried to shake her off. Mercy had sincerely never noticed that one kind of people sat in the back and she wasn't that kind. The heat of the day pushed against Grace's skin, made worse by slippery, tired twins. The heaving machine that jostled them through town was filling with people and their heat and smells. For the briefest moment, when Grace saw Mercy, she thought she'd been given a miraculous help. The briefest moment. The time it takes to see just one man watching as Mercy clambered her way towards the back, a smile spread across her face in total ignorance. She had nearly made it to Grace, which would have been a disaster, when the man who had been observing her offered his seat.

"Miss?" He'd said as he rose from his seat. "May I offer you this seat here, right next to the open window?" It wasn't a question; he took hold of her elbow, wheeled her around and plunked her down in his seat before she had a chance to reply. Then, he struck up a conversation from which even Mercy could not extract herself.

If Grace hadn't needed the help of her hands, if it had not been a detour at her expense, she might have found it within her power to laugh. Except Grace didn't care what color the hands that wanted to help her were and she did care to be kept from her friend because of someone else's stupid ideas.

So the girls learned that getting to the river separately was the kind of thing that chafed but saved time and hassle. It was just easier. Though they hated it, they lived according to public sentiment. Until they got to the river. Nobody told anybody what to do at the river.

Tulsa sits at a bend in the Arkansas River; right where you'd put your hand on the crook of a staff. Grace and Mercy watched them build the first bridge to cross, built to carry trains of workers and supplies to the oil fields south of the city. The girls were small when they assembled the trestles. Mama had walked them down to the banks on cool mornings to watch. The boys were especially interested in the grubby hands and sooty faces of the men who rose and fell on pulleys. They watched the heaving beams being raised into the grey sky. For a while. Eventually the girls had applied themselves to testing Mama's limits. They edged closer and closer to the water, anticipating a holler from Mama to get away from the lapping ripples against the white rocks.

As the bridge ascended and reached its steel arms across the breadth of the riverbed, their limbs stretched and lengthened. The friends wanted to dance along with the current, wanted to wade out into the flow. They wanted to reach the sandy islands that poked up from the bottom of the bed during dry months. The older they got and the longer they could maintain their balance, the harder it became for Mama to keep them close.

It was Mercy's idea, the first time they tried to reach the very middle of the river. Mama was busy feeding lunch to the twins, who were not interested in eating anything but the mud they squished between their fat fingers. The girls took advantage of her inattention, taking off their shoes and wading out into the shallows. Mercy went further than they had before while Grace hung back, stealing glances at her mother on the bank, her back turned to the river. Mercy plunged ahead, splashing wildly, nothing stealthy about her, while Grace followed like the loyal puppy.

"I wish I thought to bring a stake. To make our claim." She got to the sandbar first, and was plotting her world takeover as Grace scrambled up to her, her feet thick with mud from the bottom of the river.

"Well, it wouldn't stay anyway, Amelia."

"That's hardly the point, Know-it-all," she waved off the objection.

"Okay, Fancy Pants. What's the point?" Grace pushed back.

She bent down and scooped up a handful of the grime, letting it run through her fingers as she crouched there. Grace backed away a step, looking for shelter and reaching for her own handful of goo. Too late. She had flung the mud before Grace registered the glint in Mercy's eye. She always underestimated Grace, though, and was surprised when Grace was already preparing to throw back. By the time they heard Mama shouting from a hundred yards away, mud dripped from their faces, covered their once-clean blouses, filled their ears and noses and hair.

That was the day Amelia became Mercy.

They trudged back through the water under the glare of Mama's burning eyes while she stood resolutely on the shore. Mama ground her fists into her hips, dimpling her silhouette. The twins, who were barely old enough to feed themselves, seemed to understand the trouble the girls had wrought. Perhaps they noticed the grinding muscles of her jaw. They dipped their heads seriously, avoiding eye contact, holding their small arms behind their backs. Their posture distanced them from the naughty girls.

Mama called out as the girls broached the shore, waddling toward her in submission. "Grace and *mercy*! What were you girls thinking?" It was clear, in the way she asked, that a reply was not required, or even suggested. She supplied the answer. "I'll tell you what you were thinking. Nothing." Here, the finger wagging began and Mercy, formerly Amelia, dipped her head mimicking the boys, but she bowed to hide her brimming smile. If Grace had looked at her then, she'd have been clipped that night for sure.

Mama carried on in a similar fashion for quite some time, the boys retreating up the bank, Mercy cutting a wide swath between her and Grace, removing herself from all culpability. Grace, meanwhile, consoled herself under Mama's outrage, knowing Mercy would get hers as soon as they showed up at the back door of her house, filthy.

"Are you laughing, Grace Marie?"

"No ma'am."

"Because you better not even be smiling." Grace lost the rest of her words. Mama had turned to pack up the picnic, round up the boys. She muttered a breathless stream of words, pausing every so often to glare at her muddy child. Grace had tried to rinse off in the water with poor results and did her best to help Mama get the boys ready for the walk home. Mercy was on her own, and she chose to leave an impressive amount of the Arkansas smeared on her white legs. Grace knew exactly why. Anything to make her mama itch.

The walk home was decidedly quiet. Grace fussed with the boys, asking them questions about what they'd seen and listening as their small voices rattled on about their adventure. Mama punctuated each step with certain intelligible words. Grace avoided the spittle that accompanied Mama's screed. Mercy strode confidently like the self-appointed queen of Tulsa. Nothing stuck to her, ever.

Miss Willie spotted them before the troupe had made it to the back door. She stood on the back step, having laid out a large basin of warm water and a pile of fresh towels. One hand on her hip and one clamped to her forehead, a visor against the afternoon sun. Unmoving, utterly silent. To Mama's credit, she did not look away from her boss. She held her gaze, her fear only betrayed by the shaking picnic basket in her straining knuckles.

Mercy appraised her mother. Grace recognized the dare in Mercy's eyes, in her happy stride. Grace did not want to be there; she wanted to shrink into the dirt and slink home, get clean and never come back.

The only problem with going home was the promise of a come to Jesus conversation with Mama upon their arrival.

The five of them stopped where Miss Willie stood. Mama peered up at her, waiting. When nothing happened, when Miss Willie did not speak, Mama drew in a sharp breath and prepared to speak.

Miss Willie cut her off. Not with words but with a howl of laughter that rose from her trim pink self in such a surprising manner that the filthy wanderers froze.

Wiping the tears from her face, Miss Willie shouted, "What have y'all been doing? Did you take a bath in it?" Those covered in mud and those in charge of those covered in mud blinked at each other while the knowledge crept over Miss Willie. She realized that's exactly what they had done.

Mama was the first to erupt. She dropped the basket and braced her hands on her swollen knees. She laughed a solid and nearly silent, wheezing kind of laugh that brought tears blooming to her eyes like wells. The boys, though innocent of the humor, threw themselves in the grass and split up. Mercy was the last to get the joke. Her heart was so set on a decent row with her mom that she clamped down on her face, hoping to avoid the contagious smiles. She eventually gave way. They all did.

Sitting at the table after Mercy had bathed and Grace had rinsed what she could in the basin out back, the girls listened while the mothers kept up the story. Mama drew that tale out so long Mercy and Grace became embarrassed and then bored. Miss Willie noticed her daughter grimacing at the table, picking pits out of cherries and throwing them into a bowl. She walked behind her and rested her palms on Amelia's shoulders. "Sounds like you got a new nickname, honey."

Amelia, whom the rest of the world called Mercy, screwed up her eyes. Grace shrugged. Amelia searched her mother's face.

"Huh?" She grunted.

"You meant to say, 'Excuse me, ma'am,' didn't you?"

"Excuse me, ma'am?" Amelia sighed.

"I like it, Amelia. It's perfect for you two. Always up to something, it's almost ironic." Miss Willie beamed.

Amelia shook her head, uncertain, suspicious

Miss Willie patted her warmly and Amelia melted under her gaze. Just like Mercy; no one ever knew what Miss Willie was going to do. Grace realized she'd been holding her breath, certain the fuse was lit. She exhaled when Amelia relaxed.

"Mama. I don't get it. What new name?" That cost her something, admitting ignorance.

"Grace and Mercy. Rachel told me all about it."

Grace trilled with understanding. "Oh! I get it!" Mercy, nee Amelia, tossed her ponytail around to look at her. "I love it," Grace gushed, catching her ambivalence and trying to convince her. "Don't you? Mercy?" She prodded

"Hmph." She resumed pit-picking. "I could get used to it." Grace caught Mercy glancing at the mothers, who were themselves exchanging their own satisfied looks.

4

The bridge that helped build Tulsa ascended in parallel with the girls. When they were finally old enough to go unsupervised, the river was nearly always their destination. That Thursday was no different. Grace carried a cold flask of lemonade and a packet of sandwiches Mama had fixed for them. She'd handed them to Grace with a wink and a reminder to be home by nine. Always nine, even in the summer, before dark. She had her reasons.

Mercy and Grace had plans for that summer, and it all started and ended at the river. Grace arrived first, and found their spot. Down a short embankment, hidden by a thick copse of greening trees, she scrambled. At the flattening joint of earth, she cleared away a pile of branches that revealed a small opening, a shallow cave where the two watched the water coursing. They had repurposed castoff planks of wood from Mr. Williams' lumber yard into makeshift stools. Grace had absconded with her daddy's Army duffel, filled with a blanket, some old jackets, a few magazines. On rainy days, they sat and listened to the sound of water on land, wind through the trees.

Grace laid out the blanket, set the sandwiches on napkins, not the linen ones they had just spent the afternoon folding. As she poured lemonade into the lid of the flask, she picked out Mercy's unmistakable approach, lumbering through the snapping branches. Seconds later, her wide open face burst into the cozy space.

"Ta-da!" Whatever antagonism had passed under her skin in the kitchen had washed itself out. She flounced in, all kinds of joy.

When Mercy was lightness, Grace found it easy to want to be around her. Sometimes, though, Grace wondered if she spent most of her time finessing the edges of the world that butted up against her gangly friend. Grace was determined to keep her friend in that lightness. Grace shrugged to herself, thinking about Mercy's tempest, hoping Mercy blurred the edges around her world, too.

Together, they set out their small meal, mapping out the summer again. They enjoyed the repetitive task, since they had scrawled out their summer dreams nearly every day for the last few weeks. Rehearsing, anticipating and practicing the excitement they so much expected was almost better than the arrival of the thing itself. The girls had a slew of parties and gatherings slated for the weekend which would keep them apart. They bristled at a separation of three whole days.

Grace was to spend her time at Booker T., getting the school decked out for graduation. Her friend Esther had volunteered them for the decoration committee; they had been making tissue paper flowers and cutting out letters for the graduation dance. Poor Mercy. Instead of kicking dirt at the river, she was to fill Mama's kitchen shoes. Mama and Grace had no small measure of trepidation about this plan. If Mercy's napkin folding looked as if she'd done it with her feet, why, her cooking and baking were on a par below Mama's.

The First Church women, of which Miss Willie was a peripheral member, were throwing their annual Memorial Day picnic which required a pie for every man, woman and child in attendance. Miss Willie, with a zealous hope of veering her child into more social involvement, had volunteered for this task. She had failed to consider her inability to coax a pie crust from a pile of flour and a splash of ice water. It fell to Mama and Grace to get Miss Willie ready for baking. They had made as many crusts as they could anticipate, leaving them rolled and wrapped in the icebox. Cavernous bowls of fruit and sugar awaited their kind attention. All Mercy and her mama had to do was assemble them. Mercy and Grace belonged, body and soul as they say, to their mothers, subject to their domestic demands.

Aside from decorating at the school—a vacation Mercy could not enjoy—the girls had the strictest schedule for the next four days, until Monday. Mama granted Grace one small thing: She had promised that Grace didn't have to find a job until then. Mama knew that, no matter what happened after graduating, Grace had a long life of work before her. Four days she could give her. Four days were a mercy.

"So, after our picnic on Monday, you'll meet me down here again, right?" Mercy said.

"That's the plan."

They tittered. They felt the small joy of pushing against the rules, as if they were such rebellious girls, taking advantage of their parents' distraction long enough to sneak to the river at night, after curfew. Still, risking a surreptitious walk to the water was the wildest adventure they could imagine. That naïveté would ignite like paper, turn to ash on their tongues before the four days were over.

"I wish I could just come with you to your dance." Mercy flicked Grace's hand. Grace flicked hers back.

"Yeah. That'd go over well."

Grace did not reciprocate this wish, and she knew enough about her friend to keep this information sealed inside her. Not for the first time, a glint of guilt flared up against Grace's ribs, like a match igniting and extinguishing. She felt the shadow of the feeling if not the solid heat of guilt itself. She knew that Mercy didn't exactly conform at her school, or anywhere really, so there weren't a whole lot of parties for her to attend.

Mercy resumed her campaign in lieu of Grace's absent answer. "Don't you want to just sneak me in? I'll be so bored." Silence edged into their cavern, like a sneaky fog that portends rain. Grace worried the edge of a napkin. She had no answer.

Mercy picked the scab again. "You promise you'll be here?"

"Of course." Grace answered quickly, relieved to have something to say. "Where else am I going to go?"

"On a moonlit walk with Jack Thomas." Mercy's voice lengthened and sharpened in pitch, playground taunting Grace.

"Be quiet, you." Grace tossed a bread crust at Mercy. "Besides. Jack Thomas doesn't know who I am." A beat. "Yet."

They laughed, finding footing on the cusp of teasing, skating through the obvious thing that kept them apart. The river floated by. Behind and above, they heard the honking of horns, the heavy, distant roar of steel on steel as another train made its steaming way through the flats along the banks, pushing outward and away. A scissor-tail flycatcher landed on a rock in the river, pecked against the stone, then flew off. The sun cast the long shadows, the alarm clock that told the girls when it was time to scatter on back to their places.

They sat, quiet in their little den. No one bothered them there. Grace's mind circled back to Mercy's wish, to go where Grace went. Guilt itched at her again as she thought of the names they called Mercy at school. Not at Grace's school. Her school friends didn't care about Mercy, any more than they cared about any other white kid. They cared at Mercy's school. Good thing she was such a stubborn mule; only Grace saw the way the words broke her.

Grace didn't want to, but she sighed, "I have to get. My night to..."

Mercy broke in. "Make dinner. I know. It's Thursday." Her shoulders, the first thing to soften after a mood, good or bad, fell. "See you tomorrow?"

Grace smiled, tossed the napkin at her. "You bet." Then she ran off, making her way home, skirting town, taking the easy route.

5

Back home, Grace helped her mama start dinner and waited for Daddy. SamandJacob smacked a baseball in the street between the houses. Every few moments, the crack of wood and a crowd of small voices rose to the windows. Mama set out the pie Miss Willie gave them while Grace scrubbed potatoes at the sink. Waiting for Daddy. When she was just a little thing, Grace sat on the floor pushing toys about on smooth planks, listening for the clang of the trolley as Mama cooked dinner. The baritone chorus of men done with a long work day crescendoed through Greenwood, and Grace felt the final jolt of anticipation that had been building all day.

Daddy walked home from the trolley stop with his neighbors. In almost every season, with the windows open, Greenwood wives heard the low waves of male voices riding over the hill, picking out the sounds that belonged to their men. The trolley let them off at the slice of Greenwood and Archer that formed the southeastern border of their city inside the city. Where they had ridden in silence at the back, once they stepped off and began the hike up the rise to their place, the men became garrulous and fun. Especially on Thursdays.

Nothing beat Thursdays in Greenwood.

Thursdays in Greenwood were a weekly family reunion because live-ins like Jules got that night off. The confectionary, the beauty shop, the barber and Dreamland all stayed open late; men bunched around the storefronts one-upping each other's stories. The women looked after the kids, who ran through the streets playing ball, buying candy, standing in line to see the picture showing at Dreamland. Grace and her friends tried several times, unsuccessfully, to sneak into the upstairs of Dreamland where couples went to dance.

If Grace wasn't at the river with Mercy, she enjoyed the walk home on Thursdays, because Jules usually walked with Grace and her mama, and Jules usually had some scandal to share about the House Next Door, where she worked. That Thursday was no different, and Grace counted on her mama to tell her anything juicy she may have missed. She had imagined, as she had walked home, how Jules would thunder on about those crazy people.

As Mama puttered with dinner, she recounted Jules' story. It seemed Jules had thwarted Mrs. Whitehurst again. Mrs. Whitehurst's sister was coming all the way from Jefferson City. According to Jules, Mrs. Whitehurst said it like a song, like words that looped together, like all-the-way-from-Jeff City was a kind of spell one used to conjure up sisters. Jules had washed, scented, and ironed a white cotton coverlet and its matching sheets for the guest room Mrs. Whitehurst reserved for said sister from Jeff City. She had dressed the wide bed, and as a special touch had used the box-pleated bed skirt. Jules had wanted to clip some hydrangea from the garden for her bedside table, but since they weren't ready yet, she placed a small tea cup with a basil seedling peeping out from the dark soil. She cleaned the water decanter, filled the closet with fresh towels and placed a small basket of toiletries for the sister from Jeff City.

Mrs. Whitehurst turned the livid purple of a shiner when she saw it. "Jules?" she hollered. "This will not do. Simply not." Jules stood waiting to absorb the lashing, to hear Mrs. Whitehurst explain what particular abomination she had committed now. The woman of the house had continued.

"Basil seedlings. I see what you're trying to do here, Jules, and it's not going to work."

Jules wanted to defend herself. "Ma'am. I was just trying to spruce it for your sister from Jeff City."

Mrs. Whitehurst eyed her, trying to catch Jules' angle, and truly, there was usually an angle with Jules. "It won't do. Simply won't do."

"Yes, ma'am."

"If you make up the bed before she gets here, I'll never hear the end of it. You must rewash all of these linens, iron, fold and then, when she arrives, you start ironing them again. Not until I tell you.

Then you make up the bed." Exasperation blasted past her fat lip. "I can't be doing everything, you know!" Jules bowed to hide a smirk.

Mama repeated Mrs. Whitehurst again to Mama. "She can't be doing everything, you know." While telling the story on the walk from the trolley, Mama said Jules' laugh had rippled like her belly. Jules' laugh was loud and low, and it tripped over itself escaping her body. Grace thought she'd like to laugh with anyone who could laugh like Jules; her laugh just made Grace want to laugh right along with her.

"Switch out the basil. Hydrangea from the garden. Yes. I know it's not ready yet. Just cut it the day she arrives. She won't notice it anyway, unless it's awful."

"Yes, ma'am."

"Jules? Next time, you check with me first."

Jules had nodded. The times she did ask, the times she didn't ask, it didn't matter. Mrs. Whitehurst had a way of changing her mind, almost as if she was just thinking of ways to keep Jules busy. Almost.

The potatoes baked in the oven with a pan of meatloaf. They sizzled and made the house smell like family. Grace filled her nostrils with it, that smell made her antsy for everyone to be back in their own four walls again. Mama laughed about Jules and Mrs. Whitehurst.

"Made for each other, those two."

The long table lay open before her, where, for the second time that day, Grace folded napkins, when she heard the baritone chorus of men done with a long work day, nothing that happened with Jules could sustain her interest anymore; she and her stories were a way to pass the time while waiting for Boyd.

Grace didn't talk about this part of her day with anyone, not even Mercy. It was nobody's business how much she loved being with her parents. She harbored a secret shame that she was probably too old to still find something exciting about the first sound of her daddy's voice, plucked from a caucus of many, tumbling down the street.

The habit evolved, like those best family traditions. When she was too young to be running down to the river alone, Daddy swept into the house, and whatever griping he'd been doing with his friends dissipated. Throwing open the door, he beamed and laughed, throwing himself on the floor to crawl around with the twins. As if he'd never been anywhere but with them all day. When Grace was old enough to help Mama in the kitchen, an age that Grace had always felt was too young, she was long past the playing stage. When Boyd wandered in, knocking Sam on the arm and tousling Jacob, he listened to Grace's stories. Mama smiled and let Grace tell Jules' stories, stories about planting tomatoes with Mercy behind the garage, and stories about who sat on which trolley and when. When Boyd got home, Grace's words poured out of her like she was on some kind of pressing schedule and had to use her entire daily allotment of words in record time.

His first step into the yard landed softly. Then the first step on the front porch. Then his hand grasping the knob, pushing open the door. Grace held her tongue and listened for her silent daddy making his silent way home. She could never pick out his voice among the crowd, because keeping his lips closed was like his religion. Grace could always guess, rather, who was coming by their footsteps, the sound of the gait and the breath. While Daddy's was like laying bricks, intentional and ordered, her mother's took some liberties with cadence, sometimes groaning from the aches that afflicted her. The boys, of course, were like scrabbling monsters careering wildly. Grace waited for him. Every single day. His step was a favorite song.

Daddy was a horrible liar. His smile was empty that day. Like two rubber bands stretched from his ears to the corners of his mouth, holding a grin in place, and badly. Though a smile flickered on his lips and in his eyes while he surveyed his wife and daughter working, the women noticed a shadow, a layer of worry hooding Daddy's face. Instead of turning on the faucet of stories, Grace finished scrubbing the potatoes, and gave Mama a glance. She nodded, and Grace knew it fell to her to keep the twins outside until called.

Mama and Daddy expected their daughter to hover near the front door, fishing for a nibble of the news he was about to deliver. Grace didn't catch much, though. As she made her way slowly out the door, she heard him say, "You'd think, after all we did, things would have changed. Am I dumb to keep expecting that?"

Mama reached her arms around him, caught Grace's eye and waved her off.. Mama's hands flattened against Daddy's broad back. Disgusted by this display, Grace picked up her pace.

The simple fact of her presence outside signaled JacobandSam that they were under surveillance and prohibited from the house for the foreseeable future. It wasn't a message they needed. Those two never went in until Mama had called for them more than once and Daddy stepped on the porch to holler. Grace suspected it wasn't that her parents were worried about the boys overhearing. They didn't want her to hear. Grace heard everything; her ears like a net, capturing all the information that might prove useful. It wasn't just the hearing, though; Grace could dissemble the whispers. Grace would know what Daddy was talking about when he said, "After all we did."

Grace held court on the front stoop on another important day. She had pressed her palms against the smooth grain of her skirt, drawing the fabric taut around her legs, then she curled over herself into a comma, listening to the wind flip through the American flags that cluttered their small patch of green. She had wanted to strike an imperious pose, but she was too anxious. Too hopeful.

On that day, Mama had warned the boys to stay near the house. The four of them had spent the whole week getting ready for Daddy's return. Mama carefully led them through what the boys thought were silly conversations. She had asked them what they remembered about their daddy. Mama filled in the gaps since the boys struggled to remember if they had eaten breakfast, being too busy with balls and bats and scuffed knees. Grace hovered near her mama, trying to still her anxious pacing. When Mama shooed her off, she took up her post and settled her mind on the same worries her mama had: some snafu would hold up his arrival, or he wouldn't remember her, or he'd be so different they'd trip around like strangers. Grace felt that her lungs had ceased to function properly, that they could only inhale infinitely, filling her with hope like an overinflated balloon, ready to burst as she waited for the day to arrive. When the day came, the hours and minutes ticked so slowly it was as if the hand of God reached down and made seconds extend for whole days.

In the years since he had returned, Grace troubled herself not infrequently with memories. She wanted to put a finger on the exactness of the changes in her daddy, to loop a tidy bow around the precise thing that was her father before and after. She wanted a clear and unadulterated picture of this man. What bothered her was the truth: that she had been too young when he left to know how going to war had changed him, if it did at all. Grace was just stretching into her limbs when he flew away, and no matter if people live under the same roof or across the world, change is going to happen in a year or two. When Daddy came home, his smile was less broad, but his eyes were as bright as Grace remembered. A man has a way of looking at his child. When he left, Grace was ten, no baby, old enough to know that the men had expectations. Everyone in Greenwood had expectations.

He said once, after being home a few weeks, "I'm so happy to be home, and I'm so disappointed. I should have known better."

"Disappointed?" Grace had asked. "You're home, Daddy. With us." As if that's all he ever would need.

He laughed. "I'm not disappointed to be home. I'm disappointed to be wrong."

He sat down at the table, where she rolled bits of leftover pie crust into pinwheel logs, filling them with cinnamon sugar and butter. She pushed the wooden pin over the dough, careful with the edges, expertly calling up a perfect rectangle from a simple ball of unused crust. He watched, quiet for a while, then chuckled.

"It's like those pinwheels you're making, Gracie. You put the spices together and bake them. You expect them to stay together when they come out of the oven. In this case, we just came out of one oven and right into another, separate in every way."

Sitting on the porch, trying to catch crumbs of her parents' private conversation, she understood. Nothing had changed after the war. They were still stationed by convention and precedent, if not by the military. Told where they could shop, eat and work. Marooned in their own part of town. There was no equal about it. Grace spit in the grass, impressing the boys as they ran in circles in the street.

She stepped off the porch careful not to make a sound, removing her shoes before her feet touched the grass. She hunkered over and crept under the open kitchen window, crossing her fingers they'd still be there.

Boyd was talking. "It's frightening, Rach. They're rounding up anyone who doesn't fall in line. Even whites. That man last year was just the start. Don't forget about the wobblies, either."

Mama murmured something Grace didn't catch, and Daddy rumbled back. "I have to think about it, Honey." He paused so long Grace figured he was done talking. She was unsatisfied, caught in an unpleasant suspense. Mama did not bang pots in the kitchen. Cicadas did not sing a summer hymn. The boys in the street froze in time and space.

Then, "He was lynched."

Nobody used that word unless he wanted to make a point. Not in that house. Not in that neighborhood. Not at their jobs. Nowhere. Grace's stomach lurched but she pressed herself closer to the window. Mama continued clucking and tsking, her voice a backdrop to Daddy's talk, listening and fixing dinner at the same time. He continued.

"It's getting worse at work with Tucker. He is all over Dub, so then Dub gets all over us. Tucker's always creeping behind a corner, waiting for mistakes."

She must have wandered closer to the window, maybe she was looking out for the boys because Grace could just about pluck her mother's vocal cords as she tried to lighten her husband. "I guess Tucker was around today."

Again a pause. Finally, Daddy conceded with a joyless bark to let her know he heard, understood the attempt. Dub, Mr. Williams, Daddy had told Grace, was a good boss.

"He's a good man, that John Williams. He's fair and not dumb. Knows a thing or two."

Grace believed her father. She would have believed anything her daddy said, especially about Mr. Williams. He was Mercy's daddy, and Mercy was Grace's heart.

"I made some cuts for a customer. Dub had given them to me himself. I took my time, measuring and checking, but trying not to take too long. Any excuse, or they'll make one up. I brought the beams directly to Dub, who was talking with the customer, guy I didn't recognize. Dub took them from me, even said, 'Thank you.' Looked me in the eye."

Before the beams had touched the ground, that man decided it was wrong, all wrong. He started getting loud, throwing his voice and his weight around, like I don't know how to read or do math or cut wood. Been doing it my whole life." He took a breath, maybe a sip of something. Grace waited. The crack of the bat, the high pitched yells from young boys filled her ears, and she was lost in that sound.

Daddy picked up again. "Mr. Tucker chooses that moment to make customer satisfaction his reason for being. Walks over, takes the beams from Dub, throws them at me. Tucker's staring at Dub, but when Dub opens his mouth and says he trusts me and knows the cuts are right, Tucker won't let him finish. Tucker says, 'If you can't get good workers, and treat them how they need to be treated, ain't gonna get far. Maybe you need to start looking for a new boss.'"

Grace knew Mama had put dinner out of her mind because all Grace heard was their voices. "I'm sorry, Boyd," Mama said. She didn't offer anything else. Mama's sorrow hung in the air between them, powerless.

"Dub nearly doubled over with a look of shame. I shrugged it off, for him. Endured his halfhearted chewing out and sent me to cut the beams again. Reminding me the cost was out of my pay. As if I'm like to forget that."

JacobandSam ran toward Grace stationed under the window. She dashed toward them intercepting them in panic. "What were you doing under that window? Whadja hear?" They demanded. Grace wondered how two boys could make as much noise as a trolley full of people.

Grace learned how to shoo from her mama, and she shooed her brothers off now, drawing then into a suspiciously long game of hide and seek. Not without reluctance did she leave her eavesdropping spot. Grace liked Mr. Dub, Mercy's father. He called her Grace-Like-a-Rock and smiled at her like they shared a secret. Grace didn't know what he meant when he called her that, but she liked it. Kindness streamed out of him when he spoke to her. She wanted to understand how the Mr. Dub she knew could let that stupid Mr. Tucker take a walk on his backside. Like most secrets adults think they conceal, Grace knew why.

Sorting through the colors in Tulsa was like trying to see to the bottom of the Arkansas after a rain. It wasn't clear to anyone, and everyone did this herky-jerky dance around what had been and what was to be. Mr. Dub was different. He didn't seem to care. To Grace, he seemed to want to kind of reach in his hand and stir it up, rankle up the dirt and sludge and water more. Picturing him, that smile he gave her, made Grace feel special. Maybe it's nonsense to see rightness in eyes, but that's what was there. A quiet rightness.

Mr. Dub didn't look like much. He didn't look like the kind of man to raise a fist to the city bully. His skinny legs hid inside wide-legged trousers, bent at the knee from wear. His shirts bloomed around him. He might have been sturdier after the war, but his face was vaguely hollow, like a shrunken jack o'lantern. Gaunt, Mama called him. Gaunt described Mr. Dub exactly: dried up by the war, and boiled down to the base of his person. He only said words he meant to say, and he did everything with a calm purpose. He might have seemed weird to others. People want noise and laughter and happiness. Mr. Dub could do noise and laughter and happiness, but it was quieter, almost mechanical. Only the warm, browned butter eyes said he was genuine.

People talked, of course. That's what they do. The yelling leaders with their bullhorns and bannered cars made a big deal out of how great the city was, and how high people could rise. They talked and talked about growth and jobs and economy and all that nonsense. They proclaimed Tulsa the Magic City, a bastion of promise. That's the trouble with promises. None of their blabbering changed anything. None of what they described sounded like the city the Ironses lived in.

People talked, too, about the Grace Irons and the Mercy Williams. No one was in any danger of utterly forgetting where the Irons family belonged. Dub Williams knew how to keep his job, and Daddy knew how to keep his. Grace knew Mercy was her left foot, her opposable thumb. She was what made Grace hold her head and disregard what they two called other people's nonsense. But she also knew this was not exactly a favorite town ideal. Appearances kept them all spinning, rotating in a social parade designed by someone else.

As much as Grace might like Mr. Dub, and as much as Grace's daddy tried to defend him, make it easy on him, everyone knew the truth: Mr. Dub would never understand, even if he was a smart, kind man. All that time walking around town, all that time in her backyard, Grace had heard everything. Grace had seen everything.

She thought she did, anyway.

Dub

6

Every man has days when to go home is to tuck his daily shame away like a name badge or the tools of his hands. Dub was having more days like that under Tucker, who was determined to bring Dub to heel, bent on making the Williams family as miserable as his own.

The thing about men like Tucker is that they are usually placated with a reverence that men like Dub can fake without feeling they've doused their souls in hell water. A bully wants to know he's the boss. Dub would be fine with that if Tucker would just let him do his work his own way and in peace.

Dub knew how to keep his head down and his nose clean in Europe. Watching his superior officers peacock, their faces just as lineless as Dub's, their bodies dense and strong like Dub's, confirmed in him his lifelong aspiration to be a follower. He had no desire to be responsible for the lives of these boys. No will to report to men with pectorals as large as melons. No need to have a bigger gun. Dub was content to dig the ditch, dig the latrine, carry whatever was asked.

Dub watched the boys fall. Then he watched his commanding officer try to write letters to the soldiers' loved ones. He'd rip page after page apart, unable to explain how this soldier, this child, who had only recently been a pulsing mass of veins and thoughts and movements, of laughter and fear and pain, was now nothing more than ground meat. To hear his commanding officer retching up the bottles he'd drunk trying to write the letters nearly caused the same reaction in Dub.

Willie understood her husband. She guarded Dub's perimeter like a sentry when he returned home from the war. She waited until he granted full access and then she came in like a whisper, like a blanket, like the silky wrap of surrender and temporary peace. She didn't need him to be the president of anything; she didn't long for a commander with so many medals pinned on his chest. She wanted him to be happy, and she wanted him home.

Dub's first night back, and in many nights to come, he slept on the floor next to their bed. When he woke screaming, like all survivors of the war did, she wrapped him up, held on tight and waited for him to find sleep again.

Weeks passed and he wandered the house like he didn't know how to fill it with his body when he felt so small. Dub took to sitting on the porch most mornings, watching the housekeepers arrive for work. Waving at the ice truck as it made the rounds. The neutral domestic echoes of normalcy sounded, for a while, fake, staged, like a radio show. It just didn't seem possible.

Willie watched Dub relearn how to be home. He mimicked her putting her napkin on her lap, using her fingers like pincers on a slender knife and long-handled fork, slicing into dinner. He remembered to shake hands firmly and force eye contact with everyone at church. He smiled with emptiness and false pride at their well wishes.

He didn't want to leave the porch. Dub didn't have make any decisions on the porch other than when to get a hot cup of coffee or which way to set his chair. Willie waited longer than most wives would have. She brought him a steaming mug one day when he'd been home maybe a month.

"Nice out here," she said.

He nodded. Looked at her. Rocked his chair.

"I can see the appeal," she said.

Dub had to give her something. "I like watching what happens. I don't know that I ever noticed."

The silence settled. She sipped her drink, clanking the ice against the glass in her hand. "What did you think we did all day? Lounged about?" She reached for his hand and tickled the hairs around his wrist. He felt her eyes watching his fingers as try to pry him open, but she'd not use force.

"Nah. Just like it. It's relaxing."

She laughed a string of pearls. "Glad it's so relaxing for you. Sure isn't for the rest of us." She made a show of wiping her forehead, then she leaned forward and rested her elbows on her knees like a roughneck.

"Don't stop."

She didn't know what he meant.

"Don't stop laughing. Best sound I ever heard."

Dub didn't embody the entirety of his skin then, but he started to fill out the empty edges. She squeezed his hand, hard. Her eyes grew hard, a kind of promising hard. She stood up, wiped her hands on her pants and stood behind his chair. Willie's eyes told truth, and her body curving around his confirmed it: we'll be all right, she told him with her body. We'll be just fine. Like that, her laugh resuscitated him. Dub's main thought, in Europe and in his own home, was that a man could do anything if he could hear the genuine laughter of a woman like Willie. He knew without thinking that when he told her his mind he was getting a gift, a present he knew he did not deserve. She had this way of just taking it in, like a meal, and working through it.

Walking in the door that Thursday, Dub was relieved that it was just the three of them. He looked forward to talking to her.

"He's pushing me, Willie." He roped his arms around her body and sagged onto her; it wasn't fair to drape his weight on her, but she received him so readily and strong, like she was made of rooted timber, a spine like a trunk, bearing the limbs of so many. Dub assumed that Mercy must have been her usual ball of fury that day, because when he released Willie and she turned into him, resting her hands on his hips, just above his waistband, slipping two little fingers just inside, giving him that steady thrill, she had weary fury in her own eyes.

"Oh, don't tell me now, Willie."

"Just Mercy being Mercy. Some days I think she's just like me, and other days, I think she's just like your mother."

"I do not have an opinion on that matter," he laughed.

She pushed him away, turned to slap some food on plates and shooed him into the dining room.

"No drink?"

"Fix your own," a coy pout over her shoulder. He followed, her pet.

Thursday dinners normally calmed him. Having the means to provide help for his wife elicited an uncomfortable pride in Dub. He swallowed his privilege like hooch because he liked Rachel. And Boyd. And their kids. But Dub didn't always want Rachel hovering over their food and their house and all their stuff. That Thursday, though, after listening to Tucker pontificating and humiliating all day, Dub was glad Rachel wasn't at the house. Telling Willie was one thing. Telling her something that Rachel might overhear was another.

Mercy slammed around behind the doors. She was a clumsy puppy, agitating to hear what her parents were saying. She was Dub's child, and he loved her, but she was nothing close to subtle. Dub eyed Willie, who nodded. His wife would hear everything he said, and everything he didn't. Leaving out as many details as he could, he told Willie about Tucker and Boyd.

They sat in a pair of chairs they had brought from St. Louis, wooden framed thrones covered in a deep blue fabric Willie rolled her R when she called it brocade. There had been a lack of space in the wagon for nonessentials but Willie was resolute about the chairs. When she said *brocade*, her eyes laughed, and the swath of her voice fluttered in his ear. Damned if he'd let her see his knees buckle. Dub found room on the wagon for the encumbrances. He half expected they'd be fuel for fires they lit along the way, over which she would cook rice and beans or mushy corn gruel. Willie, Anne Richardson Banks of the St. Louis Banks', their little joke, was not above slinging hash over a campfire. "My daddy taught me," she had explained.

Anne Richardson Banks was not from a family of any notice, and Dub readily admitted he didn't really know what he wanted until she walked up and told him. Dub had been on enough dates with enough society girls to know he'd be challenged to find a wife in that group of vacant skulls. He needed—he wanted—solid, smart, and sharply witty. How does a man not become a smitten fool for that?

Dub did not meet Willie at a cotillion. He could not imagine her draped in frippery for the life of him. Even her wedding gown was simple and elegant, not an ounce of whalebone or crinoline in the swingy thing. She caused quite a few of his mother's friends to catch some flies. Dub had never been more in love or more proud. She had asked her aunts to help her create a trousseau, and they had conceived a white satin suit like St. Louis had never seen. When they left their wedding reception, she wore long, wide pants and a short, boxy jacket. A long string of pearls swung from her neck and framed her flaming red lips. She was stunning. Wearing pants. Dub had said, "Woman, what will people think?" She had laughed and poured herself into him. "Shall we go, Mrs. Williams? Mrs. Willie Williams." She took his arm and they left.

As they settled into the chairs, Dub recalled how falling into one of them had become part of their evening ritual. A drink decanted into crystal tumblers, a few quiet minutes before dinner. Willie had cried the hot tears of loss sitting in those chairs; unnumbered losses, whispered condolences, uncertainty about future children. They were not unnumbered, of course. Dub knew. He counted each one. Mercy was to be the only one. On days when she was particularly precocious, he tried to remember that.

Mercy often had joined them when she was younger, launching herself into her father's lap the moment he plunked his glass on the side table. Give her credit for timing. She had the pliable limbs of youth that allowed her to wrap herself into any position, clinging to a leg or a chair, begging for one more story. When she got tired of being close, Mercy threw herself to the floor and squatted in front of wooden blocks or she pushed fat pencils around on paper while Willie and Dub talked. Those days had passed.

She was growing up, too busy conquering T-Town, that's what the bosses called Tulsa, to give her parents a second glance. The fact that a Negro was his daughter's only companion gave Dub no small amount of worry.

"I just miss Mercy."

Willie plucked his hand from the chair arm and stroked his fingers, her fingertip smooth and hot along the map of veins on his hand.

"I miss her, too, Dub. It's good she's got Grace."

Dub dropped her hand and pushed himself up. "That's just it. You know I like Grace, but those two are asking for trouble."

The Magic City lived up to the stories. Even in the time since the Williams family had been here, the turn of the century, the city had changed. When Dub and Willie had arrived, everything was dirt and dust and clanging machines, but the buildings sprang up from mythical soil, enriched with oil and money. The Ironses of the world stayed within their limits, except at the Williams' house. That's what worried Dub.

They weren't naive. Boyd and Rachel Irons didn't expect anything other than the separation that they had found. Still, at the Williams' home, there was at least a show. A sort of willingness to blur the lines. Here, the lines were carved into the earth. The Frisco railroad tracks on the south marked white Tulsa from Greenwood. Greenwood was surrounded on all sides, by the river, hills and more tracks crisscrossing the red dirt.

Dub never understood, was it the negroes who built Greenwood to insulate themselves, or was it the whites who forced them to build their own town. That idiot Tucker argued that they should stay there and who cares why; he ranted and raved about them taking up the best land and how dare they get uppity. Dub saw the wise economy of blacks staying in Greenwood. If they were restricted from white businesses, it was just good sense for them to have their own. He just could never figure out which was the chicken and which the egg. They have to get their laundry done somewhere, their hair cut, their cars. Good for them.

He always figured if a man could do his work, provide for his family and think for himself, what difference did it make what color his skin was? Coming to Tulsa on the wagon was risky; he and Willie didn't know what they'd find, but they were sure there would be work. They wanted to claim the promise of the Magic City, just like every one they met making their way West.

Tucker's business had grown with the city. He was a main distributor of building supplies with a network, Dub suspected, of back room agreements. Everything Tucker wanted seemed to sprout from his hand, as if he had some kind of green thumb of industry rather than botanics. Dub regretted his cynicism about Tucker's methods. Maybe Tucker just happened to get in at the right time. After all, anyone could figure out that the roughnecks and the oilmen needed places to live. They needed to eat and they needed to wash, and they demanded to be entertained. Even before the big Ida Glenn oil discovery, even before the train merged the two banks of the Arkansas, before thousands of barrels of oil pumped out of the earth every day, the people had needs.

Tucker was one of the first men to establish a business. Dub didn't fall to coarse language, not very often anyway, but Tucker's success made Dub wonder why the good things happen to the assholes.

Dub tied his hopes to Tucker's success anyway; he rose as Tucker he did. Dub's success enabled Rachel came to work at Dub's house.

Tucker talked. In the early days, it was just the two of them cutting and delivering lumber all over town, giving Tucker ample time to talk. Tucker thrust his calloused paws at his customers, pumping their arms priming them for future sales. His eyes sparkled at everyone. He was a natural.

Once, they had dropped a load of supplies at Greenwood and Archer, when the negroes were building Dreamland. Dreamland promised to be a big structure, with seats for something like 700 people. Tucker shook hands with the owners, but he didn't work too hard to hide wiping his hands on his pants. When the men drove away, Tucker left his goodwill at the curb.

"Niggers building theaters. Only in Tulsa. Makes me sick." A wad of phlegm rose in his razor-scratched throat. Dub swallowed his words and buried his thoughts. He gave way to Tucker's powerful force and allowed Tucker to erase the lines Dub had drawn in for himself. Dub coated his skin with shame like grease; he protected himself by keeping his mouth shut. Tucker had punched Dub's shoulder. Dub's silence was his agreement.

Dub had trudged home to Willie, bringing his guilt offerings. A gold necklace, a cameo, a ruby ring to match her full lips, each gift a sacrament their so-called progress and his shame. Each tiny wrapped box cradled a badge of his silence. Tucker bought Dub, and Dub knew it. Let him. Willie wore the trinkets only to church. She, wise woman, saw the trembling hands that offered the gifts, the forced smile and the blank eyes. She understood. She wore their complicity. It tasted like milk going bad. Willie had no need for gems and baubles, but when she wore them, it sealed a promise between her and Dub, that they wouldn't be like this forever. They shared, too, an undercurrent of fear. They suspected that they would never have the spine to be anything more than bauble-buying chumps.

Dub congratulated himself for hiring Boyd; it was the smartest decision Dub had ever made, after marrying Willie. Smart, kind, prompt, thoughtful and, *son*, could that man take a tongue-lashing. When Tucker aimed his fury at Boyd, and he did so often, the better man listened, agreed and did as requested. Meanwhile, Dub shuffled his shoes, impotent to stop it, change it or say anything that would be any kind of salve. To anyone.

Dub liked working alongside Boyd. He didn't run at the mouth, like Tucker. Curious, Dub had asked him once, how could he work all day without saying a word.

"Used to it, I guess."

"How'd you get used to it?" Dub wanted to know how he managed to keep it all, his whole self, buttoned up like a uniform.

"The war. With the French. Didn't understand them. They didn't understand us. You get used to someone else doing the talking." He had hoisted a beam and hauled it to the sawhorse. Dub was impressed by Boyd's muscular stride as he moved; Boyd carried the burden with a surprising ease.

Unspoken rules. Men like Boyd and Dub didn't talk about the war when it ended. So Boyd's reply only gave Dub more questions. Dub was patient, as his wife had been, content to let the answers come over time. Sure enough, they trickled out from Boyd's crumbling crust as the men learned how to approach the other. That kind of manly solidity, a concreteness, Dub felt, was deficient in Tucker -- one of the reasons Dub didn't trust his boss. A man so sure of his opinions displayed a stubborn inflexibility. Not the kind of rigidity that would get a man elected, necessarily, but the kind that could pit him up against his peers in an infinite game of King of the Hill. Dub suspected that Tucker did not know that game never had a winner. Tucker's unceasing blather spared no room for anyone else, but Boyd created space around him, like a big circle of trust people wanted to walk into and enjoy for a while.

The day Boyd asked Dub to consider hiring Rachel, Dub was at once proud and unsettled. Tucker had been buzzing in Dub's ear about getting help for Willie. Willie didn't want it; Dub sure didn't want it, but Tucker was persistent. "Plenty a negroes to do your work. Get one." As if it was a matter of simply selecting a new stove or picking up some groceries. Dub imagined a warehouse full of shelves, and on the shelves, rows and rows of black people, waiting to do his laundry.

Boyd was smart; he had a family to feed, and he was in this city for the promises everyone chased. "My wife Rachel's looking for work. Heard you might be needing a laundress."

Boyd did not look away from Dub. He spoke deliberate words. It was the first time Dub had considered it. "Be great if she could bring our little one."

Before he knew it, Dub had agreed. She would be at their house the next day.

Willie was furious. "I don't need any help. How *horrible*. We aren't hiring a *servant*. No. I won't have it." That woman had an ember for a temper, just waiting for a gentle gust to blaze up.

"I'm not saying you need help, honey." Dub stammered. "And she's not a servant."

"Then what? What's the point?" Then: "Dub. You're making that atrocious man happy, aren't you? You're doing this for *Tucker*."

"Can we just try it?" He slumped, beaten on all sides. Boss, negro, wife.

"Fine." She walked away.

They had a quiet dinner. Knives and forks scraped across plates, lips smacked and throats gulped, but no one spoke. Dub cleared his throat before offering to tidy up dinner, and Willie refused, taking three plates to the kitchen. Dub retreated to the garage behind the house and shuffled around clusters of oil cans and wrenches. Dusted off the workbench he never used. Touching the slick, cold steel of his tools and smelling the tang of chemicals did not give him the courage to enter his house, *his house*, again. Looking through the small window out over the tiny grass patch behind their house,, he saw her in the neighbors' yard.

Jules. She lived next door and hung out their laundry. Poured their coffee and tea, set their table, made their meals. They seemed so happy to have her, and, Dub told himself, she had a job, away to earn money for her family. Dub wondered if she had a family. She mesmerized him.

Jules' strong arms reached toward the clothesline with a calming rhythm. Her deft fingers pinched open the clips and dropped the laundry one piece at a time first into her arms, then into the basket that she nudged along with her foot. Dub listened. She hummed a song that conflicted with the late evening birds but that seemed to belong there anyway. She was large and obvious, but she was also graceful and intent. Dub felt he could have watched the routine for hours. She bent to lift the basket, and her feet whispered in the grass. She disappeared into the House Next Door.

That night Dub wrestled with sleep, wondering what Jules would be doing at that moment. He imagined what it would be like to have some stranger lurking about his house, doing things he was capable of doing. He understood Willie's point. She was a fantastic cook and didn't have but Dub and Mercy to care for. Dub was curious; he wanted to know how it worked. He wanted to know how Mrs. Whitehurst and Jules worked around each other.

Dub woke early to greet Rachel at the door, unsure how Willie would take it. He was pouring a cup of coffee when a tap came at the back door.

"Rachel?" Dub pushed open the screen door. "Pleasure to meet you." He thrust out his hand. "I'm John Williams. Call me Dub."

She smiled and reached out her hand. "Hi, Mr. Williams." She blushed.

Dub invited her in and started to pour two cups of coffee when she interrupted. "Mr. Williams. I can do that." She shooed him away, taking the pot from his hand, pouring out two mugs and then enjoying a long sip. "Have you eaten breakfast?"

She poked around in the cabinets, pulling out the skillet, the eggs, bread, plates. Right before his eyes, hot breakfast appeared. Rachel had just slipped the plate in front of Dub when Willie entered the kitchen. She looked shy and tentative; Dub's heart might've cracked a little if he didn't find it so charming. He might have cared more if he didn't have that full plate in front of him.

Dub stood up to make introductions, between two grown women who looked as nervous as if it was the first day of school. They mirrored each other, like boxers unready or unwilling to throw the first punch, uncertain, weighing the opponent. After he introduced them, Dub focused his attention on cleaning his plate. They made small talk and drank coffee. Having shoveled away his meal and drained his mug, he found himself sitting in an awkward feminine silence. He hugged Willie and breathed into her ear: "Just give it a day. She's to help you. Whatever you want. If you don't like, it we can fix it." He kissed her cheek and let the door slam.

Somehow they worked it out.. It took longer than he expected, but they figured it out. Willie found time to read and sew and volunteer because Rachel took on so much of the household work. She enjoyed putting the money into Rachel's hand at the end of each week, pushing extra bills into her palm, smiling at her.

"I feel like we help each other be women," she had said, after a month or so.

"What do you mean?" Dub asked, sidling up to her, ignoring the impulse to declare his idea an unmitigated success.

"She can earn a living, which is something her grandmother couldn't do. I get to help her with that, and . . . ." The end of her sentence fell into her lap. Dub waited. "I like that I can spend some time doing other things. It still feels strange, sometimes, to have someone doing jobs I should, could be doing. Mostly, I don't want her thinking we're uppity. I just can't stop thinking we're just like everyone else." She threw down the sewing she held on her lap. "Am I justifying having a black woman wash my dirty laundry?"

Dub understood then. Willie walked the same kind of line he walked, buter world was full of dishes and linens rather than pine planks and nails. Willie grew up hiking back roads with her papa, setting up tents where he'd preach about the divine rights of man for a day or a week. Willie's papa had argued for the integration of society and preached about the evils of systematic oppression. When he got sick, Willie moved to St. Louis to live with The Aunts in their boardinghouse.

The Aunts required that Willie put in a full day's work. She emptied her chamber pot, washed her sheets and cooked once a week for everyone. "Everyone" could be a group of rail workers heading west or a mother and daughter traveling east after losing their men in the territories. The Aunts' home was open to anyone willing to work for room and board.

"If I sat down to read, The Aunts found me another job," Willie said, usually to Mercy as Mercy attempted to wiggle out of chores. "Or if I sat down to read, they made sure it was 'right proper' reading: The Bible, *Common Sense*, or primers they prepared to send to Africa."

Mercy did not believe her mother had ever bowed to the rules of another, even if it was The Aunts.

"Mom, tell about that time when you told The Aunts the servants could do something for a change." Mercy had a particular interest in tales of her mother's youthful rebellions, when The Aunts wore down her pride and when she refused to do her chores. Dub chuckled over these stories, too. He imagined her skinny legs triangled over the blue chairs, reading something improper, waving her hand at the servants. He pictured The Aunts, too, rising up imperious and aflame, bringing Willie to attention by the little pink edge of her tender pink ear.

She didn't tell the story often. It embarrassed her.

They were wedged into Tulsa. Wedged into their house, and into a set of expectations that didn't fit them, a badly tailored but bespoke suit that could not be altered. After the city burned and the tents went up, Dub would try to imagine if there had been another way. He thumped himself, wishing he'd had the courage to refuse. They could have hired a white girl. They could have avoided hiring anyone at all. Dub could have rejected Tucker and his agenda. He could have been stronger. He could have changed things. Leastwise, that's what he told himself on vacuous nights when a smell or a taste kicked something loose in his memory, when he'd get to feeling responsible. It was no solace, the fact that the burden did not rest only on his shoulders.

When Rachel brought her daughter to work with her, the daughters twisted around each other like two strands of hair braided together. The women followed their lead. Instead of simply wandering the edges of the same house, they began to take their tea together, to sit on the porch for a spell after lunch. They found an easy routine and kept to it, and it occurred to Dub that Willie was more comfortable with Rachel than she ever was with the First Church ladies. That was later. At first, though, the two circled each other for a few weeks.

Early in her time with the Willie and Dub, Rachel showed a practiced eye. When Mrs. Whitehurst came to call, Rachel brought tea on the good china and then removed herself to the back of the house. She used the right words, like "yes, ma'am," while ducking her eyes downward.

The day arrived when it fell to Willie to entertain Mrs. Tucker and the Ladies' Auxiliary. Rachel prepared and served tiny cookies on tiny plates and pastel drinks in tiny cups while Willie's ambivalence turned the cookies and drinks sour in her stomach.

That night, she met Dub at the back door. "I can't do this. I love Rachel, but I can't keep her. We have to let her go."

She said the Auxiliary had lobbed their ugly ideas *right in front of Rachel*. Willie described how these fine, Christian women had talked about black domestics as "theirs." Willie had drawn in the soft tissue inside her mouth and clamped her teeth over it as Mrs. Whitehurst declared that *the Bible tells us how dumb they are*. She flared her nostrils as Mrs. Tucker burbled her assent.

"Willie, that's their problem. You just go on about your business." Dub wanted his embrace to have power, a force that could erase those words and women from his wife's mind. Dub's first thought, always, was to get her close to him. It was so easy to do. She pushed back that night.

"I hate the way they look at her. Look *through* her. It's worse than how they look at Mercy." The tears arrived.

Amelia, their Mercy. Sweet and strange child, pushed at every edge she encountered, as if any obstacles in her path existed solely for her to bulldoze with her outsized will and mental effort. When she was little and pestered adults, her parents smiled it away. They could say she was stubborn, or that she had a mind of her own, which, strictly speaking, was the truth.

The older she got, the less cute and the more annoying her contrariness became. Especially when it came to Grace Irons. "Why can't Grace stay for dinner? Can she stay over night? Can I go to Grace's?" Mercy was a wrecking ball, and the indulgent eyes of the adults had long since replaced indulgence with suspicion. When Willie wasn't watching, Dub swallowed bicarbonate of soda, trying to assuage the ball of anxiety in his gut. He was not equipped to regulate this daughter with her questions and her ideas and her total lack of regard for the way things were done. Because the truth is, he liked it. He wanted to be like her. Dub wanted to thumb his nose at Tucker. He wanted to retrieve his spine and his dignity and do things his way.

Dub would say his daughter was the spark that inflamed the plan. Willie and Dub had seen the reports from across the country. Dub found himself tempted back to the floor next to their bed. The entire county, the country, had a penchant for violence which banged against his skull, a daily nightmarish reminder of the war. The Great War. Was there such a thing? It was plain to Dub that violence was all the country knew how to do since Europe had detonated. Now it seemed the fuses were lighting up, ready to explode their own world. Willie's fretting about the ladies and Mercy's uniqueness made Dub want to protect, in his meager, silent way.

"It's coming this way," Dub had said one night, splayed in his chair and peering over the paper. Willie didn't ask what was coming. She knew.

"Yes," she said. "It is."

"Don't like to think of that stuff affecting Mercy." He had meant to say what she heard; he didn't want the violence to rip into the home of their friends, the Ironses. She heard him admit their private truth: that they were too small to change anything. Mercy was the only way Dub knew to articulate it, but he never dreamed how intimately Mercy was to become acquainted with what was already well on its way. He didn't think she needed that much protecting. He was awed by a strength in his kid that he knew he could not match.

Willie had said, "There's that space above the attic." Dub had filled in the rest. God, that woman gave him too much credit, too many chances to be the man he wanted to be. For as many times as he didn't get the hint, his relief that he understood this one surged through him.

The shame that he had tucked in daily was the noose he wore for years until that conversation. In a few short words, she had pried it loose and pulled it off him. Shame wears on a man. He can't rinse it off in the bath. He can't drink it away. God knows Dub tried. As much as his work with Tucker gave him a useful way to spend his days, and made him useful to Mercy and Willie, this project added purpose to his nights.

Dub collected cast off beams, spare bits and bobs from the lumberyard. Boyd helped him install a partial room divider above the attic. They carved enough sleeping space in the attic to separate adults and children. Each time he hammered a thumb or slammed his forehead on the ceiling on his way up the ladder Dub resolved again. Dub raced a half imagined mob. Willie sewed up old sheets into curtains for the window. She hung a long drape in a corner, and tucked a chamber pot behind it, left some paper, a few bath towels, a pitcher and basin.

Sometimes it felt like Christmas morning. If Dub saw Grace waiting out back for Mercy, he checked himself. He wanted to pull her aside. He wanted to show her; he wanted to say *see what we're doing.* Each time, she turned her full face on him, her eyes open and ready to understand, but her feet always sort of angling another direction. Ready to run if need be.

When he surrendered, again, to Tucker's bullying, he joined the mob. Tucker had not ordered him; his job didn't openly hang on the balance of Dub's decision, but his participation was strongly recommended by Tucker and the boys. Church held no sanctuary for Dub, either. Like a hive of old ladies, those guys, whose kids went to school with Mercy, hammered at Dub, a nail refusing to angle rightly into the wood grain.

"It's not right, Dub," Rachel and Boyd had said.

"You gotta come. Just once. You'll love it," the Williamses had promised.

No. Boyd thought. *No, I will not love it. I will hate it.*

They never stopped.

Dub bought another gem for Willie's crown of shame and tucked his own between his legs.

When Dub had confessed to being swayed by Tucker, she rolled off his stomach and curled into his arms, her hair like spun sugar and her smooth forehead slick with spring heat and effort. She lay there so long Dub thought she had fallen asleep or was thinking of a way to divorce him quietly.

Finally, she lifted herself on twin columns, her arms braced against him. She leaned over and took his face in one hand; if he had closed his eyes, he knew she would have appeared like a tattoo on his eyelids, burned there in lucid color. She kissed his forehead. She touched her lips to each of his eyes, each cheekbone lit up with her touch. Her thumb grazed the space of loose skin just under his eye sockets, wiping away a tear.

Willie put her head into the bony space of Dub's collar, and soon her breath was rhythmic and calm. He lay awake, staring at the ceiling, embarrassed by his riches.

Friday

Grace

"Flogged, Tarred and Feathered
Modern Ku Klux Klan Comes in to Being; Seventeen First Victims"
Tulsa World, November 10, 1917

7

Later, when Grace followed the arc of the mean days in her mind, certain things stood out like excessively bold colors, as if a child had colored too hard with a crayon too bright for the picture. A red slash, outside the lines, noticeable to anyone but the child with the crayon. She didn't know she would want to capture every section of the day like a strip of fly paper, to stick the residue into her head and make it stay there. When she realized she wanted that, that she needed to be able to recall with precision what distinguished one moment from the next, the colors had already faded. She knew she would shade them far more wildly than the mundane day required. This is the way with memory. Do we ever remember anything the way it really happened, boring, like a grocery list, without the assigned meaning of subsequent events?

After Mama and Daddy let their children back in the house, after JacobandSam shoved food into their mouths like underfed predators, after they washed up and told stories, they strolled down to the corner. Thursday nights in Greenwood buzzed.

Friday pressed on Grace's eyes before she was ready. Mama forced open the blind in Grace's room, loudly and with conviction. Mercy slept soundly in her bed, Grace knew, for another hour, until a small stroke on her shoulder and a whisper in her ear brought her to Friday. She told Grace about it once, how Miss Willie had this way. Sounded like perfection on a platter to Grace as her Mama rattled and banged around her room. The way Mercy described it, though, made it sound like horrifying torture.

She'd said, "You're so lucky." She said this often, and Grace responded in kind.

"You can be so dumb, for such a smart person," Mercy had said.

Mercy shoved her lightly, and Grace imagined the same way her mother might have shoved her, with just enough force to make her presence known, but not in any way menacing.

"Okay. Tell me again how lucky I am. I keep forgetting."

Mercy whined, "Your mother doesn't startle you awake. She doesn't get her face all up close to yours and make you breathe her breath to wake you."

"Again, how does this make me lucky?" Grace wondered.

"It's like she's getting her scent on me, like she thinks I'm a baby, and she won't let me grow up."

"You could look at it that way." Grace said, knowing it was easier to let Mercy navigate to these conclusions herself, to let her understand her ridiculousness in her own time.

"What other way is there to see it?" Mercy demanded.

Grace waited. They sat behind the garage, pulling weeds from a patch of red soil where the tomatoes grew. The act of pulling weeds pleased Grace. She liked the way the underground grasp of roots prizing loose from the reluctant earth made a slippery pop. Her fingers added a sort of hesitating percussion against the shiny stems, the dirt crumbled, then the weeds were free. Again and again.

"You probably think it's nice or something."

"Or something."

"Grace. You're not listening. She walks in there all quiet like a dream and whispers my name in my ear. She presses her hand on my arm and calls me up from the place where I want to stay."

"Uh huh. Sounds awful."

"Grace!"

"What? You're telling me you hate that your mother lets you sleep in, then wakes you gently because she loves you? You're saying that you resent waking up. Everyone wakes up. Most of us resent it. Every day. Some of us have to do it the hard way."

Now it was Mercy's turn to grasp the weeds. The first clump came loose with her fury, fast and loud. Watching her snapping at the grass, Grace knew Mercy simmered hurt and misunderstanding. Finally, her hands slowed and her breath followed suit.

When Mama hoisted the blinds, they rattled against the thin panes and the birdsong knocked about inside Grace's head, as if the absence of the blinds made all the difference in volume. Mama touched Grace's shoulder, too, and she whispered "wake up, honey," in her ear like a psalm. Morning sounded like fading music in the house. Daddy's feet padding across the wooden floors, Mama's skirt already fastened, trying to walk the dishes quietly in the kitchen. Their voices low. Seemed like they were always low talking. Kids know that means something.

That morning, it meant that Grace was supposed to do as told and get ready to walk with Mama to the Williams' house. She didn't expect to see Mercy. She had church meetings, and when Grace was done fixing up the rest of their pies, she had her own plans.

Mama pulled the door behind her. She and Grace were last to leave. They walked on soft feet toward the end of their street and joined with another cluster of women walking toward the trolley line. More low greetings in the rising day, most of them tired from the night before, remembering what they'd said and done, who they'd seen, not ready to release that coveted time. Jules bordered on angry because she'd only had enough time to wash her clothes, kiss her family and go back to the apartment above the garage of The House Next Door. Fridays for Jules were like other people's Mondays.

By the time they reached the Williams', Mr. Dub was already gone. The women pushed into the kitchen through the garden door and were greeted by the shrill rebellion of Mercy, from upstairs.

"Mother, I am not wearing that!"

Mama and Grace blinked at each other. "Best get working, Grace." In other words, "Butt out."

Grace hung her cardigan on the hook behind the door and wrapped an apron around her frame, adjusting it to fit her small body, doubling it over at the waist. She tied a ribbon around her hair and washed her hands. Mama asked her to start in the living room near the front of the house, as far away from the bickering women as possible.

Grace started dusting, picking up the brass bookends, the framed photos of Mercy from each grade of school. She opened the windows after a few minutes and let her mind follow the wind, the street a quiet hum of domestic work. Branches brushed against each other as she fell into a rhythm.

When she went to the kitchen for a bucket of water, Grace surprised Miss Willie, who had been casting her usual absent gaze out over the back lawn. As Grace pushed into the room, Miss Willie turned, her fingers clutched a mug of coffee.

"Excuse me, ma'am." Grace gestured toward the sink, and Miss Willie drifted away.

"Can't talk sense into that girl," she said, pulling Grace into that gap between them that she had no interest in bridging.

"Yes, ma'am." Grace filled the bucket with water, silence stretching beyond comfort while she grasped for something to say. She occupied more than one space between them. As Mercy's friend, her duty was to Mercy; Grace took her side, championed her cause, came to her defense even when she knew Mercy was wrong. Which was often enough, but, her mother was Grace's mother's employer, and therefore Grace's employer. Miss Willie and Mama had found it easy enough to settle into a routine, but Grace had yet to find that balance.

When they had first started working there, they didn't see much of Miss Willie at all. It was her practice to have a list, in order of priority, ready each morning. She wrote in precise capitals, with an unusual way of making A's so that they almost looked like triangles. Grace used to practice making A's like that until her teachers made her stop. Miss Willie came to the kitchen when Grace and Mama arrived, handed the list to Mama and asked after her family.

Mama: "Fine, fine. Everything's fine, Miss Willie. You all doing all right today?"

"Yes. Yes." So it went. When Miss Willie patted the hair at her temples, smoothing imaginarily out-of-sort strands, she announced that she had extinguished her supply of thoughts, that she needed to be somewhere, anywhere, else. "If you're all set for the day then . . .," and she was off to her paintings or her garden or wrangling Mercy in another part of the house.

Grace must have been about five when they started working for the Williamses because Daddy was teaching Grace her letters in the evenings. At work, Grace's job had been to read Mama the list; wash dishes, hang linens, polish crystal. She drew tiny boxes next to each line, checking them off as they worked.

In the beginning, Miss Willie had busied herself in other parts of the house. Grace strained her ears listening for footsteps, for any sound that they were not alone. To Grace, the house was gigantic. A dining room and a kitchen with two entirely separate eating areas, two distinct tables where they ate. A porch that wrapped three sides of the house and more than one bathroom, plus a cellar.

At lunch time every day Miss Willie appeared in the kitchen to gather lunch, check in on Mama, murmur of few words. If Mama needed to know where the dust pan was or to ask about washing rags, she asked then. Mama said Miss Willie's preference for cold lunch told her all she needed to know about her. Mama didn't mind being left alone to get about her business, either.

"We're gonna be just fine, working here, Gracie," Mama had said.

Later, when Grace picked through her fragmented memories for those soft remnants of her time with the Williams family, she liked to settle on Mama's declaration that Miss Willie was just all right. When she remembered how quickly Mercy roped around her heart, she decided this attachment had as much to do with Miss Willie as it had to do with that pesky Mercy. The whole world said that these two girls could not be friends, but there wasn't anything anyone could do about it. Maybe they never wanted to.

Grace held this thought close, believing their friendship immune to the illogical morals of others. For a long time, she had no reason to think otherwise.

"Grace?" Miss Willie called from her kitchen that Friday, looking for all the world like the need she had would extract a price from Grace.

"Yes, ma'am?" Grace hesitated; something in the tone, the way her eyes slid across the girl's face without looking at her, the step forward told Grace to be careful.

"I hate to ask this, honey." Grace cursed herself. In a three-second span, Grace imagined a slew of various horrible tasks Miss Willie might be fixing to assign. Miss Willie tucked a piece of brown hair behind her ear, ran a palm across her abdomen, smoothing the denim of her husband's slacks that she wore that day, belted tight against her small waist. Grace couldn't resist her. She had both the nerve to wear slacks, and the ability to wear them like she was born to wear them, and that was just for weeding the garden. A long scarf dangled from her head, cinched itself over her short bangs, and grazed her shoulder, so that she could flip it back, with a flick of a finger.

Again. "Yes, ma'am? Can I help you with something, ma'am?"

She laughed and pushed like a schoolgirl on Grace's arm. "Grace, you quit calling me 'ma'am!' I've told you that before, honey."

"Yes, ma'am. I know, but my parents . . ." Miss Willie knew all this."It's a habit." A kernel of confidence settled behind her voice. One part of Grace's mind panicked; this might have been the longest conversation they had ever had.

Miss Willie started to resist, waving her hands in the air, her gesture that encompassed everything. "OK," she sighed. Then, "Grace." Her body signaled surrender.

"Yes, ma'am." The bucket was full, steam rose toward their faces, filling the room with heat it did not need. "Was there something else?" Grace pointed her toes away from this woman, ready to run away regardless of the water that would have sloshed all over their house. While she dreamed of running, she stuck her feet to the floor and made herself meet Miss Willie's eyes.

Now it was her turn to hesitate. Grace stayed planted.

"I just wondered. Think you could talk to Mercy?"

"About what, ma'am?" Grace stepped backward.

Miss Willie fluttered and blew out a gust of air. "I need her dressed for the Ladies' Auxiliary. We're decorating the church today . . ," she trailed off. "The point is, I need her to wear what I have selected." Her voice shrank, like she was putting it into a jar, to save for later. "If I have to watch them eye her up and down again today . . ." She shook herself. "Would it kill that girl to wear the dress I chose?"

Grace listened, incredulous. She knew her child as well as Miss Willie did, and that meant Mercy had already decided what she was not wearing. Grace was wondering how Miss Willie had concluded that Grace had the negotiating skills to convince Mercy when she realized that Miss Willie had stopped talking. The kitchen was still around them, and they could hear Rachel knocking about in the dining room.

"What do you think, Grace? Can you help me out?"

Her first instinct rattled out when she shook her head, even while her mouth said, "Sure, ma'am." It was pointless to refuse. Miss Willie's hand clutched at Grace so fast that Grace didn't register its warmth and firmness until she was released. Miss Willie walked from the room while Grace felt the pressure of that small hand, its small pink fingers surprisingly heavy, as if settling into her bones.

"Miss Willie?" Grace called her back before the full thought arrived like a speeding train in her head. She prayed Miss Willie had not heard. Some prayers are answered with a resounding, "No."

Miss Willie turned, holding open the door, a dark space behind her. Her whole body was a question.

Grace looked down, wiped her hands on her apron, took a step toward her. "Are they . . .," Grace balked. "Are they talking mean about her still? Or again?"

Grace's voice was a strand of ribbon that had once been buoyed by a balloon but now dangled aimless from a high branch. She was well aware of how much the church ladies disapproved of Mercy running around with *the little negro girl*. Many of Mercy's other actions, Grace knew, were rooted in an explicit desire to spite. Grace prayed for the day when Mercy acknowledged that this only made her the subject of more chatter. Wearing mismatched socks, playing kickball in the alley with boys, letting her hair down like a swamp of curls in the summer. Mercy didn't care. Mercy did what she wanted.

Grace cared. Mercy's mama cared.

Miss Willie gazed at Grace long and soft. A space widened between them, a pool of understanding, and the girl saw, without recognizing what it was, how Mercy's mama had fallen so easily for Grace. A tiny tilt of Miss Willie's chin was enough. She turned to leave.

The words puffed out, unbidden. "I'm sorry, ma'am."

Without turning, Miss Willie raised that small white hand, a volume of words. There was no blame. Watching Mercy casually release convention provoked dueling impulses in Grace. Her boldness attracted while her disregard for the rules caused tension. It felt like doing that exact wrong thing on purpose, then waiting for discipline while trying to decide if it was worth the coming punishment.

Grace pushed open the bedroom door. Her prayer that Mercy would not hear the knock had been answered with another "No." As lightly as she knocked, Mercy had heard. "Get on in here," came her voice, annoyed.

She was sprawled on her bed, dressed in one of her dad's old button-downs and a pair of dungarees rolled up at the hem, exposing her skinny, pale ankles. Grace reflected that while her friend did receive many of their mother's fine features, she was also the sad recipient of her father's fish-belly white, bony legs. Mercy flipped the pages of the paper, carefree as you please. She threw her words over her shoulder and, in that moment looked just like her mama had down in the kitchen.

"I know what you're doing here, Grace. Tell you right now, it won't work."

"OK." Grace took a seat at the dressing table. She had cleaned this piece a week ago, dusted and polished, straightened the hairbrushes, the ribbons, the barrettes, the photos tucked into the crack between the mirror and the frame. She had removed the white lace cloth on which her small mirror stood and bleached it in the sun, ironed it to starched perfection and returned it to its place without Mercy ever knowing it was gone. Grace wondered if Mercy understood where all her clean things came from. Did she think they were simply always clean? Did she think there was some house magic that tidied up all of her personal effects at her convenience?

"I'm serious, Grace. I'm not wearing that."

"OK."

Mercy eyed Grace with suspicion. "You should see it. It's hideous."

"Show me." Grace wandered around the room and plopped onto the bed while Mercy rolled off, stomping to her closet. The paper the Williams' read might as well have been from New York City, as different as it was from the Tulsa paper Boyd and Rachel read. Different stores, different news, different everything. Grace marveled, ignoring her attitude.

In a huff, she shuffled some garments around, hauling a blindingly vibrant confection from her armoire. Her mother had chosen a confection. There was no other word for it. Lace at the modest hem, the skirt bloomed out like an inverted tulip. A shiny black ribbon circled the waist and drew the eye to the bodice, tailored but not curvy. A scalloped collar looped around the high neck. There was no mistake: this was what the girls would call her first Big Girl Dress, normally a happier occasion that Mercy presently allowed. Grace herself had never owned a dress so lovely, and she resisted the impulse to pet the swirls and bows. She wondered exactly what kind of decorating those First Church women were getting up to that required such fancy dressing.

Grace's mouth gaped open. "It's beautiful!"

Mercy tossed a strand of pearls at her in disgust.

"Are you looking at the same dress?" She demanded. "Do you see the color?"

The color. She was mad about the color. Bright pink, like an obscenely gorgeous rose, the one hogging all the sun and attention. Nothing in Mercy's history to that point indicated a desire to dress in this particular shade. Her mother knew it. Grace knew it. Both girls knew that was why Miss Willie had chosen it.

"See?" She demanded.

"I see." Grace conceded. She was hoping to sound neutral, but her statement rose in pitch at the end, more like a question.

She was on guard again. "You're on her side!" Mercy threw the dress on the bed, crossed her arms on her chest and assumed a warrior stance.

"That is not true, and you know it." Grace raised her eyebrows and lowered her chin. "Yes, she asked me to come up here, and you know I had to listen to her. She only asked me because we're friends. Be glad she at least knows that."

Grace turned toward the mirror and pulled a face at Mercy in the reflection. She returned the grimace.

"Some days I just can't stand that woman. I mean, pink, Grace!" The color was a cuss on her lips.

"Yes."

They were quiet. Mercy stalked around the room, fury in each step. Grace straightened the table, imagining the room was hers and that Mercy was there to clean. She pictured Mama presenting her with an elegant dress for a fancy party, where ladies sipped tea and ate small cakes that dissolved in their mouths, their delicacy a fantasy.

"You know, don't you," she tried again, "that she's doing my hair?"

Miss Willie wanting to curl her hair only meant one thing. These two were in for a long morning. Grace shook her head. "Sorry, Mercy. She wants you to look presentable."

She grumbled. "It's stupid. I don't care what I look like. I don't care what they think of me. It's stupid. And another thing," she filled her lungs with air and let loose again. "What a hypocrite! She wears whatever she wants. They lift their penciled eyebrows at *her*, but she whistles on by. It's a double standard. That's what it is."

She had a point. She had a few. Mercy didn't care about decorating the church or herself. She didn't care about princess seams and white gloves. She didn't care for other people's rules about her life. She also didn't see the look on her mama's face down in the kitchen. She didn't notice the sideways glances, the hands held to mouths as she walked by. She didn't hear the whispers.

She had no idea what her carelessness did to her mama. Or to Grace.

"She loves you," Grace said.

Grace sat at the mirror, wishing the right words would slide across her tongue, past her lips, some short and pleasant blessing to blunt the hurt. They didn't arrive. She sighed instead. "I gotta get back to work. Be good to her?"

"Fine." Mercy huffed and grabbed the dress as if it were no more than a dishrag.

"OK. See you later." Grace hovered near the door. "Want me to tell her, or you want to just come down when you're ready?"

She stuck her tongue out. "Be down in a minute. I'll find her."

As Grace pulled the door closed she heard it. "Thank you, Grace." Grace kept moving. Didn't hurt to let her think her words missed their target.

In the hallway, the air was cooler and certainly less riddled with feminine nonsense. For once, Grace was happy to chase dust and wipe tables.

Mama and Grace didn't mind working when Miss Willie and Mercy were at home. They were faster and had more fun when they weren't, unless Mama was in a generous mood and let Grace run off with Mercy, which was by far the best way to spend a day. Inside the

Williams house, with Miss Willie and Mercy revving each other up, their friendship could not be primary.

Back in the kitchen, Mama asked, "Got a preference? How about finishing the bathrooms and the laundry while I get started on dinner?"

Grace heard her singing from the kitchen, bursts of song with the percussion of pots and pans. She had her own way of doing things, and when Miss Willie wasn't banging around in the same room, Mama found it easy to choose her way over her employer's. The truth is Miss Willie never knew the difference. If she did, she never said anything.

The spring day tempted Grace outside to hang laundry, a job that was neither especially strenuous nor mentally exhausting. Tugging the wet load outside, she planned the rest of her Friday. She strategized. If she got this all sorted early, she'd have extra time to decorate the gym for prom.

To Mr. Dub arriving home for a late lunch or to Miss Willie staring out the kitchen window, it might have seemed that Grace stood in their yard, hanging their clothes, but her mind traveled north and then east, twisting right at the river, then around town and quick up to Greenwood. She was there, at school, laughing with her friends, her other friends. A smile yanked the corners of her mouth as she met Esther and Shelly, Martha and Agnes, and they blushed at the names of the boys they hoped would ask them to dance.

Suddenly, Jules' voice boomed through the neighborhood, recalling Grace's mind to a union with her body. No sooner had her attention diverted to Jules, than it was rerouted again to the noise coming from the kitchen. The Williams' kitchen. From the sound of it, Miss Willie was just tickled to see her daughter looking so fine. Mercy was resolutely unwilling to just let the woman have a moment.

Grace slipped into Mercy's pretty shoes. If Mr. Tucker was not exactly kind toward Daddy or even Mr. Dub, Mr. Tucker's daughter made Mercy's church experience more like the very bowels of hell itself. Eliza Tucker was not exceptionally beautiful nor was she particularly smart. Anything she knew about human interaction and leadership had been gleaned from the antisocial preening of her father, which put her at a distinct disadvantage. Then again, she'd been able to command a central role in the society of children at Mercy's school. Grace thought that just went to prove natural selection. The strong survive, and if they're mean enough, they prosper, besides. Mercy was both the perfect target and the worst. Eliza was the reason for all the primping in the house.

Grace had been working with Mama in the kitchen the day it started. Miss Willie had agreed to host some church meeting. A whole horde of women traipsed across the Williams' threshold, prim heels gliding as if something inside the shoe might break with too firm a plant. Skirts swished, clouds of perfume jangled together in the hall, overpowering the smell of the luncheon they had prepared. Grace was too small to do much, but later she remembered peeling cucumbers for those ridiculous sandwiches. Miss Willie had determined to get Mercy involved with church, or anything. Toward that end, Miss Willie asked Mercy what she could contribute.

"Anything," she had promised Mercy. "Anything you want to make."

For days, Mercy pored through the books. She pestered Mama. She poked through the cabinets and made lists of her favorite things. Finally, she hit on it. Mercy had decided to make the cinnamon pinwheels Mama had taught her to make from leftover pie dough. Mercy insisted she make them herself, her first real cooking job. She had asked Mama to tie an apron behind her, and she piled up her hair, roping it together with a scarf, just like Mama wore. She had watched Mama and Grace make them for years, so she knew all the steps. She waited patiently for the castoff bits Mama didn't need. She dusted the table with flour, dusted her hands with flour, then began to roll out the dough. Now, Mama'd been cooking since she was in the womb, so she could roll a crust into a perfect circle without trying. Mercy had rolled a crust that more closely resembled a perfectly shapeless mass, but Mama had reassured her and they continued.

She had melted the butter carefully on the stove, swirling the pan when it bubbled. She didn't have the intuition to know when to take the browning butter from the heat, so her butter had carried the faint smell of singed hair. Again, Mama reassured her, and Mercy had continued. Mercy poured the melted, scalded butter onto the dough, and then heaped a mixture of cinnamon and sugar in the very center of her blob. Mama nodded, and Mercy used the back of a spoon to spread the crystals, covering the surface of the dough. She knew the whole thing was supposed to roll up into a tightly formed cylinder before being sliced for baking. Her efforts resulted in a more organic form. Upon closing the oven door, Mercy promptly forgot about her baking project. Until she smelled them burning.

In the end, the pinwheels were misshapen, overcooked sweet treats. Mercy arranged a tray with them, angling the bites into fanned stacks. Then she used her scrawling, fanciest handwriting on a white tented card to highlight for their visitors that she had made her "extra special cinnamon pinwheels, with thanks to Miss Rachel."

The women came in pairs and quartets; Mr. Dub's tattered joke was that these females always, always travelled in packs, a fact that filled their men with a vague and unsettling fear. When Grace heard the doorbell ring, and the feet tramped into the front hall, she had to agree, and she appreciated his observational skill. Voices tumbled on top of each other like puppies as they entered, but after Mama had served the buffet, the women got serious.

Though Miss Willie was hosting, Mrs. Tucker appointed herself grand marshall and proceeded to corral the women under her order. Her voice rose and fell while the rest of them emitted the sounds of consent. All mutterings stopped at the sound of a crash and a subsequent cry. Footsteps, louder voices, the door to the kitchen forced open, Miss Willie appeared.

"What is it, ma'am?" Mama had asked.

"Nothing, Rachel. Mrs. Tucker's daughter spilled the candy dish. It shattered."

Mama moved toward the broom closet but Miss Willie reached it first. Mama wrapped her hands around the wooden handle and pulled it toward her. Miss Willie was defiant.

"It's fine, Rachel. I'll take care of it."

Mama dropped her chin, but raised her eyebrows, meeting Miss Willie's gaze. "Ma'am? May I suggest you allow me?"

"Don't be silly. It's your lunch. It's just a little glass. I'll get it." She was out the door and barreling back down the hallway. The smallest shake of her head did not escape Grace's gaze. The words poured over her shoulder and stuck to Mama like spilled honey. Shortly, it began. Mrs. Tucker suggested that Rachel should be doing this work. She had raised her voice loud enough to punctuate her point.

Before that mess was tidied, before Grace worked her way into a spot in the hallway that afforded a decent view of the sitting room, another crash ruptured the tenuous peace. This time, Mama walked down the hall.

Unable to stymie her curiosity any longer, Grace crept into the hall, just a few steps, and peered into the commotion. She saw something that instantly reminded her of a creature whose picture she had seen in one of the nature magazines Daddy brought home. Grace knew it was Eliza the minute Grace spied the child. She looked like a frill-necked lizard, this little girl, practically being swallowed by crinoline and pleats, hiding behind her mother's skirts, sneering at Mercy and her mother.

Mercy had been standing near the candy dish as well, as she relayed the events later to Grace. She was showing Eliza the stupid cucumber sandwiches they thought were so silly, but Eliza was too busy shoving lemon drops in her fat face to care. Mercy had touched her hand and Eliza had reacted loudly and suddenly. "Don't touch me! You play with that *girl*!"

"What girl?" Mercy demanded.

"That *colored* girl." Eliza wiped her hand on her skirt as if wiping sewage from her skin.

"So?" Mercy demanded again.

"You dress funny. Everyone makes fun of you. You're too busy playing with her to notice."

"You're too dumb to realize that I don't care." At which point, Mercy reached to touch Eliza again, prompting a loud shriek and a hand flying too close to the candy and the dish crashing to the floor. Eliza, seeing her mother distracted by the candy dish, and intent on leveling another blow at Mercy, had flipped over the tray upon which sat Mercy's crazy pinwheels.

When Grace peered around the corner, she witnessed Eliza grind her patent encased foot into what Mercy had made. When she saw Grace watching, she pointed a plump finger at her. An accusation.

As they left, Mrs. Tucker mumbled some halfhearted apology, something about Mercy being so clumsy, and Miss Willie made that smile she used to make that told anyone paying any kind of attention that she was decidedly not smiling on the inside.

The Tuckers had been a cross to bear for so long. Mercy hoisted most of it. Grace assumed Miss Willie remained ignorant of the devilish frilled child. Only later did she learn what all Miss Willie knew. Grace assumed Miss Willie was too friendly, too kind to measure the cost of their friendship. But Miss Willie knew. She knew every penny of pride they stole from Grace, from Mercy. From her. Miss Willie kept a full accounting of exactly what she paid. She didn't care so much about appearances as abiding and that woman tied all her love onto Mercy, a sack of hopes and heartache. If Miss Willie was going to have a kid, that kid was going to be herself, but she did care to abide in peace with her neighbors. She used to say, "Mercy, please. I'm just trying to stay in the still waters." She was asking Mercy to personify her name.

So the thundering in the kitchen about Mercy's hair was to be endured, and eventually, without Graces's intervention, Mercy succumbed to her mother's desire, just that once, to look "appropriate," just for Miss Willie. Mothers and daughters. If ever there were a more complicated relationship, Grace hadn't heard of it.

8

The girls met at the river on Friday night, too. Mercy arrived as herself, in rolled up pants, her daddy's old work shirt, hair tied with a piece of ribbon and not very well. Locks of caramel and sorghum spun about her head, nearly uncontained.

"Did you run all the way here?" Grace laughed, seeing her hair disheveled.

Mercy reached up and patted her head. "Oh, hush. It was a long day. Never been so glad to get out of my clothes. They must have put extra itch powder in that abomination."

Grace handed her a tin cup of lemonade. "So. Tell me all about it?"

She groaned. "That stupid Tucker was there. Well, two of them. The female ogres."

"Did you leave well enough alone?" Grace asked, a sense of lurid interest rising. Any story involving Mercy and Eliza was bound to be good.

Mercy took a long swig of lemonade, wiped her mouth with the back of her hand and burped.

"She started it." Then she laughed and regaled Grace. From the way Mercy told it, Eliza had been in training for that day. Eliza, under her father's careful tutelage and her mother's indistinct parenting, had learned the art of not getting caught. Mercy bit into her sandwich. "Dumb girl pulled at the hem of that stupid dress." Mercy chewed with her mouth open, bits of food flew from her lips. "I tried to ignore it. Really I did." She stopped to swallow, as if to punctuate her point. A smile simmered on Grace's face as she listened. "Finally, I swatted at her, and 'course, I was the one got caught. I had to bend and bow and genuflect. I did it. Just to get it over with." She ripped off another bite.

As she finished her tale, sucking bread crumbs off her thumb, she said, "Really, it was a little bit of everything. A smorgasbord, if you will. Everything from my dress, which, if we're being honest, was much prettier than hers, to my hair to how I taped the bunting to the church stairs."

She tipped her head back, emptying every drop into her waiting mouth.

"What'd you do?" Grace asked. "You're here," she gestured a hand around their little hovel, "so you must not be in trouble. How'd you manage to hold your tongue?"

"It was not easy, tell you that. I pretended she was a gnat that I didn't want to get stuck in my teeth, so I kept my mouth closed."

"She is a gnat," Grace mumbled and laughed, but she wanted to know something. "How do you stand it? How can you listen to her constant buzz and not want to wipe that perky smile right off her face?"

"Don't you think I want to? Course I want to. I wanna throw one a her mama's perfect pies in her perfect little face. But that," Mercy sucked a crumb from her pointer finger, "would be a waste of pie." She filled her fingers with a scoop of dirt and they both watched it stumble out of her hand, landing in soft plumes on the dry dirt. "I hate her, Grace. I hate her."

This was as strong a word as Mercy ever used. Grace nodded, seeing that Mercy's eyes were open in shock and relief. She continued. "I hate her so much and the stupid things she says. I hate what she says about you and your family and your . . . ." Grace did not interrupt her. She needed to find the word she wanted to use. "Neighbors." She finally found it, or one that was nearly as accurate.

Grace knew what she meant.

She meant, people like Grace. She meant, "Your kind." Which was to say, people from Grace's neighborhood, which was to say, black people. Who don't look like Mercy. Grace nodded again. It was all she had. Some mechanical assessment.

"Mercy, you can't fight that fight." Grace couldn't say, didn't say, but longed to say. At fifteen, Grace didn't possess the words to say what she felt or thought about this whole situation. *Call us negroes or niggers or coloreds,* she thought. Words are just letters all bunched together to try to make something complicated easy. Easy enough to put on paper. Easy to forget. Easy to distill. The letters don't make up the word, though, and they don't fill a heart. They don't make it easier for one person to serve while the other dunks cookies in tea.

Grace didn't expect Mercy to do anything other than defend herself, especially around Eliza Tucker and her adoring crowd.

"I don't care, Grace. She can say whatever she wants. Doesn't make it true."

It used to be easy. When they stuck their feet in the mud and crawled up the banks of the river. When their shorthand head nodding conversations were an inviolable contract. Grace sometimes looked for signs, waited for it to happen; waited for the whole piece to clatter to the ground, and for the world to grind its foot in the broken pinwheels. Later on, she wondered if it had to happen, if some cruel force was trying to do them a favor, keeping them from the increasing tension they couldn't erase with mud and lemonade.

The far bank of the river hid in shadows as the sun dipped lower. Grace tightened the cap on the lemonade while Mercy folded their napkins, locked their box and stowed everything for their next visit. As they pulled limbs and greens in front of the gash in the hill, they heard the unmistakable and surprising beat of a drum.

"Sounds like a parade," Grace whispered. Mercy's eyes glowed with curiosity. She turned toward the street and pulled Grace with her as she ran off in the direction of the sound.

Grace hauled Mercy back by her blouse to hide behind a massive oak. The drumbeat crashed louder outside the cave, and even louder where the girls stood. When they poked their heads around the tree, they expected anything but what they saw. Grace had heard Mama and Daddy murmuring about the newspaper articles. Groups of men formed loose groups of common hate and swept through towns. The reports said the men were interested in justice and clean communities. Boyd and Rachel knew what they meant by *clean* and anticipated a similar movement to arrive in the West. They hoped, though, that because the city was already divided, maybe Tulsa would escape this particular plague. Having an organized group was redundant in a city like theirs.

Twenty or so men, shirtsleeves rolled up, faces obscured by white hoods, trudged down the middle of the street. They pushed a single man along with them, like an abandoned boat on a stormy sea. His arms slanted awkwardly behind him. Grace and Mercy shared a realization: He wasn't simply holding them there, as if he merely enjoyed the position. They were bound. Two large men flanked his sides, alternately shoving him along while the bound man stumbled and struggled to remain on his feet. As men approached Grace and Mercy's hiding spot, the girls shrank down, becoming as small as they could, looking for shadows to hide their bright summer skin.

His face. Grace knew him. Mercy covered her face with both hands and shook her head. "No."

The word was so small in the copse of trees, such a powerless noise from a powerless person. The darkness, the leaves heavy with spring, the gruesomeness of their imaginations swallowed her word before it traveled to any other ears. The men could not have heard over the noise they made, but the girls cowered nevertheless. Mr. Baker, the shopkeeper from the end of Mercy's street, lurched with every shove from the men. Dried blood smeared his cheek, and his nose jutted sideways at a sickening angle. The worst, for him, had just begun.

Before the group of men had passed, Mercy clutched Grace's hands, squeezing to staunch her fear, to stop the images that threw themselves uninvited against her mind. When the group was nearly beyond their hiding spot, Grace became aware of the pain in her hand and patted Mercy to release her grasp. Grace wrapped an arm around her and pulled her close, and together they crouched low in the woods. After catching their breath, and straining their ears for the all clear, they crept out. They jumped back and froze.

A pair of men had left the group, were hanging back. A streetlight cast a wide net of light that reached too close to where the girls cowered. Grace silenced Mercy with a finger on her lips; they stuck to the forest ground just as they had fallen. The girls were a tangle of limbs and worry, watching the men approach.

They were shocked enough when they recognized Mr. Baker. One of the stragglers slowly approaching the hiding spot lifted his sheet back, bent over and vomited so close to the girls that they heard his spittle landing on fallen leaves, could smell the mess of his sickness. Then they felt their own. It was Mr. Dub.

Grace's mind pooled with a slurry of images and feelings. She didn't know which thing she felt was right, or which thought she could latch onto as an anchor. His face swam in front of her, and she tried to figure out how she could possibly be seeing Mr. Dub in a white hood, with another man who surely had only seen the beginning of his beating. The questions flew so fast she could not capture one. By the look on her face, Mercy had the same problem: her daddy. With them.

Grace experienced her first blast of regret. She learned that she could not reel in the words she had thoughtlessly blurted. She discovered that bruises fade, but the slicing ache of brutality never dulled in a memory. Grace rewound and replayed the scene for years, each time ending the scene a thousand different ways. In her revisions she was impossibly kind; she granted herself an aplomb she could not have summoned then, in the dirt by the river. She edited her words, pretending that she did not drop Mercy's hand like a glowing hot poker, or slap Mercy's face. But Grace could not imagine hard enough to create a new and different, a better ending. She could not re-imagine that instead of pushing Mercy down, Grace picked her up. She wanted to. She wanted to do all of those things. Truth to tell, Grace also wanted to do what she did. In her surprise. In her fury. In the face of this knock-her-off-her-feet revelation, Grace relished the give in Mercy's tender skin as it collided with Grace's palm. It felt good to know the weight of her body as Grace placed her hands against Mercy's shoulders and sent her flying. At home, in her bed, Grace flushed with shame at how thrillingly true it had felt to make her best friend hurt.

The small measure of satisfaction that the physical pain provided was not a strong enough balm to still the drops of acid that filled Grace's belly. Hurting Mercy did not end Grace's shock or change what they had seen. It did not stop the tears, the shame, the panic or the frustration. It did not stop anything. It did not change the world. It did nothing. Hitting Mercy was like putting a burned finger in ice water; the throbbing only returned, coupled with the sting of cold.

Grace left Mercy on a blanket of yellowed pine needles near their small patch of solitude. She stomped off leaving Mercy to walk home alone; Grace fumed as she ran, then walked, through alleys and side streets, trying to get home unseen. The menace, the creeping hate they expected had snuck into town while they were looking the other way and knocked on the backdoor. Getting home alone in the dark had never been something that fretted Grace. She used her brain and a generous helping of caution. She avoided certain places, but mostly because she had a circuit of short cuts seared into her mind. That night, her fear startled her. Her heart raced though her pace slowed. Her mind skimmed faster still. Every hoot and whistle and clang she heard skipped over her in surprise. The worst part was that she didn't have her best friend by her side.

Tucker

9

Son of a bitch, that boy put up a bigger fight than necessary. Tucker could not understand the ones who didn't just lie down and take it. Made his job harder, too. Swinging the truck into the drive, his arms throbbed with effort, but he was satisfied to see his lawn and home illuminated by the swath cut by his headlights. The light in Eliza's room on the top floor flicked off. His fist was seizing up, but the gashes on his knuckles marked him rightly. That one learned a lesson he won't be forgetting soon.

There was a kind of height the boys got when Tucker imparted his cruel lessons, like a thirst that ached. Tucker didn't want them messing with their women, so he warned them before they split up for the night. Told them to go down to the twenty-cent houses in town rather than rough up the wives. He don't want to hear about their visit there, and if he ever seen any of them there, they had these rules: no eye contact and never any mention of it in church or whatnot. Some of them were shifty with the eyes, and Tucker found drilling a hole in their skulls with his eyes served to remind them. Usually took just the one time.

Tucker's wisdom came with the force of his fists. Way he saw it, he was doing a community service, teaching and leading young men. If he'd run his business by letting other people tell him what to do and when, well, he would still be a delivery boy. He muttered as he approached his grand home, *look at me now, standing on this patch of grass my wife would call a "lawn,"* stretching her mouth wide, like she was letting the word wash up around her teeth. Up to the boss to show the way; Tucker was the boss, so he showed the way. He believed there was, like the Bible said, a time and a place for everything. The time to smack your wife sure wasn't after taking a man down a few rungs. Bedroom stuff, in Tucker's philosophy, was a blurry line; do what you want, but he best not see any bruises on Sunday morning. The fellows could get a little out of hand after a party like that, so that's why he sent them to town.

The kitchen was dark but the missus had left a glass of milk and three cookies on a platter on the table. He slept better when he got his milk; the cookies were a womanly touch. Tucker made a show of wiping his mouth on the cloth napkin, leaving a trail of someone else's blood on the linen before setting it aside just so she'd know he'd touched the thing. He made sure to drop enough crumbs to give her something to do in the morning. She likes to be useful.

Tucker headed for the laundry, expecting her. She liked to see him hang up the strop and the whip in the closet back there.

"Did you get him, Daddy?" Bare feet, white gown, long hair. What a beauty. He ruffled Eliza's head and kissed her forehead.

"Yeah, baby. We got him." Tucker held the strop out.

Eliza ran her fingers over the soft leather, her face open and willing. "It's not hot anymore." Disappointed.

"Shit, honey, I can't bring it home hot all the time. Sometimes it takes a while to shoo off the boys."

Head bent, she sighed. "I know. Wish I could go."

She had him asked so often that it was their song. She said *I wish* and he said *no way in hell*. Every time.

"I wish you was a boy." To look in her glassy eyes, Tucker just knew she'd be precise and deadly with any weapon in hand. She'd make those idiots he was attempting to lead look even dumber.

"I don't have to be a boy; I can handle that strop. Edmund down the street just got his first whip. Showed me after school."

Tucker laughed and moved away. She followed, jawing the whole time.

"Eliza, hush your mouth. You'll wake your mama. She hates that talk."

"Eliza, the whip is easy to use, and I know you'd be better than any boy at lashing at one of them niggers. Still. I can't have a daughter of mine given to that."

More of the same argument from her. She held forth: I can run the business when I'm grown. I don't need to marry for that. Daddy, these boys are stupid and ugly and I don't want you giving your hard work to them. Think about it, Daddy. Teach me.

Same stuff as always. That girl. "Get to bed, Eliza."

She didn't know how it pained her father. He'd thought about it nearly every day since she was born. His recovery, after seeing his expected son was a daughter, was slow as the Arkansas in summer. When it rolled, he was surprised by his fierce drive to protect his family. He was as proud of her slinging his old whips in the backyard as if she was a boy who could throw a ball.

She was on the stairs, her feet like statue's, white and solid, when she turned. "Love you, Daddy."

His heart, that girl. "Get."

She winked ran to bed.

Tucker found his worn seat in the study overlooking the lawn. A bottle of hooch waited behind the ledgers on the shelf. A long pull righted him. Nothing like the burn of rotgut holy water to freshen a man. Mrs. Tucker'd done fine by leaving the cookies, but they didn't satisfy. Tucker reflected on the men they'd visited; the way the shorter one yelped out had reminded him of a guy they ran off four summers ago. One of his most beloved memories.

Agitators, more than a dozen of them, had come to town to protest Tucker's business and all them others. Sonsabitches messed with his bottom line. He could not tolerate it. Called themselves the IWW, but Tucker called them fucking wobblies. A smile cracked a gash in his face as he recalled that day. It was as delightful as seeing Eliza flicking a cat o' nine tails or throwing her first kidney punch. Sheriff told Tucker he'd stand down, told the boys to do their business on the other side of the river, that he'd keep the trail clear.

Always good to have friends in the right places, with the right kind of values. Tucker's boys had rounded up the lot of them, kicking them all the way across the Arkansas, taking their sweet time enjoying the learning. Tucker licked his lips and swallowed another throatful of liquor, feeling the hazy glow of memory and drink. Like a gauzy numbness. Tucker sometimes wished he could feel like that all the time, suspended between stark boring sober and falling down drunk. She got to, the missus, with her potions, she spent most of every day in a dumb stupor. She didn't have work to do, and she claimed it hurt.

Four years ago, Tucker had sent a group of fellas over to get the tar cooking. The consistency had to be just right, so it stuck to skin like a rubber suit. Maximum coverage, maximum pain. A fire roared around a steel drum, and the boys turned its contents with a long paddle. Summer nights were hot; those boys earned their booze and whores manning the fire.

Probably fifty of Tucker's compatriots rode in whooping; this was back in the early days when membership meant showing up, when organization meant everyone brought his own weapon. They shoved the wobblies off the flatbed with the butts of their rifles, with the steel toes of their boots, with fists. The wobblies landed in mud, bushes, sprawled in the sharp grass. Tucker's men arranged them in a circle and stripped off their shirts.

The howls. The yelling. It made Tucker weak and high and excited. It stirred up a furious burning inside him that might concern a weaker man. Those fellas had been whipped pretty good by the time the tarring started. Tucker dipped the paddle deep into the drum, gave it a good turn, pulling the hottest stuff up from the bottom. He dragged the heavy heat onto the paddle and carried it to the nearest wobbly. He whimpered and ducked his head, oh how perfect, Tucker had smiled over him.

"You think you're big time, coming here and riling people up?" Tucker kicked him, but not hard. He wanted the agitator on his knees and bowing to Tucker when he dripped the tar onto his back. That bastard had looked at Tucker, he looked right in his face. And he spit. Spit at Tucker.

Another pull from the hidden bottle and the face of the kid rose before Tucker, seated casually in his home. He was young, maybe twenty. Blonde hair, nearly white eyebrows, and this face, a sweet little baby. If he had been Tucker's son, he'd have known better; he'd have been out there with the boys, instead of having the shit kicked out of him. Tar flooded onto his back, the thick hot blackness covered his shoulders, and he bit his lip, closed him mouth, kept his eyes right on Tucker, drilling.

In Tucker's house, on his *estate*, four years later, something filled him, something he didn't like. Thinking about it, about him, that boy, that stupid boy, used to calm Tucker. Mulling over his steel-edged justice used to be like the drink; but now it never seemed like enough. Tucker lacked the ability to see the boy's face anymore; the carved jaw, the angled cheek bones, a cowlick dipping over his forehead. It angered Tucker that he had to work so hard to recall this face. Used to be, thinking back to that kid's defiance brought the bubble of anger to his heart that cycled up into determination and action. But now the boy's face had softened, flattened, and Tucker could no longer see the blue of his eyes in his blood smeared face. When Tucker did manage a sight at the edges of a solid image, the face turned to laughter. If Tucker tried to force it, if Tucker could produce the ghost of him in agony bowed before him, the boy directed joy back at Tucker. Joy. Like they were on some damned picnic.

Tucker pulled on the bottle but only drops trickled onto his tongue. The window overlooking his lawn swam and his ears rang. He heard her turn upstairs, Mrs. Tucker, rolling under her fine linen sheets in her stupor. Maybe not.

What difference did it make? Whether she knew and wanted it. Tucker wanted it. He hoisted himself upstairs and washed in the bathroom. See that? A bathroom, with running water and a flushing commode. They said he'd never get anywhere, no one believed he'd rise far out here, or anywhere. Tucker showed them.

A lamp in the corner lit her curves turned away from him. He loosened his belt, dropped his trousers on the floor for the negro to pick up in the morning, threw back the sheet.

"Mrs. Tucker, I'm home."

She rolled toward him, her eyes unfocused and a soft, drugged smile played on her thin little lips. "Not good, honey." She rolled away from him, thinking she could dismiss him easily.

Tucker forced her onto her back and exposed her hips, pushing her gown out of his way. She opened her eyes and stared. She didn't say no. She didn't put up a fight. She lay there and took it. He rocked into her hard and miserable. Her head tipped upward, exposing her long white neck. She tried once to cover herself, to roll the cotton past her thighs. Tucker threw her open harder, rocked. Her face locked on his, and he absolved himself. She wouldn't remember in the morning. That's what she was for anyway. She moaned, and he knew it was not pleasure. He slapped her and a tear settled in the deep well of her eye socket, glinting on her shadowed face. She tried to tell him to stop, but her words slipped and slurred, incoherent. She lay still and soft and dead, like a fish on the shore. Tucker curled his lip when he grew cold and dead inside her. When he rolled off she heaved a sigh, touched his back. He slapped her away.

"Feel better now?" She whispered.

"Shut up."

In the morning, the birds sang like blessed angels, the house hummed to life at his say so. Sheets tangled around his naked legs, and when he sat to unwind the mess, Tucker was confronted with his sins and his humanity. Spots of mud flecked his ankles. Funny how a man can wake up like a blank page and in moments his mind is off on wild hunts. The mud called to mind the night before. He licked a thumb and wiped away the mess, seeing maybe for the first time the legs of an old man. Red vines trickled up around his soft ankles. His knees resembled bruised melons, swollen and somewhat repellent in ripeness. Tucker didn't feel old but his legs told a different story. One he'd like to hide.

In the kitchen, the girl put a plate in front of him, poured coffee. Mrs. Tucker lounged back in her chair, legs open wider than appropriate, her head lolling on her neck like a dead woman.

"Pick yourself up, woman."

She rolled her head to look at her husband. Reached out an arm. "Morning, sunshine," she slurred.

Tucker pushed her arm away, told her to eat.

Eliza came in then and judged her mother with a look Tucker had taught her. Her eyes were dark and lidded; her expression wished away the presence of her mother. Still, she was taught proper so she put a hand on Mrs. Tucker's shoulder and said, "Morning."

Tucker smacked a hand on the table, pointed to his mug and the girl poured more. Eliza sat next to her daddy and smiled.

"Hey, guess who was with us last night?"

"Who?" Her eyes sparked.

"That girl you go to school with, what's her name? The weird one?"

"There's lots of weird ones, Daddy."

"Oh, you know, the one always hanging out with that colored girl."

Her mouth fell open.

"Shut your mouth," Tucker grunted.

Her smile was wicked. "How'd he do?"

"Lost his lunch at the end, but he'll be all right."

She laughed, slapped her leg.

"Be kind, Eliza. Some men aren't born strong. They have to get there."

She chewed her food like a doll, barely moving her lips. How could something so delicate also be so savage? She stood, twirled a circle in the kitchen, perfect like a dancer, spinning out the layers of all that nonsense under her skirt. She smelled like life, bright and alive and ready. Tucker envied her. He was proud of her.

"Have a good day at school, kiddo."

She popped out the door, throwing a kiss over her shoulder. The door slammed behind her.

Saturday

Grace

"Free Interred Negroes: Red Cross is in Charge"
Tulsa Tribune, June 3, 1921

10

The night before, when Grace pushed open the door, Daddy sat at the table in the kitchen, just his still silhouette, head bowed over a mug. His hands curled around the cup, tiny hairs on his neck and arms like sentries. He did not lift his chin towards her when she pressed the door into place quietly, listening without breathing for the click of closure.

She tiptoed toward the table, toward him, unsure of her voice even as the questions boiled inside. He didn't move when she pulled out a chair, sat down and leaned forward mirroring his posture. She sat there with him, on fire inside from what she had seen.

The house chirped its nighttime song. Creaking boards, the slang of wind on windows, the groan of bed springs, the jabber of the boys asleep and dreaming. Listening to the house helped Grace slow her breathing. After the scene on the river, after her maneuvers home, her heart throbbed in her arteries like a maze of wounds. The relaxed, comfortable rhythm of this place stilled her. Home, they say, is where you can be yourself. Home is where your heart is, they say. Home, Grace believed, is where a girl can bring her dirt to be swept up and put away by hands that care. Under the moans of the house, beneath the slap of limbs on the roof, Grace distinguished the rhythm of her father's breath. He inhaled, exhaled, repeated. A slow cadence of comfort.

It must have been ten minutes or more they sat like that, neither acknowledging the other but aware nonetheless. Finally, he reached out his hand, touched hers, a graze of his long, rough index finger on the inside of her wrist.

"You okay, Grace?" Her parents could read her so plainly, as if she was a language they invented themselves. Grace was only beginning to understand the secrets parents hide. Mama and Daddy read and translated their daughter easily. Mama said it was a matter of paying attention; you just had to know how to look.

Grace let his question work into her, and she practiced different possible answers, the silence ebbing. Daddy didn't rush her. He took a swig from his mug, returned it to the planks on the table and wiggled it into place inside the circled stain of previous drinks. Waited. Grace struggled to order her thoughts. Her head felt like a catalog of a system Grace couldn't decipher. She searched for the thing to say that would condense it, release it, destroy it. Nothing. He tilted his head, once, reluctantly, when she shook off a sentence that had formed, one she refused to say. Shaking her head erased it. He watched her for a minute, then returned again to gazing at his mug, breathing in and out.

She managed a question of her own. "Daddy?"

His head pivoted up and forward, his eyes hovered on her face, the Spirit over water. His gaze was soft and serious at once.

"What if you found out someone wasn't who you thought they were?"

He nodded. Her question wasn't the one she meant to ask.

"Daddy?" She tried again. "Is Mr. Dub ever . . . Does he ever . . . Daddy, are you sure you know him? Are you afraid of him?"

His eyes asked several questions of his own. Grace read them there and ignored them because he ignored them.

"I want you to hear me, Grace," he said with the low rumble of his voice, the deliberate tenor he used made his words heavy. "I trust Mr. Dub." The four words hung in the air between them, a sacrifice, a blemished offering. He continued.

"What you think you know might not be true." He stood then and walked to her. His hand on her shoulder unlocked the doors of her tension, and while she did not truly understand what he meant, she wanted to believe him. "I love you, Grace."

"Love you, too, Daddy."

"Get to bed."

"Yes, Daddy."

The pressure of his touch, which in the kitchen had felt like comfort, dissipated in the room Grace shared with the boys. They grunted and pushed each other, even in their sleep. Feet sprawled. What had been the sweet sounds of slumber from in the kitchen were loud gongs in the same room. Each noise, each turning limb twisted Grace back to the river. She joined them in the shuffle and prayed for sleep.

Her body tingled with physical reminders. The way Mercy's malleable skin gave way to Grace's palm, the way the tender leaves turned angry against her sweaty bare legs when they fell. The smell of his sickness rose around her. The angry thump of a drum punctuating cries from the mob stole silence from the room. It was a nightmare she was awake to witness. In her room, the window was open, and a heavy breeze tugged at the cotton curtain. The wind carried phantom sounds with it, confining Grace in aggression.

She awoke in a cool, summer morning bliss that crashed around her when she opened her eyes. That one sweet moment that spanned the place between sleep and awake fled before she was alert enough to resist. A blink was all it took for her to remember. Daylight did not erase anything. Grace had seen her best friend's father wearing a hood. Her friend, reeling in her own palpable way, went sprawling under Grace's force, and Grace had left her in the woods to find her own sniveling way back home. In Grace's room, in her bed, the rewinding scene in her mind portrayed an anger she didn't understand. Her father's midnight words clashed up against her anger like a single dull sword of defense.

"Don't think you know," he had said.

Anger is the strangest thing. Anger is visiting a horrifying fun house, without the fun. It is like wearing glasses in the wrong prescription or walking through life upside down. It is an ugly mask, a veneer of venom that covers the open sore of hurt, disappointment, betrayal or misunderstanding. Anger is alive and destructive like no war that ever was.

When it pounced on her that morning, fresh and unsuspecting out of that sleep she didn't know how she found, she was weak meat. Grace surrendered without a whimper. She lay in bed, letting it have its way with her. She gave herself over to the ferocity that thrummed in her veins. She stewed and steeped in the heat until she had trained herself not to wince. She said goodbye to Mercy.

The day would not wait. She forced herself out of bed, not sure how to have a day that didn't include Mercy, equally sure that seeing her again was about as high on her list of things to do as taking tea with Eliza Tucker. The burn started low in her gut, a hot pile of embers. Each moment awake fanned the spark. In the hours since she had last seen Mercy, this other half of herself, Mercy's alive and explainable presence became a jagged silhouette, scribbled over with images of what they had witnessed the night before. Over night, while Grace slept, Mercy was amputated from her, excised from her awareness. In her place, Grace felt the handprint of loss, a thundering cleaver slicing them apart in a way their skin color had never been able to do.

Mama was in the kitchen, dressed for work. Daddy stood at the door, between two places, his face ready to shift from his home face to his work face. His work face looked like someone pulled a shade down on him, or applied an invisible layer of concrete over him. He didn't knit his brow with concern or smile easily with pleasure. At work, he was flat, a blank piece of paper. At home, he was a pliable ball of emotional dough. He watched Grace making the same transition as she stepped from her quiet room to the community space of the kitchen.

"How you doing today, girl?" He offered a raft; she could use it or ignore it and tread.

She pulled a face and grunted, shuffled forward. Mama took in her daughter's clouded face, didn't see what she wanted, so she pivoted toward Daddy. She wanted the script; she wanted to know what story those two were telling without her. He ignored her gesture and winked at Grace.

"Love you, ladies. See you tonight." He was gone.

Now it was Mama's turn to take up the monologue. Mama's way of gleaning information involved more, much more, talking than Daddy's. His contented nod and gaze injected questions into the air. Mama fished for Grace's every thought. She started almost right away.

"Daddy says you got in late last night," her statement was the long flash of a fly rod cast over a teeming school of fish.

"Yep." Grace had no plan to nibble on her lure.

"Do anything fun?" Mama cast again.

"Not really. Just hung out."

She nodded, pretended like she didn't care, that her inquisition had ceased due to lack of interest on her part. Grace rolled her eyes when she turned her back to make toast for the boys who had slumped into the room, wiping sleep from their eyes.

Grace chewed her toast without tasting it. Drank her milk only to assist in swallowing the crumbs. Dust on her tongue, no words to wash it away. The boys chewed like they'd never experienced the delicacy of toast before; smacking lips, loud gulps, groans of intense pleasure. Grace's temper flashed; It was toast, for Pete's sake. The sound echoed through the kitchen and she flung back from the table.

"Will you two just shut up!" she hollered at them, their eyes full of curiosity, their full mouths gaping like the barn door Mama's always going on about. Mama swooped toward Grace and the boys ready to intervene. She saw the glint of a smile on Jacob's face, which did nothing to allay her anger.

"What are you smiling about?" Grace demanded. "Huh? You two chew like animals. It's disgusting."

The boys exploded in laughter and Mama moved between Grace and the boys, shooting them the Church Look. They ignored her. Of course. Grace recognized that kind of laughter with another stab. She had once shared laughter like that with Mercy. One of their mamas would tell them to hush, but the girls, so overwhelmed by their humor, could only laugh with more abandon in the face of reprimand. The more they tried to stop, the more tears ran down their cheeks, their stomachs clenched with spasms of laughter. Then? That day? The boys well-knit camaraderie only expanded her anger. She was a shored up dam, and each of their peals broke loose another gap; she was a sieve threatening a flood.

Grace ran from the room before Mama could see the tears that burned her face, before she gave the boys something else to laugh about.

She got the day off. Mama had planned to use Grace for weekly silver polishing. When she pushed open the door of their room, having sent the boys out to play, she slid over the boards to Grace's bed. The tears had stopped until Grace felt the pressure of Mama's hand on her shoulder blade. Until she heard her soft cooing words, coaxing information or pleading to comfort, Grace had only lain still, concentrating on feeling the breeze, the buzz of a fly as it smacked ignorantly and repeatedly against her window. A small distraction, a constant drone that Grace focused on. Anything to distract her from Mr. Dub in a gang.

"Gracie, what is it? What happened?"

"I don't want to talk about it."

"You want to hang around here today, minding the boys?"

Grace nodded into her pillowcase, relieved.

"Okay," she said. Her palm rounded over her daughter's scalp, each finger a texture, a meaning, a sentence she thought but wouldn't say, didn't need to say. Grace gleaned all the right words from her mother's solid, firm application of a hand to a head. Her hand told Grace what she needed to know: Rachel loved Grace, she didn't understand but wouldn't push, she wanted her to smile, and she knew Grace would in time.

"Why don't you rest a little? I'll let you know when I'm leaving."

"Mm hmm." The pressure of her hand took some of the weight with her, and her feet retraced their prints to the door. Her fingers pulled the knob into the jamb with a click.

Grace cried.

11

Those kind of tears wear a girl out. She cried tears that threw themselves out of her body and hurt the space between ribs and skin. Those are the tears that turn a person to the inside, raw. She felt as if her belly had been hollowed out and dried like a gourd, good for nothing.

Grace woke sweaty and confused, but the painful emptiness that had lulled her to sleep had become a bland emptiness that she could only try to fill. Mama had not notified Grace when she left, and judging from the height of the sun, she'd been gone for some time. Grace listened, searching for the sound of the boys playing or squabbling anywhere within range. Nothing. The neighborhood hummed its daytime story; comings and goings announced by the distant crash of doors, faraway voices of people hanging laundry, catching up, working in their yards. No children's sounds. The absence of yelling was the only impetus Grace had to crawl out of bed. She worried about SamandJacob. Those two could dash off and find trouble faster than Grace could dust a room. It was the one thing she had been tasked with, and she felt her failure.

A piece of paper fluttered on the kitchen counter, underneath a grey rock from the street. Mama's rigid handwriting scrawled across the page, each letter a controlled line, meeting precisely as though the blank paper had been ruled with invisible ink. "Boys are with Mr. Jenkins. He's got them hauling trash. Let them be. Go decorate school if you want. Home by 9." Then, as if she'd been unsatisfied with her note, an imperfect, hastily drawn "xo" danced across the lower corner of the page.

School. Grace didn't want to go to school. She didn't want to leave the house. Neither did she want to be hanging around when Mama got home filled with questions or news she might have culled from her work day inside Mercy's house. In the bathroom, Grace held her wrists under the cold tap. She patted her neck and forehead and fixed her hair. She dressed carefully in a pressed black skirt and fitted button-down; Grace appreciated the crisp look of a white shirt tailored for a woman. She admired her figure, curved and trim, in the blouse. She replaced her usual birthstone earrings with the tiny faux pearls Mama and Daddy had given her on her thirteenth birthday. A spritz of rose water on her neck and knees cooled her skin if not her nerves.

Grace mused that two days ago, she had been excited about decorating. Before school was truly out for the summer, they had to send off the seniors. When she dreamed about graduation during the last few weeks of school, she imagined a bright Saturday like this one, skipping to the building with the rest of her friends, giggling and carrying on about who knows what. Never once in her daydreams did she walk alone and in such a funk that she barely registered the passing cars. She walked not with the light steps of freedom but with the clomping tread of a dry anger. When she thought she had reached the crest, another wave crashed on her. That this was supposed to have been a fun day and was now ruined was one more dancing injustice.

When the high school came into view, Grace was almost running in her fury, and she clenched her hands like a punishment. Seeing the school, she caught herself. She didn't want to walk in there all shades of mad. She controlled her gait and opened her hands, spreading her palms wide to the wind. She forced herself to feel the coolness of air against slick skin. It felt like prayer to roll back her shoulders and fill her nostrils with spring. Grace learned that trick from Mama, too. When things got to be too much, Mama closed her eyes and fell inside herself, into her chest and her veins and into the beating of her heart so that she could breathe. When Grace was little, and sick or mad at the boys, Mama touched her shoulders in just the right way. The touch, like a bird lighting on a branch, pulled her back from the brink of hysteria, the small weight of her pressed in towards the heart, then relaxed. Maybe not all the way. Maybe she still had some raging to do, but the touch signaled something to her. Mama's breath told Grace it was okay to let go. Grace pointed her fingers straight down, let her arms dangle at her sides and let gravity bend her shoulders, so that she could take one mighty gasp and enter the building.

Booker T. Washington High School was filled with people. Prom and graduation brought the kids to the edge of anticipation. Esther spotted Grace walking in, though Grace clung to the wall in the hopes of finding a solitary job.

"Grace." No chance. "Gracie!" Esther called across the cafeteria and people parted like the Red Sea to make a path between the two, their eyes surveying the scene, hoping for the next interesting topic of the day. When they discovered it was just two underclassmen, no one remarkable, the voices spilled again, lifting their excitement of the big events to newer heights. Esther broke through them all and found Grace.

"I can't believe you're here!" She shrieked. "Your mama let you off?"

Grace forced it. "Yeah! I'm as surprised as you are. She never lets me off."

"How'd you swing *that*?" Esther bumped her hip playfully into Grace's.

"Not sure really." Grace shrugged. "She just told me I could come."

"Well, I don't care how you managed it," she eyed Grace, not believing the story, which was made more unbelievable by the tear-swollen eyes and unconvincing smile. "I'm just glad you're here."

She dragged her off and put her to work with the rest of their familiar group, making tissue paper flowers. Esther pushed a fat pencil into Grace's hand and set a wad of blue tissue squares on the table. Grace wrapped each piece around the flat end of the pencil, then dunked the end into a plate covered with paste. Finally, she attached the gummed up flower to a wedge of cardboard in the shape of a B.

They wrapped and dunked and plunked until their fingers had taken on the color of the tissue, working toward spelling out Booker T. Washington. The letters were large, almost as tall as a person, so that the finished words could be seen from every angle when the principal called the names of the graduating class.

Though she had come reluctantly, and though she added little to the conversation, the repetitive, thoughtless motion calmed Grace. Chatter flooded her ears and drowned out anything unrelated to that moment, that room, that school, its students. No one demanded anything from Grace. No one needed to hear her voice. She was content to sit and dunk scraps into glue.

Simple chores are done simply. Mindlessly. If you want them to stay mindless, you have to really work at it. You have to stay focused to stay empty. Grace didn't stay focused. Something about the plucking of the tissue, the sound of paper against wood, the sense of finishing a job well done reminded her of her mother and how she spent her days. Thinking of her inside the cavern of the Williams's house, pent up with them all day, Grace felt guilty. She was suddenly aware that she was making flowers instead of polishing silver. Polishing silver was one of the first jobs her mama had taught her.

The first time she had polished silver, years before, rain had been bouncing against the windows, and another grey day kept Grace and Mercy inside. Mercy had helped Grace hang the laundry in the cellar, accepting that the laundry was unlikely to dry in the dank space under the house. They had begun preparing lunch and dinner. Changed all the beds. Dusted the floorboards. All their normal chores were done, and they were getting squirrelly. Mercy kept up a steady brook of questions as she followed Grace from room to room. Her babble was as light as a stream and as unpredictable. She was going on about the color of grass when Mama, tired of her voice, lit up.

"Hey. You girls want to do something fun?" Now, the way she said "fun" made them suspicious. Mama was not the kind to strike upon impromptu games as a way to shirk the job. Fun, the girls reasoned, must have had a different meaning. She sensed their reluctance. "Come on. This used to be my favorite job when I was your age." She walked off and they followed, Mercy practically levitating with eagerness.

"What is it Miss Rachel? What are we gonna do? Huh? Oh, I bet it's not really fun at all. I bet its gonna be a chore. Huh, Miss Rachel? What is it? I can't wait to find out."

Their first stop was the rag drawer; a large cupboard at the back of the house held the broom and dustpan, a fly swatter, and a mountain of Mr. Dub's old work shirts cut into crooked squares. Mama had selected two large swatches, one for each of them, Grace guessed. Her eyes glowed. Then, from the highest shelf, she had brought down a white tub wrapped with solid black letters Grace couldn't make out. Then they marched on Mama's heels toward the dining room.

"The dining room?" Mercy questioned her. "Why did you get two rags? Can I have the bigger one? I wonder why Daddy doesn't wear these shirts anymore. Are we staying in the dining room, or is that just one more stop?" She didn't pause for an answer, and Mama didn't make an effort to give one anyway. Mama clucked and Mercy kept on making noise.

Mama pulled out the chair at the head of the table and gestured for each girl to take a seat near her. Before sitting down, she made three soft steps to the china cabinet, bent over and pulled from the bottom drawer a wooden box. She used both hands to carry it back to the table, her arms bulged with effort.

With the box on the table and her sleeves rolled up, two girls pulled their chairs even closer. She was going to reveal the secret of the box, and it was going to be good.

She fooled them.

She opened the box and two sets of eyes that had been preparing for awe instead looked confused at the woman at the head of the table. When the box creaked open, all they saw were piles of silverware, all jumbled up in heaps. Soup spoons mingled with dessert forks. Knives sat with their sharp teeth pointing every which way. Most glaring of all, the pieces did not shine. They were kind of tired and dirty looking. Nothing special at all.

They looked at mama. Had she suddenly taken complete leave of her senses? Mercy spoke first.

"Don't hear this the wrong way, ma'am. You know I don't mean to be forward. Is it possible to do so much laundry that you get kind of nuts?"

Grace flinched. She might have thought her mother had been too long exposed to the harsh odors of chemical solvents. She might even have said it later, to Mercy, in private, but never in front of her mama. That was just asking for a stern sit down. Maybe Mercy really did have special powers because Mama did not discipline Mercy with her eyes, neither she did unleash a verbal reprimand. Instead, she threw back her head and laughed, the kind of laugh that scared Grace, because it looked like she was crying. She laughed so hard not a sound came from her. Grace relaxed when she saw the way Mama's belly, soft and small, jiggled like a poorly executed gelatin mold.

"You are too much, Mercy," Mama said when she had recovered her voice.

"I know, ma'am. My own mama says that all the time."

Mama looked at her, calm now like a cloudless sky. "I know she does, Mercy. I know she does."

Nobody had anything to insert into the pause that enveloped us, we were nearly itching with the awkward clench of it.

"Grace, sort this flatware by type, into piles on the table. Mercy, you get all the serving utensils out. Lay them flat in front of you. I'll be right back."

She returned carrying a dish of white powder and a bowl of water.

"Tsk," she shook her head at Mercy's pile which she had not bothered to sort or straighten. From her position across the table, Mercy took in Grace's neat rank and file sets of spoons, knives, salad forks, dinner forks, dessert forks. Twelve of each. When Mercy saw her soldiered up spoons, she attempted a swift call to order, but Mama stopped her, touching her hand.

She showed the girls how to use damp soda and the white cloth to polish each piece. Dipping the fabric first in one dish, then the other, they applied the abrasive to the silver, rubbing, finessing along the tines, pressing their nails along the spines. The first spoon

Grace shined filled her with a giddy desire to polish more. She wanted to uncover the luster under the deep scars of use. Seeing the one spoon glinting in the light was like rubbing the dirt off their feet after a day at the river. A little ritual of clean-making. Everything seemed brighter when a shaft of light reflected from a singular point.

That was one of their most perfect days. They sat and rubbed and talked. They wove a web of language that Grace saw mimicked in varied sororities the rest of her life. In the months after the parade of funereal goodbyes, the women she knew shared the distinct but vague language of grief. When speaking of their loss, that special one they loved, their thoughts were cast out into the world, carried away by the wind of another thread, caught up and secured to the lintel of her bones, her memory a structure supported by what they could remember.

As they persistently say, time makes it easier. That's only true if you become constantly distracted by the press of life so much that your mind cannot always be busy thinking of those times you want so much to cherish. By the time Grace got to college, back in Alabama, she had grown accustomed to delaying her thoughts. The web-spinning words of women continued through her life and in all the women groups she would come to know, the ones where she said what she really thought instead of painting the gloss of appropriateness on everything. These are indeed gifts, these friendships of freedom. Grace discovered profound comfort in two things. Her daddy for reading to her, and those women whose words spoke the gentle subtexts of femininity. She studied words and then made it her business to teach words to others.

Of course, Mercy managed to mangle the job. She left bits of dried soda on the forks. She forgot to wet her cloth to rinse the bowled ovals of the serving spoons. Her ladle. Oh, her ladle looked like she had tried to lick it clean with a mouth full of caramel. She entertained them all the while, Mama and Grace slouched over the table, taking their time rubbing out the grime, smiling into the light.

Mama had used some white paste from the tub she had brought down. That was magic paste. She didn't have to work so hard or long at polishing her silver. When Grace asked her why she got to use that and they had to use the soda, she smiled. That was her way.

Mercy told them that day about Mr. Tucker's daughter. Mercy told how the animosity grew between them. Once, when Eliza Tucker and Mercy Williams were still pretending to be friends for the sake of their nervous parents, Mercy had arrived early at Sunday School. This was notable in itself, as Mercy operated under her own standard of promptness; which is to say she lived by the assumption that nothing started until she arrived. On that particular Sunday, Eliza had plans. Big Plans. She had received a dress in the mail. Not just any dress, but a dress from her Aunt, who had traveled by train to New York City. This aunt, having successfully secured herself employment answering telephones in a towering building, sent Eliza an extravagant, flouncy gift and matching socks.

"For indeed," Mercy clucked, mimicking her mother, who was not in attendance, "this is the true meaning of church; causing an uproar of envy and spite in our neighbors."

The way Mercy conjured her mama into the dining room with her voice, the way she flipped out her hand then rested the elegant limb on her birdlike hip, the catch in her throat when she said the word "neighbors" as if she didn't quite subscribe to that term herself, it seemed almost blasphemous, if it weren't so laughable. Grace scanned the corners of the room for any signs of Miss Willie; her laughter felt disloyal.

When Grace looked up, it was not into the eyes of her mother and her best friend, but into the puzzled faces of her classmates, who had managed to carry on a conversation about Jack and Grace without one rebuke whatsoever from Grace. When she did respond, it was with laughter, at something having nothing to do with the people in the gymnasium at Booker T.

"What's so funny?" Esther hollered from the other end of the table. Grace fought an urge to cover her ears. She had not noticed before how loud Esther could be. Then, just like when she learned a new word, the knowledge seemed to be everywhere. Instances of Esther's extreme volume pummeled her mind, called forth as if by some spell. Unlike with a new word which provides plenty of opportunities to highlight, the knowledge of her loudness only grated on Grace. It seemed as if Grace had missed an important clue only to be confronted by it too late.

"Just thinking." Grace bowed her head and prayed that Esther got the hint.

She did not.

"About Jack?" The taunting loudness. The presence of so many others angled against Grace, making her central to all prom activities. A rush of heat started at her hairline and poured over her face, climbed from the backs of her knees upward, like two paths of lava ready to collide. Her ears rang and she felt the first stab of panic. Esther's voice lofted above the din as she rallied their friends to continue the mockery, which some part of Grace understood was borne of intimacy. The sting of it, and her lack of real knowledge, and the flood of visions from the previous night were too full a battlefield to fight; Grace could not find any humor.

"I'm not feeling too well," a weak offering, Grace willed her voice to steady even if her knees could not.

Esther's face changed. There. Grace saw it. A flash of recognition that this wasn't the time. Esther rushed toward Grace just as she pushed away from the table, the odor of drying glue, wet tissue, and people coupled with the heat in the room forced Grace to swallow. Her gag reflex kicked in viciously when Esther reached her.

She took Grace by the elbow, but Grace resisted, flinging off her fingers. She tried again, a touch to the small of Grace's back steered her toward the ladies' room. "Grace!" She heard a shrill whisper full of reproach. Grace stormed ahead, calming her stomach which burbled precariously, but throwing grease on the fire of her anger.

They reached the hallway and a cool gust helped the tummy problem immediately. Grace leaned into the tile wall, rolled her forehead against its cold surface and waited for the queasiness to subside. As Esther paced behind Grace, Grace was trying to decide if Esther was a protector or a jailor. A group of students walked by, barely noticing them. Grace heard a girl's voice ask, "Is she sick?"

"Nope. Just taking a break." Esther answered them cheerfully, too brightly. Then, in her ear, "Grace. Grace? What is your problem?"

Grace turned to face her. "I'm not feeling well," hoping her lame tone begged enough to warn her off.

"I can see that. But, the whole laughing thing, spacing out," she waved her hands in a general way to indicate that all of Grace did all of something all wrong.

"I had a long night. Didn't sleep well. I'm tired." The litany of complaints did not answer Esther's inquiries. She twisted her face, asking more questions than Grace cared to answer. "Okay. Look, Esther." Esther, by her bothersome staring, had cracked a hole in Grace's boundary.

"I was just remembering something from . . ."

"From her. From them."

The silence was enough. Esther was the only one from this place who knew the extent of the friendship between Grace and Mercy. She didn't know all of it, but she knew enough.

"Yes. Well, no. I mean. Yes, from her, but it's not, I don't think it will be a problem anymore."

More silent questions. "Don't worry about it, Esther. Let's just say I'll be around here a lot more often."

"Good." She sounded relieved and resolute. Like they managed through giant effort to put something terribly awful behind them.

The hallway felt like a hothouse and even as she leaned against the wall next to her, the air was sucked from the building, from Grace's lungs. Some ghostly hand reached for her, folded her like reckless origami, crumpled her like waste paper with nothing that needed saving scrawled across it. Grace buckled and fell to the floor, her face rearranged into some pantomime of feelings beyond her ability to control.

Esther folded down beside her, draped an arm across her shoulders and let Grace fall into her, accepting her weight like a chair. After her family and Mercy and Mercy's family, Esther got the bulk of Grace. They had been walking to school together since forever. Their relationship had achieved that kind of ease which allowed them to walk unbidden into each other's homes, through the back door, to rummage in the cupboards for food, to enter without knocking into each other's bedrooms. Their borrowed clothes from each other like they hung in the same cabinet.

Earlier that spring, Grace had grown bold. Esther had always peppered their walks from school with questions about Mr. Dub and Miss Willie. She had heard the same talk as everyone else, how Grace's parents were different, how they didn't seem to fit in, but no one could lasso what was so peculiar about them, saving their peculiar daughter.

"So, what's it like?" That was how Esther usually began.

"What's what like?" Grace had smiled at her knowingly.

They walked side by side, Esther hip checked her, teasingly. "Seriously, Grace. Like you don't know."

Grace feigned ignorance. Sometimes Grace got a kick out of pretending to be dumb, other times she just didn't feel like talking about it.

That day was mostly the latter. "It's like what it is. Nothing. Everything. They're just a family." A sort of dare slid through Esther's words, and the challenge had stirred something in Grace, like sugar from the bottom on a glass of iced tea. Swirled her into confusion and indecision.

"Come on, Grace. Everyone talks about them. What makes her so peculiar? They say she might be . . . deficient somehow. Like she's got a few screws loose?"

Before she could defy Esther's claims with an outburst about Mercy's goodness, an image of Mercy had floated by, chasing away the outburst. Grace thought about Mercy then, and how she challenged her parents on nearly everything. How she'd run down the lumber yard to meet her daddy for lunch, barefoot and her hair down. How her mother forced her into twirly dresses that she'd ruin by kicking off her shoes the minute she rounded the corner of her street and walking through puddles. It occurred to Grace then that Mercy took stands on things that hardly mattered, and the thought confused her. Mercy was her friend, wasn't she? If she was a friend, why hadn't Grace let anyone know? Grace had always kept the friendship shrouded out of instinct. Now she wondered why she did, or if she did.

Truth: Esther's logic was tight. Everyone who thought Mercy might be addled somehow came to that conclusion by observation. The girl provoked people.

Grace made a decision.

"Tell you a secret?" They had continued to walk, and Grace kept her voice loose, sliding her eyes to gauge Esther's reaction. They walked half a block before she answered.

"What kind of secret?"

Grace took a turn letting their footfalls fill the void. "Just a plain, old secret. Nothing very scandalous." Then she added, "I guess."

They had stopped at the corner, waited for a few cars to rush past. Esther took Grace's hand, and together they dashed across the street. Then she turned to Grace. "OK."

"I promise," Esther said, "not to tell anyone."

Grace looked at her, hard, like she could see more than just this whispered half promise, deep down to the inside of this other person. It had spilled out like a balloon let loose in the wide sky. Grace's story took the same trajectory, whisking this way and that in no particular order as she careened through the tale of her friendship with the weird white girl from the other side of town. Grace didn't defend her. She didn't color the truth with her own wishes about her character. She painted, she thought, a close replica of the girl she knew. They had reached Grace's yard as she finished.

"So, there's this way about her that catches in my throat," Grace had said, "this sort of lightness." She struggled to explain precisely how Mercy, foreign, alien and just plain weird owned her loyalty. "I don't know, Esther. She's my friend. She's crazy and weird and wild. She lets me down all the time. She forgets that I don't live her life, and it drives me mad." She blurted, "I love her. As much as I love you or anyone."

Esther had led Grace to the backyard and found two apples from the basket on the back stoop. They sank into the shade under a pear tree and crunched.

Grace had expected to feel relief. She had expected to feel further emboldened. She had expected to be free from the heaviness of forced privacy. Instead, she was disappointed to feel unsettled and, too, to feel the very tip of a sharp blade of anger. The apple tasted too early, bitter on her tongue, sour in her stomach. Esther munched hers without expression while Grace questioned the quality of hers. She peered at it with suspicion, waiting for Esther to decide how she'd respond.

The sun shifted behind a cloud, the leaves whispered and tickled their bare legs, drying the light sheen of sweat on their foreheads. In the brief respite from the early spring sun, Grace closed her eyes, until the sun roared back into the sky with conviction and purpose.

Esther spoke. "So you and this girl, Amelia?"

"Uh huh?"

"You been friends for how long?"

I shrugged. "Long as I can remember."

"Never thought to tell me? Tell anyone else?" Esther's question did not surprise Grace. She had waited for it, and there it was, the shadow of accusation.

Grace had rushed to an answer. "It's not like I tried to hide her, Esther. Not at first. At first, it didn't come up. What reason would I have to tell anyone? It was like a separate life. Here and there. You know?"

She was quiet.

"Esther. You knew. You can't pretend you didn't know."

"Mmm."

Grace chose to hear her speaking agreement, so she continued. "Then, it just seemed more . . . " *More what,* she wondered. "More prudent," she continued, "to keep them separated. Like keeping the salt from the sugar."

Esther blew out her breath, "Oh, so which one are we? The salt or the sugar?"

"What? It doesn't matter. It was just an expression, a way to explain."

"Mmmm. Fine. So, this girl, you trust her?"

"Of course."

She had tossed the core of her apple into the weeds rimming the yard and wiped her hands on the grass, then on her skirt. "What's her last name again?"

Grace answered, and Esther blanched.

"You know her daddy's in that club? The one that rounds us up? Takes us out to the train yards? You know that, right?"

"No." Grace had laughed. "There's no way, Esther. Got to be another Williams. There is just no way. None."

"You sure?" She wasn't sure; not at all.

Grace scrambled up and stood over her, threw her apple core away, looked down at her. "Yes. I am one hundred percent sure. Her daddy is a good man. I know it."

On that empty Saturday, in the airless hallway of her school, on the day she had been planning for weeks, Grace felt sick, and sicker every moment. Obnoxious heat pressed on her, and the questions felt like acid in her stomach. She looked at Esther and was relieved to see understanding on her face.

"It's gonna be okay," Esther said, but Grace was unconvinced.

12

Knowing the back ways and short cuts saved Grace. She wandered home slowly, taking switchbacks and alleys in a distorted effort to elongate her walk. She made lefts and rights, wandered down alleys she hadn't visited in years. Back at the school, Esther had led her to the washroom and splashed her face for the second time that day. She had hugged Grace and sent her home. "I'll call around later, okay?"

Grace had waved her off and walked. Despite her fixed purpose, the walk home did not end with a sudden revelation of wisdom. It did not wash her with peace like a river. Instead, summer gnawed at her bare legs, and sweat trickled under her blouse, soaking the band of her skirt, which squeezed her like a bodily noose. She huffed up the low graded hills, her tongue thick in her head, a hunk of diminishing meat. The swoon from the school had passed, but the sun brought another. Thirst and anger propelled her. The burn under her skin matched the flame in her chest that gonged against her ribs, percussion keeping time with the tangled thoughts. Corded muscles cramped in her legs, they twisted behind her knees, up around her thighs and sent shock into her hips as she thundered through the streets and alleys. Grace deserved the hurt.

The dust kicked up her limbs, turning her socks from white to dun, meeting her mood and sifting her anger into a kind of morose sadness. Grace chased her thoughts. The dust on her feet reminded her of mud at the river. Mercy's face rose, swirling in the dusty remnants before Grace, like a city-sized phantom hanging over the rising buildings of Tulsa, suspended from clouds, behind which the sun blasted and blazed. Mercy was too much all at once.

Grace did not learn the domestic secret until she was cemented with Mercy. Too late. They were not simply the children of women who navigated their own tenuous friendship. Mercy and Grace were, they knew, equals. Nothing complicates things more than a lack of pecking order.

Grace's great-grandmother knew the secret, or so Mama had said. Mam had worked at the Big House in Alabama from the time she could snap beans. When she snapped the beans wrong, Missus pinched the baby fat on her arm, right there by the armpit. Mam snapped beans wrong so often she had a permanent welt on her arm, a bruise inked with cruel fingers in the color of ownership. It was, she had said, "Their brand on me." Mam took to wearing long sleeves even in the dead dull heat of summer.

She worked up from bean snapping and garden chores to the out-kitchen, keeping the cook fire burning through long work hours, on into night when the wild sons of Master didn't bother to eat with the rest of the family. If she wasn't restocking the wood pile, she was shaping dough, shucking corn, dipping honey.

Missus, Mam had said, was robust in figure, with the grand bosom of her European descent, the frozen eyes that calculated the worth of a side of beef or the strength in a man's back in a glance. She spoke with wide lips that featured her brown gums, the greying enamel of her large teeth. Mam used to imagine that the teeth on that woman could swallow a fully dressed turkey as if her jaw unhinged like a snake's. Mam said she had nightmares, abated in time by the secret she learned, that Missus' eyes glowed a yellow, unsated hunger. Mam did what Missus told her to do mostly because of the nightmares, and the pinches. That was the way of it.

Mam saw her way to being thankful for pinches. When she made it back to the clutch of tiny shacks tucked miles away from the roads, the farm and the Big House, she saw what the others endured. She had seen the purple tightness of swollen skin over an eye socket. The yellowing ridges of a bruise across an otherwise luminous face. She had seen, too, the meaty red mess of a man's back flayed open, flecks of leather and stone clinging to the puss, flies buzzing near, tasting death. She learned to dislike roasting meat for Missus; the smell that would have been so tantalizing to anyone else only recalled the scent of skin burned with the prod for cattle, the tongs from the stove, for nothing more than cruel delight.

Mam walked a more tightly drawn line that Grace would ever know. Before Grace was born, before they could flee those parts without fear, Mam had perfected the theater of service.

Mama had plunked Grace down after a bath one night. She picked bits of grass from her little girl's hair and combed three strands. As she plaited, her fingers had tickled Grace's neck, wafting the scent of clean skin. Grace focused on Mama's breathing, closed her eyes, let Mama tug her head as she worked. "I wish you could remember Mam," Mama said.

"Mmm." Grace sighed, settling in; she was about to get a Lesson. When SamandJacob were older, they teased Mama about her Lessons; the children saw no obvious schedule to them, but the lessons were a thing of sporadic regularity. As they grew, they honed their observational skills, so they came to recognize certain gestures as precursors to a Lesson. Like Mama being uncharacteristically quiet at dinner, or if she got a sudden whim to visit the library, checking out more books than she could carry on any topic that caught her fancy.

This Lesson caught Grace unprepared, and without the boys as a buffer. Too late to get out of it, Grace was already relaxed under Mama's ministrations, lulled by the light touch of hands on her scalp.

"She was a hoot, my great granny." She had paused and Grace did not break into it. Stories about Mam were surprises; but if she got too impatient for them, Mama told the story too fast, and left out all the best details. When Mama started talking about Mam, no one interrupted her. Grace closed her eyes again and waited.

"She was quite the actress."

Captured by curiosity, Grace interrupted.

"An actress? No, she was not."

Mama had nearly finished braiding, but she slipped her hands over Grace's head, starting from the hairline at them temples and back toward her ears.

"You didn't know? Oh, yes. Destined for the stage." Grace imagined she heard Mama's eyes crinkle with knowing, a kind of joy at the telling, an anticipation of her own for the listener who does not know.

Mama's fingers pulsed behind Grace's ears and then glided to the sinews coiling up the sides of her spine, into her hair. She pressed on these cords with her thumbs.

"Mam had Missus fooled. Mam *mm-hmm*ed her way through that job every day."

Her thumbs pressed and Grace rolled her head to indicate where she wanted more. Mama told how she had learned to act, at her mother's knee.

"I remember when Mam told thesecret to the ladies at the shacks one night. We had gathered around one Sunday afternoon, a cool spring day had brought us out,. The sun sizzled on our arms, and then the clouds cooled us off again. It was the first time I realized such a thing was possible, to not give someone all of you."

Mama told about sitting with her friends, darning socks and mending shirts as Mam told the story. Mam had been serving tea to Missus and a group of her lady friends when Mam knocked over a glass of tea. Missus glared at her with her too-pink gums and her fierce eyes, but she had only given her the vaguest remonstrance. As Mam left the room to fetch a towel and a new glass, she heard Missus brag.

"Oh," she had said, "they are the clumsiest bunch, but I do love them so. I'm rather careful with them and want only the best for them." Mam could scarcely get from the room before hooting.

When Mam reentered the room, another woman was agreeing about how one must take care of one's possessions. Missus took up again.

"Indeed. Why, just the other day, I sent home food with this one here for her litter." It was not hard to imagine the Missus' giant head lurching,   toward Grace's great-grandmother, while her chins continued awavering.

"I let them take breaks, even give them some days off." She had fixed her eyes on Mam. "Isn't that right, you?"

"Mm-hmm, Missus. Thank you, ma'am." Mam had forced a smile and even a slight bow. "Anything else, ma'am?"

Mam tucked every bit of the story into her mind, carrying home her story with a smile on her face that Missus could never remove.

As Mam sat with the women telling her story, she slapped her knee.

"Can you believe that woman?" Tears ran down her face, she wiped them away with a stout finger.

When Mama had told Grace this story, in their living room in Tulsa, Grace didn't get the joke. Seemed like Mam had been put in her place by a mean old lady. Grace pawed her way through the story, looking for the beginning, like a messed up ball of yarn.

Mama had turned Grace around and opened an arm for Grace to fall into. Their weight drew them together as the worn ends of the sofa raised up on either side, making a kind of arcing smile of the furniture.

"That woman. How dumb could she be? Mam perfected her act over time. When Missus asked after Mam's family, she gave the vaguest answers. Eventually, Mam took to concocting an entirely fictional family. The other slaves hid their faces, knowing Mam was telling tales, even while Missus drank it up like a kitten."

"Oh!" Awareness broke across Grace face, and she understood.

To draw a bow on it, Mama said, "She did what Missus ordered and exactly nothing more. Mam always said her family was her business and no missus who paid for her could know a thing about any thing."

A shadow flitted across the window, a bird returning home at dusk. They followed the bird's trail in the sky, and Grace reviewed her mama's behavior at Mercy's house.

"Mama?"

She murmured and nudged Grace, ready to listen.

"You act, don't you?"

"That's a question."

Grace laughed. "Yes, Mama. It is a question. What's the answer?"

She laughed and nudged Grace again. After a time, she said, "I suppose in my own way. It's not because I don't trust her, or Dub. The work we do, it's like," she stalled, searching. Always precise with language, Mama and Daddy were careful talkers. They did not speak a thing unless they meant to say it.

"Making someone else's food, doing someone else's wash, why, it's like seeing the secret parts of who they are, without any skin around it. It's like seeing too much of something."

"I know what you mean. Being close without being close."

"Yes, That's right. I guess I act my part because I don't want to share all my secrets with anyone. I don't want her to see *my* wash or *my* kitchen."

After that talk, Grace made a study of her mother at work, whether she was setting the table or putting up jars of garden vegetables. Mama gave just enough information or a full enough response to Miss Willie as was genial, friendly, even, but for every sentence she said, ten sentences remained, banging around inside her.

It was too late for Grace to learn the part. Her adoration for the Williams family, all of them, made her a wide open heart. She concealed nothing from them. When she thought about it, she didn't really want to know how to dance that dance. That would have meant a trade, giving up Mercy for safety.

Because Mama and Grace were often invited to take tea with the Williamses, to eat lunch at the same table, and to use water from the same sink, Grace noticed them. She adored them. She did not hesitated to tell Miss Willie an entire story, never thought to keep a part of herself back. She was a girl, and guileless. She had known them forever and mistrusting them had never occurred to her.

But now everything had changed. Each moment Grace had polished and declared precious was stained or spoiled. Every memory of tea on the porch held the vague odor of Mr. Williams' vomit. Every story Grace had ever told Mercy about their lives in Greenwood felt like unwanted gifts, tucked in the far corners of a closet, still shrouded in tissue, found when looking for the Christmas decorations. Grace sickened to think of Miss Willie, Mr. Dub and wild Mercy pulling out the stories now and having a good laugh.

Willie

13

It was a nightmare. Willie knew it would be. Mercy marched into the meeting at the church full of forced bravado. Her clomping feet and her clear animosity did her no favors. After the dress drama and the hair hoopla, Willie cranked her smile brighter and wider. Pulled between Mrs. Tucker's hazy meanness and her own child's pig head, compounded by the sharp tension from Dub's work, Willie prayed for the forbearance to endure pie making and banner hanging without chewing holes in her tongue.

Mercy had her way of cooling the friction inside her. After all the babies Willie had carried and lost, she stopped expecting one of them to arrive. She didn't expect her. Certainly, she did not expect such a tempest. Willie sculpted an ambivalence around her heart with each loss. Pregnancy, for Willie, meant tears. Every month, as Willie's belly distended and she giggled to feel that flicker of life inside her, she held her breath, and clutched her heart.

Willie's shame was not just the losses, but the way, and she would never breathe this truth out loud to anyone else, on the hardest days, Mercy was her burden. Willie's sorrow was the private horror that she had prayed that the quickening would stop. Willie had wanted it to end. The more she felt the child moving, the sadder Willie became. Her vibrant rosebud lips fell downward, a collapsing, awkward parenthesis. Letting go of a tiny seed Willie had conjured up into a child had to be easier, she figured, than releasing a thing with limbs that could kick and clamber and crawl around inside her. She knew it would end. Eventually they all ended that way. No way around it; Willie was angry. Angry at the baby for prolonging the torture, at a God who made a woman hurt so. A body could easily pass a tiny unformed thing, could even handle the subsequent grief, but the ache they left in her chest, well, that never ended.

The Aunts would have rapped her knuckles for that kind of thinking.

"God does not work like that," one of Willie's aunts would say, if Willie had the courage to ever admit it, her throat evicting the words.

"Gracious, Anne Richardson Banks, you bite your tongue!" The other would agree.

Their eyes focused on Willie like they were telegraphing some deep well of understanding. Willie did not have the code to translate whatever knowledge they were foisting on her. While she may not have learned that particular language, living in that wild house with all those people coming and going, Willie knew what The Aunts were about. They did not abide a God of punishment or pain. They were about making do and doing good. Their favorite words were justice and love, and they carried them like swords.

Why it should surprise Willie that a child of hers could be just as fierce as The Aunts, she didn't know.

Among the clutch of church mavens, and still simmering in her frothy dress and contradictory anger, Mercy's arms gangled at her sides like over-boiled noodles. Her back was as straight as if she had a flagpole for a spine. She had a combative but *laissez faire* stance that kept everyone clear of a five foot radius. Willie was jealous; she did not have the luxury of forcing distance because she was supposed to be the adult, and she was supposedly making friends. Instead, Willie approached the circle stubbornly ambivalent and annoyed by a trickle of sweat messing her new blouse. Not that she cared. Willie abhorred dressing up as much as her daughter.

The Williams women carried their pie baskets into the building, following the crowd, the lot of them smelling of melted butter and sugar and ripe berries. At least that was pleasant.

Dimpleknees was in front of them, with *Squishyshoes*. This made it bearable; these secret names Willie gave the women. Oh, it was horrible, she knew, but really, if you've met one pearls-and-lace monster, you've met them all. Willie nudged Mercy with her elbow, nodded toward the rubber soles in front of them, pressing into the concrete floors of the church basement, the rubber soles rushing outward with each step, the sound bouncing off dark walls.

Hairpins and *Sourpuss* came along behind with *Nylons*. *Nylons* approached with the whisper of her encased legs, syncopated with *Squishyshoes*.

"Morning, ladies!" One of them sang out.

Mercy and Willie murmured a greeting, Willie's trilled up higher, too perky. She cleared her throat and blinked.

Leaving St. Louis was easy for Willie. Living out of a wagon was easy. Building their house was easy. Trying to figure out how to step into this circle was nigh upon impossible. This was odd, though, because no one, not one of those church people, heralded from Tulsa. They all had loaded up their lives and tried to transplant them directly into this new space, carving open the earth, hunkering down and reaching out for roots, willing them to take hold and clamp down. Wanting viability and, maybe, if it wasn't too much to hope, happiness.

In the early days, when it was just Dub and Willie, when the streets were nothing more than packed dirt and the bridge hadn't spanned the two chunks of land, they clung to each other and to their immediate circle, which was small enough. All they needed they found from supply wagons, the local grocer, his boss and the negroes. Dub daily rushed home from work only to pick up more tools and throw up their walls. Willie liked working alongside him. She found a certain pleasure in how her arms grew lean with the effort, how her fingernails became brittle and crusted with dirt. The sweat of accomplishment and the thirst of determination were powerful draughts. They, in their early and quaint perfection, could do anything in this town, with each other.

Little Miss Amelia, stinkpot Mercy, came on the heels of the first real crack in Willie's heart. In those days, women were not granted the luxury of mourning each child that did not catch a first breath. Miscarriages and stillbirths were as common as horses on Main Street. People expected forbearance and a stoic slant to the face. Honestly, Willie had expected it from herself. People shored up their wounds when every normal instinct was to collapse and allow the sucking tide of grief to pull them away from the severe outlines of bloody reality. How exactly is one expected to say goodbye to someone she never knew? How to explain the ache for a being Willie never held in her arms. They persisted, each of them. Willie's family of ghost children, wisps of ideas she could almost feel, could nearly hear if she strained hard enough.

Staring out the window in the kitchen when Mercy was beginning to crawl, Willie's gaze swept over the new lawn and lost focus. The bright bulbs that rose like arrogant princelings caught her attention. She decided then that the riotous heads of the flowers bending in the gusts from the plains, these were the heads of her loss. Then she shook herself; just flowers, pushed around in the breeze. Willie plastered the stoic back onto her face, squared up her shoulders and marched, just like Dub did when he left for war. They continued to march. That is what one must do, so sayeth The Aunts. March. The window gazing became a habit. It was not uncommon for Willie to get lost in the flower heads, and in the sound of the footsteps, marching her away, pulling her along and forward.

Of course, when Dub left, Willie had Mercy, and blessed Rachel to keep her planted in the daily. Mercy opened her mouth, and the words spilled out before she had learned to swallow solid food, before her fat baby feet stuck to the wooden planks of the floor while she trundled around. Willie swore some days that child was electric; she never got tired of talking, and she never stopped requesting the exact opposite of what anyone wanted for her.

Willie conducted an experiment once when Mercy was about six. She had asked which way her mother preferred her hair.

"Up or down, Mama?" She lisped, and Willie smiled.

"Hmm." She tilted her head like an artist judging his canvas, "Let me think."

Mercy stood before her mother, walked closer, pressing her body up into Willie's, so she could see, really see her. Willie didn't get the hint. Not then. She only figured out later that to be seen was exactly what Mercy wanted. Willie missed it. She missed the cue, the plea, the offer. If she did see it, she had refused it.

Willie lived with an aching wish that she had swept Mercy up in her arms and twirled her around like Dub did, pretending she had wings and could soar; that Willie had swooped into Mercy's face and peered into her the way Mercy peered into her; that she had said, "I love you exactly how you are, however you are."

Instead, she threw down the gauntlet, because she wanted to test her theory. More than that, though. She wanted to be proved right. As if being right to a six-year-old was infallible, irrefutable evidence of her distinct and splendid maternal abilities.

"I like it up," Willie said, fully aware that Mercy also preferred the swish of the ponytail across her shoulders.

Next day, Mercy had brushed it down, let it splash across her back and graze the space between the two points of her shoulder blades. Willie watched her fight with it at breakfast, on the walk to school, and on the walk home.

"Want me to pull your hair back, sweetie?"

"Nope."

Stubborn. Eventually, she caved, but not by Willie's might. The fierce heat was the only thing that could force its way on her. Her hair, a velvet blanket, so heavy and dark, made her neck hot,and cutting it off was not an option.

It took time, but Willie learned to relax the lead she imagined she held, loose in her palm, as if there wasn't one at all. To reign her in was to ask for a battle. Other daughters, belonging to other mothers provoked Willie. Watching them did not assuage Willie's doubts about her child's normalcy. She wanted to know that this kind of constant contrariness was to be expected from these tiny people who would grow to be women. She needed to know if they were born to push against the presumed power of their own mothers.

When Willie got to thinking Mercy was within the acceptable range of behaviors for whatever age she was, Willie'd run into one of those damned church ladies and feel shame. Whatever goodness she found in Mercy, these women trumped without a flick of a diamond-studded hand. These women had perfect children, who dressed perfectly and engaged appropriately with the world. Their children had manners, and they wore clean socks, and not a speck of dirt marred their delicate silver moon fingernails.

Willie cajoled, begged, yelled. Mercy kept dirt under her fingernails with the determined intent to irritate her mother. It worked. Like the day they dressed to decorate the church.

Clicking behind *Squishyshoes* and *Nylons*, Willie tried to remember her reason for insisting on the damn dress. She stewed in her mistake. Another habit, a daily assessment of her parenting missteps. The ledgers she kept against herself revealed a complicated calculus of ifs and buts. Of two mistakes for every one triumph. A bad habit, sure, since the deeds were done. Whatever they were. Willie could not retrieve those mistakes. They were not like a broken dish. She could not pull it all toward her, piecing it together, glueing the jagged edges into proper alignment. Willie could not make it right.

Willie tugged Mercy's hand, gave her a look that begged for perfect behavior. Mercy rolled her eyes.

"Don't worry, *Mother*. I'll be good. You won't even know I am here."

That was the truth. The one they called *Sally Sue* claimed Willie to hang bunting. *Sally Sue* did all the heavy lifting, keeping up the conversation, a monologue, really, alive with a steady stream of chatter. Her pitter patter acted as a backdrop for a reflective afternoon.

Mercy, however, was grouped with other girls her age. When Willie heard Mrs. Tucker announce in her cloudy voice that the girls were going to hang American flags around the street, Mercy aimed a glare at her mother. Willie shrugged and whispered, "Sorry," over the perfumed heads in the room. She hung back as the troupe left the room laboring under swaths of patriotic fabric.

"You want me to say you have to stay with me?" Willie offered as Mercy hovered nearby.

She shook her mom off, determined.

Sally Sue grabbed Willie's hand and flounced off for the front of the church, where they were stationed by whatever commander they served. They worked for an hour or so, Sally Sue's voice like a lullaby.

"Right, Anne?" Willie heard her in-public name.

"Excuse me?" Willie stammered.

"Isn't that right, about Amelia?"

Willie ducked to hide her flaming cheeks, rifling for some kind of response.

"Oh, dear." Willie patted her hand. "Please forgive me. I'm afraid I wandered off in my mind. What is right about Amelia? You mean *my* Amelia, right?"

Sally Sue fluttered her eyes. "Well, I just was saying, I was sorry to hear Amelia isn't going to the dance."

It must have been as plain as red, white and blue that Willie had no idea what she meant. She knew nothing about any dance.

"I . . . um . . ." Willie pressed her lips together and grew warmer by ten degrees, willing herself to think. "That's right. She didn't care to attend."

Sally Sue. She tucked her head, again. "Oh, right. Of course."

"Excuse me?" Now Willie maybe took a step or two closer to *Sally Sue's* curled head. "What does that mean?"

"Nothing, Anne. Just . . . nothing."

Possible retorts, explanations, and general topic-changing sentences rushed in Willie's ears. She hurried to find one that would maybe just once present her in a fairly decent light.

"I think I see what you're saying, Sally Sue." Sally Sue looked around, trying to figure out who Sally Sue was. Willie let that go, pretending she meant it as in insult.

"You're saying of course I'm lying about Amelia not wanting to attend the dance. You think there's another reason. You think I'm lying."

"No, Anne. No. That's not it . . .please . . ."

"Let me tell you something, and you can let Mrs. Tucker and whoever else you want in on it."

Willie's tongue burned to say those words. Having it out with the Tuckers would have been preferable, but in lieu of that, Willie was willing to settle for a demeaning little chat with one of their minions. She didn't. Rather, she was stuck tight between wanting to holler at the entire world that they could just mind their own business, and trying to act like a proper lady.

Despite the words that tasted glorious on her tongue, Willie did not set *Sally Sue* straight. The two women pretended to believe Willie's story.

When she saw Mercy at the end of the day, Willie curled her fingers around the soft flesh at the crook of her arm. "What's this about a dance?" She hissed in her ear.

"Don't want to talk about it."

She let Willie hold her arm, as they made for the door, out of the church, into the white afternoon. "I was embarrassed today, dear, that I did't know about any dance."

"Sorry." One word, close-mouthed.

"Sorry?" Willie tossed back, with a smile burning a hole in her face.

"Sure. Sorry."

Willie wound an arm through her daughter's and pulled her closer.

"Mercy. Why?"

For all the nonsense that girl could fling at her mother, there was a little wedge stuck inside Willie, like a pill she swallowed the wrong way. This portion of total acceptance and utter unwieldy joy that this child, this spiteful, rueful, domineering young woman, was the essence of youth and vitality and beauty and justice. In her secret self, Willie saw that her daughter was magnificent, and Willie wanted to be like her.

Mercy didn't let that tarted up Tucker girl push her around. She didn't care two bits for any of the rules the rest of them ratified. The way Mercy was with Grace, the one thing that turned all their whispers into a crashing roar, was also her redemption. Because Grace was better. Better than them. She was Willie's antonym.

When Willie rebuilt the minutes of her days, that Saturday is the one Willie wanted back. She didn't know anything until then. She certainly did not know her child, this little seed that quickened like lightning and flashed. The one who rooted to her womb until she outgrew that space, and then she crashed out into the next space that could not contain her.

People say some ridiculous nonsense in the face of loss. A person can only endure that for so long. After a steady diet of "God's will," and "better place," and "perfect timing," Willie suspected that people didn't listen to their own words. It was as if people arrived programmed with certain phrases to deploy in a handful of social opportunities to appear contrite or excited or moved to tears when really, they just wanted to appear to be doing the right thing. It is possible to make words come from our mouths that mean nothing. They are mere sounds, the soundtrack of mourning. They sound like empty murmurings because that is what they are.

They said that about her Mercy. These people who could not be bothered to understand her when they had the chance, they said, "She was too big for this world." Willie's least favorite: "God needed her."

The Aunts would have beaten down the person who said that with a good dose of Scripture, and a whole lot of fury.

She was big. Willie liked that. She held on to the idea of Mercy's bigness like a warm rock against the muscle of her heart. The grandness grew even while the warm rock clunked around, knocking against the rest of her abrasions. She was big. She was bigger than Willie had ever noticed, and surely bigger than any largeness Willie could have imagined for herself. Mercy was bigger than her mother's heart, bigger than her home, bigger than a mother's furious love.

Sunday

Grace

"We found whites and Negroes singing and dancing together. Young, white girls were dancing while Negroes played the piano."
Tulsa Tribune, May 21, 1921

14

Sunday morning Grace was a tangled mess. The thing with Mercy blew her into anger's territory, but spending the night with friends tugged her back to safer spaces.

The dance on Saturday was a suitable antidote, if temporary. Grace had been able to shake off, for a while, the trouble with Mercy. The band thumped so loud that real conversation could only happen in the courtyard outside the building. Inside, Esther and Grace smiled at each other, tapped their toes and danced with their friends.

Esther handled her like a bruised fruit, with not a little distaste, but mostly willingness. And Jack. Jack had been dreamy. He approached from Grace's side while she was turned toward a group of girls. She read in their faces that something approached, something good.

"Will you dance, Grace?" His hand spanned half the distance between them, palm out and open and ready.

Her mouth felt like the desert. No words poured out. She merely nodded and took his hand. While the band played Paul Whitman, Eddie Cantor, Nora Bayess and Fanny Bice, they glued themselves together through the music, his warm palm resting just north of the small of her back.

He glided Grace along the familiar floor of the gymnasium, but in the dark, with the lights twinkling and the music blocking out everyone else, Grace built an imaginary world, to climb inside with Jack and stay a while.

He smelled like Barbasol, and being close enough to smell his skin felt obscenely intimate. Her mouth stayed dry while her heart thumped a syncopated beat. Jack was sure and smooth, his eyes held her when they talked. He was solicitous and kind. When he released her after each song, he asked for the next one. Any time she wanted to excuse herself and run giggling to Esther, he watched her retreat with a smile and promised to find her again. He stayed true.

Grace walked home with a kind of happy exhaustion, with a remnant of sourness at the edges of her tongue, and the thing with Mercy bubbled.

A ten year old thinks turning sixteen will make her sophisticated and savvy. That first love will glow. You think you will know. When you reach sixteen, seventeen, by golly, you think you do know. Everything. Why should't you? The world is so small when you are sixteen. Right about when things start to get complicated.

Grace shuffled through Sunday morning, getting ready for church, helping Mama dress the boys, dashing out the door in hats and gloves, Bibles tucked into their clean arms. There was so much to do Grace could neither ruminate on all the wrongs she could find in her history with Mercy nor drift into a pleasurable memory of dancing with Jack the night before.

Sundays were always like this, which probably saved Grace from a pathetic repeat of her glum Saturday. She was torn. She wanted to rail against Mercy or imagine dancing with Jack as they skirted the dance floor of the high school gym. She didn't want to be burdened with JacobandSam or the prayers and the eating and talking and visiting. She wanted to wallow or ascend.

In the minutes she had free to think her own thoughts, she was miserable. Upon rising, Grace thought of Mercy in the first moment, before she ever thought of Jack. Quietly chewing her breakfast, she recalled so many snacks in their little river hideaway. Church was a break, because everyone from the dance was there, and they talked in circles again about what had happened the night before. The music and the dancing and who went where with whom. And Jack.

"Hiya." He said as he handed her a paper bulletin.

She blushed. "Hiya."

"Pleasure to see you today."

"Oh, you say that to all the girls," Grace giggled, and winked, because of course he did. It was his job.

He blushed. "I really mean it this time."

"Peace, brother Jack," she smiled and took her seat with Mama and Daddy, who were trying not to crane their necks, trying not to listen.

In the ups and downs of church, standing for hymns and bowing for prayers and fanning themselves during the lesson, one prayer hooked around her. She had thought she was safe, that since she was surrounded by the people of her most recent pleasant past, she was immoveable. When the prayers came, and the heads bent, she listened. There's this kind of love church people talk about, but it seems like a kind of love people don't get to see very often. This kind of accepting way of looking at people, being willing to let people have their druthers. Seems like someone has to go first, and risk it all. If Grace decided that she could let people think what they wanted to think, and believe what they wanted to believe, she had the disadvantage. She'd be offering tolerance without any promise of receiving the same thing.

Grace thought of Mercy, and wondered if she had spoken with her father. Knowing that girl, she'd have picked a thousand fights with him between Friday night and Sunday, never once coming to any kind of point. In the middle of the prayer, in the center of her anger, Grace smiled to think of her. An ache sprang from her gut, like paper being crumpled, engulfed in fire. Grace missed Mercy.

She cried quiet tears. The kind a woman can manage as long as no one asks her how she's doing, if she needs anything. Those offers of kindness are keys to the floodgates, and they hurt. Keeping her head down for the duration of the prayer, all through the sermon, all through the rest of the hymns, she found a square of solace. Daddy nudged her to stand at the end of the service, for the greeting of their neighbors, before the benediction. When Grace turned her swollen face to Daddy, he acquiesced. Mama put a hand on her shoulder, and one of the boys flicked her arm with his middle finger plucked hard against his thumb, leaving a mark.

"Go the ladies' room and wash your face. Meet us in the hall when you're ready. Keep your head down and don't talk to anyone." Mama whispered, her voice a bridge between here and a there Grace could not imagine.

The rest of the day whirled past, and Grace stuck close to her parents. Friends invited her to walk home with them, beckoned Grace to join their circles after church. Instead she wound through the events lost and not wanting to be found. Accepting any curves that came, blending through them, righted again by the solid timbre of her father's voice near her, Mama's hand nearby for a squeeze.

Mama blessedly assigned Grace the task of keeping after the boys at the party that night, providing Grace with a ready made excuse for anything she didn't feel like doing. Which was everything.

On a stage at the center of Greenwood, bands blared through the night. Groups of people dotted every patch of grass. The smell of fine cooking rose from grills brought to the streets, people sharing their picnics with anyone they knew. Keeping up with JacobandSam proved a challenge, but it kept her moving. Because she was chasing them, she did not engage in a long conversation with anyone. When a short visit lagged and threatened to turn lengthy, Grace mumbled something about JacobandSam and ran off.

They played in a long alley for a time, tossing a ball with a bigger group of kids. One of them spotted a stray dog and they were off again, chasing after the animal. He was scroungy looking, skinny and not much to look at. He was big enough to track through the shadows, though, and the boys trotted after it along the Frisco tracks.

"Boys!" Grace called. They were too far away from home. "Boys!" into the night she shouted, listening for the echo of their footsteps. She ran down streets and alleys, and the sounds of the party faded so that all she heard was the thump of base. The low din of many voices seemed like nothing at all from this distance.

For a time, Grace tracked the boys by listening to the rocks skittering down the roads as the boys scurried. She wandered, thinking where a dog might reasonably travel. Then she laughed at herself. She had no experience with dogs, domestic or otherwise. Then she heard voices, low and fast, not far from her. Could have been anyone, but the boys didn't usually talk all that much; they used a shorthand like Mercy and Grace had. They only talked around others, and not that frequently.

She rounded a corner fast, beginning to worry, and exhaled when she saw the boys. They stood at a fence separating Greenwood on the southeast side from the rest of the city, and they were talking to someone through the fence. Their bodies glinted in shadows, but Grace caught a high voice, a girl's. One of the boys moved out of the way, and Grace saw her in a flash of light.

Grace smelled the picnic food, the mown grass, the honeysuckle in a distant field. She saw the boys' eyes, flashing in the moonlight, proud and happy and careless. She heard the pounding in her ears, her heart thrown into a confused rhythm. She blinked, as if to keep the tiny pieces of herself, the braided bits of her, the ropes of a history with her tied down tight, to maintain the coolness reflected on her face, to buy time, to find the one thing that was reasonable to say.

Samuel called out, "Hey, Gracie! Look who we found!"

When she found the boys were safe, she had stopped. The surprise of Mercy somehow rooted her to the dirt underfoot.

"Amelia." Her name a statement, containing everything; anger and love in one fierce and confused sentence.

"Hey."

The boys looked from one girl to the other, still in that blessed ignorant boyhood world, not understanding. It was nearly a mess too big for Grace to comprehend. She envied their blindness.

Grace kicked a stone. "What you doing down here, girl?"

The boys cried a duet, "Oh, Mercy! Did you come for the party?"

"Don't be stupid! She can't come to our party. She can't cross that fence! Don't you know anything? She's white. Look at her!" Seems like words have a flavor sometimes, and maybe a taste, like on the back of the tongue. As Grace said the words, it felt good. It was a thrilling gift, this power to hurt, and she liked it. She savored the thoughts about her stupid brothers and this ridiculous white girl. She felt hot like a necessary fire, like getting out the words would scorch and burn and give relief. If it flamed out, it would be gone. Just like that, the bitter, acrid taste of the flame at the back of her throat caught her, dropped into her gut like a blade. The bitter joy of anger flamed out, became a dull and vague and bad tasting bitterness. It tasted like guilt and loss.

"Get on back, and stay to the big roads. Find Mama and tell her I'll be along." Grace barked orders at the boys, then found a kinder tone to send them off, hoping to convey an appeal for forgiveness without having to ask for it.

Little kids have little fights. What feels like a rent in the soul is usually fixed by a glass of milk and a cookie. Sometimes a nap and an hour or two apart can be the best first aid for hobbled hearts. Before she was Mercy, she was the little girl who followed Grace around the house, while Grace followed Mama, learning and helping as they went. Mama and Grace listened in silence to Mercy's steady stream of words, an astounding amount of commentary for one so small.

One day years before, Mama and Grace had set to cleaning the windows. They gathered a stack of newspaper and a spray bottle of vinegar. Mama added a drop of lemon to the bottle before they crumpled the paper into wads, sprayed the glass and scrubbed in circles, erasing red dust from each pane and sill. The little girl, in a pink play dress and white socks, flounced after them.

"Why you doing that?" Mercy asked.

Mama had grunted back at her.

She persisted. "Why you using the newspaper?" She didn't wait for an answer. "I can show you where the rags are? Want me to get some? I can help? What's that smell? Can I try?" She had pushed in on Grace, getting closer and closer as Grace pressed against the lower panes, the ones within her arm's reach. The hem of Mercy's dress whispered against Grace's. Grace wanted to be kind, but more, she wanted that girl out of her way. Grace gave a little nudge with her hip, pushed her back a bit.

"Sorry." Mercy murmured. She mirrored Mama's movements, asking questions. Talking. "Once," she said, "once, old Jules? From next door, you know? Once, she came over to help with the windows. That was before you came here. She was so cranky."

Mercy burst out a short, crystal laugh. "Oh, she was cranky. She didn't even let me help. She told me to go talk to Miss Howard. You know Miss Howard? Down the end of the street?"

Mama looked down and murmured at her again. "Yes, honey. We know her." Mama had somehow wedged her hips around Mercy, getting her to step back to gain more room to work. Mercy and her questions overtook the room until it felt like the room was saturated, filled with letters and punctuating exclamations. As Mama moved the little girl out of the way, Grace held her.

Her words had stopped. She looked at Grace. Mama kept working while the room which had been so full of Mercy stilled. She blinked, calm and relaxed, her little pink shoulders rose and fell with her breath, the wild curls flew about like an unmanageable ball of yarn.

Glossy blue eyes shone at Grace, her face a clean, porcelain plate waiting expectantly. A bloom of freckles dotted a crazy line across her nose and cheekbones. Near her hair line, strands of pure white hair, like cotton candy, floated with their own will, as if underwater. Grace had never seen hair so white. It was nearly transparent.

Grace was possessed by an unquenchable need. She reached up to touch the white strands, not believing they were hair, or on her dark head. The silky strands floated away, her curiosity abated when she heard the screech of paper on glass, the sigh of her mother working. Grace turned to resume work when Mercy stopped her again.

"Can I please help?" Her voice was small like the smallest pluck on the highest string of a banjo, with just a twang of need.

Wordlessly Grace handed her a page out of the weekend paper and grabbed a fresh sheet for herself. She grinned when they crumpled the papers up into tight balls. Grace demonstrated how to spray at the top of the pane, to wipe in large circles expanding outward and around, to keep going until every hint of wetness had vanished.

The three had worked through the downstairs of her house like that for the remainder of the morning. They didn't talk much, except when Mama tried to get Mercy to run off and play. Each time, she said the same thing. "Don't have anyone to play with."

Mercy could only stay quiet for so long. Her courage grew again as their piles of used papers grew. By the end of the morning, she had picked up whatever thread of conversation had been pulsing through her head and began aloud again. "I never got to work along side anybody before. My mama never lets me help out. She's got these pages of handwriting for me to practice, so I can write fancy letters to my grandma, even though Grandma loves me no matter how my handwriting looks. Even though I know Grandma loves a fancy looking letter. Have you met my grandmother? She's been here. She's wonderful. She has white hair, too, like these." She pulled at the white hairs Grace had touched earlier.

"Why you talk so much?" Grace asked. Mama gasped, Mercy's eyes flew open, and then a furious wrinkle between her eyes matched the dense line her angry mouth made.

"What?" Grace looked from Mama to Mercy. "I didn't mean . . ." Mercy had flown off to other parts of the house and Mama shot a disappointed glare at Grace. She told her to throw away the mound of ruined paper rags. "Meet me on the back porch. We'll have our lunch now."

Grace crept through the house, unsure whether she wanted to see the little girl again. It didn't take her long to piece through what she had said, how it had sounded. Grace tried to shrug it off, but there was the matter of lunching with Mama to face. Her lecture would not go down easy. Grace was served something that tasted even worse than she imagined; silence. Mama didn't talk about it at all. Didn't remind her to "guard her tongue." Didn't say to find the girl and apologize. Nothing. The pair simply ate a small lunch accompanied by the sounds of their lips smacking, their stomachs gurgling, their ice clinking. Mama seemed always to know what kind of action on her part would elicit the intended reaction from her daughter.

Grace had spied her, Mercy, hovering around the doorway of the upstairs bedrooms in the afternoon. Mercy peeped in, her flying hair visible, the tips of her fingers grasping the jamb, thinking what every kid thinks; if I can't see you, you can't see me. Mama and Grace had resumed the glass cleaning upstairs. When she noticed the girl who had never spent this much time with the help before, Grace took two new pieces of newsprint and walked toward the fingertips. She tapped gently on them until the hand opened and reached through the door. She pushed the paper into the hand, and a wide-open face peered around the door, smiling.

Mercy came around, full-bodied, into the room. Grace thumped her gently with a hip as they walked toward the windows. Then, she started.

"I had a good lunch. Did you? Where did you all eat? We ate in the dining room. I hate eating in the dining room. Especially with just Mama. It's so lonely. She's so busy today. I don't know what all she's doing. She's got all these papers out in Daddy's study. She's probably writing letters to Grandma. You never told me why we use newspaper."

Instead of filling up the room, making it hard to breathe, somehow now as she talked, she was her own choir of one, a group of tiny bells, ringing out her own songs. It didn't clang against Grace's ears. It sounded like happiness.

But at the fence, Grace saw Mercy in a new way. The streetlight cast a harsh, diamond-shaped shadow from the fence between the girls onto the same little white hairs, the same dusted freckles. Grace had no newspaper or urge to nudge her.

Still.

There it was. The silence like a vacuum. No bells ringing happiness, but the quiet blast of change, a dirge.

"What are you doing down here?" Grace demanded. She planted herself on the rubble, firm. If she passed onto the strip of grass that hugged both sides of the fence that separated them, she didn't trust herself to keep the flame of anger alive.

She, oh that stubborn girl, she pushed her chin in the air, flipped her hair over her shoulder. "I go wherever I want. I wanted to come here. I came here." She cocked her head to the side defiantly. Any worry that Mercy would blow out the fire with a word of kindness melted then.

Grace didn't want to. She didn't mean to. There she was, moving forward, taking steps toward the white girl, fueled by the flame and by something hotter, hotter than the pain of what Mercy was, of what her father might have been. Grace felt ashamed that she had assumed a closeness, had presumed that they were different than everybody else. Maybe that knocking in Grace's chest was not anger. Maybe the steps she took were not the complete journey, though she stopped short at the fence. Grace bent down, plucked a handful of grass, fidgeted with a slender green blade to calm the thrashing that pummeled in her lungs and parched her throat.

Cicadas sang their ceaseless tune. Wind tickled the leaves of the trees. The distant sound of the party echoed like a memory from the empty brick buildings. Grace was close enough to see the white hairs on Mercy's forehead, caught in streams of random light, giving Mercy the appearance of being crowned with an ill-fitting halo.

"Dammit, Mercy." Grace stared at her own two feet.

Mercy shuffled closer to the diamonds in the fence, wrapped her slender pink fingers around the wire, wiggled her pointer. The defiance became begging, cajoling. Grace mirrored her, but kept her hands at her sides, tossing the grass back to the earth.

"Dammit, Grace," she said. She smiled.

"What are we going to do?"

"'Bout what?"

"You're crazy or stupid, girl." Exasperated, Grace filled her in. "About your daddy, dummy. About you creeping down here where you don't belong."

She shrugged, offered a weak, "Dunno."

Grace touched her wiggling finger, pulled away. "My daddy says he trusts your daddy."

Mercy waited. Then she said, "Your daddy's smart."

"Don't try to flatter me, you." It was pointless to protest, and Grace knew Mercy was sincere.

At that moment, Grace had no answers, except that she didn't want to breathe the flame into continued life. She wanted everything back, just the way it was, before they saw Mr. Dub in that awful white hood.

The day washing windows with the newspapers, two strangers had come to a quiet understanding. Grace knew what she had said hurt the girl. Mercy understood, when Grace approached her with the offer to help, the implicit apology. There was no implicit apology squaring off at the fence. More like an implicit, shamed silence. Even if Grace had the words, she could not rally the courage to confess the growing pile of anxiety unloading inside her. If she had wanted to, she could not have understood any kind of justification Mercy might have offered. What existed between them was a worn thread of knowing. Dancing on that frayed thread was their history up to that point.

What a ridiculous place for two girls to be. The pressure of decades, centuries settled on two under-prepared sets of shoulders. Staring at Mercy through the chain links, Grace's rose-colored lips bent into a timid smile. In one moment, the scales fell from their eyes. They were no longer blind to the place where they lived. Instead of the openness of naiveté and youth, they robed themselves with cactus skin, a false defense. They could no longer hope their fathers would be the saviors they had imagined them to be.

"So." Grace offered.

"So." Mercy replied.

Grace wrapped her fingers around the links, close to Mercy's. Mercy moved her hand, wrapped her fingers around Grace's. The hunter green plaid of Mercy's skirt winked in the light.

"Still want to meet tomorrow?"

Grace shrugged. Of course she did.

"It won't be easy," Grace said.

"That's what will make it fun." Mercy released a laugh then, like a dam busting with force and might. Strong.

The party that Grace had left, the party that she had heard bouncing through the walls came careening around the corner just then. What had been a dim awareness of something happening far away inserted itself into this short detente. A gaggle of Grace's friends from school came blaring around the corner, laughing and shouting. Before she could move away from Mercy, before she registered what was happening, they were there. Esther and what seemed like everyone else.

"Grace!" Esther shouted into the darkness, recognizing her friend, but not seeing through the fence.

"What are you doing? We've been looking for you!"

Grace shifted away from Mercy, toward the other group, hoping they wouldn't see her face on fire with fear.

"Oh, hey, guys. What's going on?" If Grace counted on Mercy taking the hint, her loud voice killed that whim. Mercy, even if she did figure it out, always did what Mercy wanted to do.

"Hi!" She hollered, trying again. The group fell quiet. "You all know Grace?"

Grace turned back to her, killed her a thousand times with her eyes. Hissed at her. She was unchecked.

"I'm Mercy!"

Grace prayed they couldn't see her glaring whiteness, hoped that Mercy was shrouded in dark, hidden behind a fence, in a place where she didn't belong. It was too much to dream they would think she was a relative or someone new to Greenwood they hadn't met yet.

Esther caught Grace's attention, mouthed, "I'm sorry."

Grace was growing used to shrugging. The other kids walked toward the voice, and when they saw her, they looked from Mercy to Grace. The echo of the pregnant quiet again was broken by Grace, working up a swallow in her coated throat.

"Grace. You know who this girl is?" It was Jack.

"Yes, I do. She's my friend."

"Your friend?" someone else said. "This girl's daddy works for Tucker. She's your friend?"

"Yes."

"You mean you work for her?" Jack asked.

"No. She's my friend." Mercy's face beamed over Grace's shoulder.

Esther tried. "Hey, Grace, you want to come with us? We're going dancing."

In the space it took Grace to decide—between Mercy and Esther, between her family and another one—the decision was made for her.

"Forget her," Jack said. "See ya." He called over his shoulder while everyone mumbled their assent.

Esther wasn't done. "We'll be there. I'll be waiting for you. Come when you can." She walked away, leaving Grace Irons and Mercy Williams in the dark.

Rachel

15

Anne Williams and her child snuck into Rachel's skin and stole her. They stole her whole heart. Keeping people in their own business and out of hers was one of Rachel's special skills, and she had many. The effect of these two people, of Miss Willie and her daughter, caught Rachel. She supposed it was bound to happen, not keeping up a gate between herself and them. Maybe the gate was kicked over, smashed in when the young ones got to be like a two-headed angel.

Rachel had determined, the day she showed up at their back door, all hung with yellow gingham and sunny like a drawing, when the child wobbled into the kitchen, that they would not suck her under. That she would not bow to those wide eyes and plain face. Those two must have had some kind of hidden charms, the way they slunk under her veins and made her care. Rachel maintained, however, that it was a grace to have known them. Everyone had the right people, good people, all bunched around them at just the right times. If Miss Willie could say she felt the same thing, Rachel did not know, but that's where she stood on the matter. They were clasped utilities like a fork and a knife. You need both to carve a meal on a dinner plate, but they tried to stay where they were supposed to be. They tried, with little success.

Before she started the job, Rachel had promised herself to stick to Mam's instructions. Mam's code for working at the Big House was simple: do your work; keep your mouth shut and your ears open; share if you must what's on your mind, but keep back most of yourself. Mam said a person could give up only what she didn't respect, and that to give too much to people who didn't deserve it was to wind up on the bottom of that deal. Mam had also chuckled and said that's how come she ended up with such a large brood. She had sung another song too: "If there's one thing you always have, it's your brain. Use it."

Mam noticed everything. That woman could recite the comings and goings of an entire family if she'd just risen from a coma. Mam didn't just watch her people. She watched the sons at the Big House, "tribe a idiots," she'd say, shaking her head. After the war between the states, when they were trying to raise their house from surrounding ashes, Mam had agreed to stay on, for pay, and with limits. Course, they puffed themselves up thinking they were doing her a big favor but Mam could have, maybe should have, left then.

"Been there my whole life. How they gonna live without me? Besides, what else I'm gonna do?" She had thundered when Rachel wondered why a freed slave would stay on with former owners. Not everything has an explanation; just look at Grace and Mercy.

Though Mam never had any education of the formal variety, she learned by observing. She learned that to stoke the fire too hot meant scorching the bread crust but leaving the center dough uncooked. She learned that to keep a platter of leftovers over the embers meant the wild boys come prowling for late night grub had plenty of choices. She learned that rolling her eyes and speaking out of turn meant pinches, bruises, or worse. Mam learned how to compress herself into a set of tasks, done quietly and as asked. Mam knew that experimentation, variation, and suggestions were not tolerated in the Big House. Mostly Mam learned the depth of human evil by watching the daily beatings in the fields. She saw the empty eyes of ownership that could scald a man's back with a leather thong without flinching at the whimpers of pain. Mam learned by watching that men don't take kindly to having their power threatened. Mam stored it all up in her body, every thump, whack and twist of skin, and she carried it back to her community. To Rachel.

Staying gave Mam power at the Big House. She taught everyone who came after the right and proper ways of the household. For a woman who didn't learn to read until one of her fifteen children taught her how, who in turn had acquired the ability by listening to the Big House children at their lessons, holding any kind of power was something. Watching those people, those fancy white people and their slender pinkies and their masks, that was her way of gleaning. Mam had said every one of them wore masks that just happened to look like their real faces. They wore the masks of civilized people, of kind people, of faithful people. None of the masks showed the true self.

Again and again, Mam had spoken one truth to Rachel. "Use the brain the good Lord gave ya."

Rachel felt Mam's lessons like a burden. Rachel accepted the reality of domestic work. It was a bridge for many of her peers from recently illegal slavery to human dignity. She understood, too, that money solved a great many of their problems. Rachel even, on stale summer nights when sleep was slow to arrive, dreamed a life unlike her own, where she had someone doing her dishes, and wringing out her dirty socks. She was not a little afraid to appear at the Williams' house, on that first day or for many months after being hired.

She asked herself often a series of whatifs. *What if today I boil the whites too long? What if I forgot to put the beef in the ice box? What if I fail to keep my mouth shut when Miss Willie makes up the potato salad wrong?* Rachel assuaged the whatifs by calling on Mam's doctrine. Do the work. Keep your head down. Keep your mouth shut. Keep your ears open.

Rachel could hardly avoid keeping her ears open, with that constantly babbling brook of a child underfoot. The Williams girl was a body full of energy and potential trouble. In her early days, Rachel made a habit of working wherever the girl wasn't. The chatter plain exhausted her. Eventually, though, Grace had solved that problem.

One of Mam's teachings Rachel didn't understand was about the masks. Then she met Mrs. Anne Williams. Willie, as the pert woman had instructed Rachel to address her, could not draw a shade down over her self if she tried. She wore her face, and her whole being, out loud. Standing Miss Willie up against Mrs. Tucker, that blank-faced woman with the hollow eyes, Rachel saw what a mask was.

It was Miss Willie's face that made the case for her. Miss Willie was solid. She was one of the first white people to shake Rachel's hand, even while it was clear to God and Rachel and anyone else who bothered to look that Miss Willie wasn't sure she wanted any other woman in her house. Course, that made Rachel like her more. It had nothing to do with Rachel, Miss Willie's pushing back. She wanted to protect her territory, and she didn't think she needed anyone messing with her system. Rachel understood that. She didn't like it herself. Saw it on her face obvious as an empty dinner plate, Miss Willie meant no offense.

The day that Miss Willie invited Rachel to sit for a spell in the late afternoon, Mam's voice boomed through her head. Rachel had accepted the invitation, of course, as a matter of obedience and manners, and not from any sort of desire. The women sat on the back steps, Rachel one step lower than Miss Willie, who had handed her a jar of tea she herself had brewed and poured.   Rachel blushed. "Thank you, ma'am," she mumbled. To her everlasting surprise, Miss Willie nudged her shoulder with the tips of her little pink fingers and said, "You stop that, now. You hear?"

Rachel had heard, but she certainly had not understood. "Ma'am?"

"Oh, between you and your child!" Her laugh was like a jangle of church bells all mixed up and being rung by a set of novice hands.

Rachel had been unprepared by Mam for a situation like that. "What shall I call you, ma'am . . . I mean . . ." She trailed off, still confused and additionally embarrassed.

"Just call me Willie. Everybody does. Leastwise, everybody I like calls me that."

Rachel was wary. The whatifs rose up. *What if her husband hears me calling her that? Or the child? Or the women who visit?* "Willie?" She asked several questions by pronouncing the name. "I'm not sure I can do that, ma'am."

Miss Willie laughed again. "Of course you can." Miss Willie leaned forward, resting her elbows on her knees, ice tickling the sides of her jar. Rachel wanted to shift on her step, to move away from the other woman an inch or two, to create a visible barrier between them, but she couldn't think how to achieve such a maneuver without being conspicuous. Miss Willie's arm was nearly touching her shoulder.

The women enjoyed the breeze and the pause in talk. Rachel swallowed tea in gulps to loosen her thick mouth and to provide a means of escape. When she drained her jar, she said, "I'll just go wash these up now, ma'am."

But before Rachel found the end of her sentence, Miss Willie interrupted. "C'n I ask you something, Miss Rachel?"

Rachel did not have the right answer to this question, though she searched the far recesses of her mind for it. She decided to sit right back down on her step and let Miss Willie talk.

Miss Willie took her time about it. After another glug of tea, and a sniffle into her white handkerchief she kept tucked into her bra strap, and a wiping of her hand across her forehead, she started. "Ever feel like, when you look at your daughter . . . ?" She paused and tried again. "Sometimes I wonder if they ever know what all goes into being their mothers."

Rachel waited, experiencing a barrage of questions that she wanted to ask in response but willing herself to stay quiet. She thought of Mam and kept her mouth closed. Mam had said you learn more in the silence between, than sometimes in the noise of, the words. She knew that if you gave a person time to get it all out, eventually they'd come to the true meaning.

Miss Willie sighed. She rambled on a bit about daughters and the general contrary nature of her own offspring, and then she stunned Rachel. She said, "I've been watching you, Miss Rachel."

Rachel cleared her throat.

"Yes. I study you. You are a wise woman, I can tell. Know how I know?"

"I sure don't, ma'am." That was certainly the truth.

"That daughter of mine will be to blame for my eventual breakdown, I'm sure of it," Miss Willie laughed and started again, and Rachel struggled to see the connection. "I like you, Miss Rachel. You don't waste any words. I can see them running past your eyes sometimes as if you were reading them on the inside, deciding whether to use them. Most times you don't. And then, when you do," she slapped her knee. "I always learn something from you, Miss Rachel."

"That's kind of you to say, ma'am." Rachel wished she had more tea.

"Do you ever feel like they will never know you?"

Rachel turned to face Miss Willie, to piece out exactly what they were talking about.

Miss Willie prompted. "Your daughter. Your sons. They have always existed in your presence. They have not known a world without their mother. But does that mean they know who we are?"

Rachel turned her eyes back to the lawn spread out before them. She watched the myrtles swaying in a breeze. "I know what you mean, ma'am. Surely do." She couldn't have stopped herself if she had tried. "My Grace, you see her here, where she's as polite and obedient as can be, but at home, she's a different creature. The world spread wide before her, without the rough patches we have earned to stop her dreams."

Rachel had not uttered this many words in one setting to any white person, least of all an employer. "Beg your pardon, ma'am."

Miss Willie applied her fingers to Rachel's upper arm with enough pressure to convey her meaning. It was all right. Nothing to apologize for.

Rachel could have said oh, my daughter thinks that because she wants to, she can have it. She thinks if she's pushy enough, she can walk right on down the road with your daughter, practically holding hands. She could have said that sure, she loves her children, and the amount of ferocity involved in loving them was enough sometimes to bring her breath up short. She could have said her worries about how they'd be, in a world where she did not exist troubled her awake some nights. Rachel understood Miss Willie when she heard her speak about her daughter.

Eventually, Mrs. Williams became Miss Willie, and both women seemed satisfied. Still, Rachel held back, Mam's instructions her guide. But the girls ended it. Slowly and by fits, Rachel eased into her work, and into the berth of connection Miss Willie had created. Rachel realized that Mam had most certainly been operating under a different set of standards, and that this home, managed by these people, the Williamses, had its own set of rules, which bordered on cultural anarchy. Rachel surprised herself when she admitted she rather liked the contrariness of these people. She found a sort of strength in their usual pushback to everything.

While Rachel would never suppose herself to be on equal footing with Miss Willie, especially under her roof, Rachel found that Miss Willie treated her that way. The more Miss Willie deferred to Rachel, the less stout Rachel's personal wall became. Before a year was out, Rachel was mildly ashamed of her crazy appreciation for the whole Williams family.

In the end, it was the girls who brought the women to recognize each other as people, as mothers, muddling through the mood-changing days of teenaged daughters. Each daughter left her mother reeling with her own insecurities. Each child gave her mother pangs of urgency to draw her close and push her away. Each child tried her mother's patience and creativity in stark new ways daily. The women needed each other.

It was the girls Rachel had continued to worry about. Mercy took to Grace from the moment they met. Grace didn't pay any mind unless Mercy was in her way, which was often enough. If Mercy wasn't talking, she was dancing or singing or just generally making a racket.

When they were little, it didn't much matter. Rachel had to take her to work, and Mercy was always there. As they grew, and started tumbling about town together, Rachel began a countdown of the days, waiting for the ugly end. Boy howdy, Rachel was right. Not the first time she wished she could have been wrong.

"Mama?" Grace had found Rachel after a bath one night, plunked herself on the davenport and shoved a brush into her mama's hand.

"Hmm?" Rachel started brushing and twisting Grace's hair into braids.

"When Mercy and me. . ."

"Mercy and I." Rachel corrected her.

"When Mercy and I walked home from the river today, how come you kept trying to walk between us. We couldn't do any talking."

"You two can go five minutes without sharing a secret, I'm sure."

"It's not that, Mama." She pulled her head away from Rachel's fingers. "It's how your eyes looked all hard and cold. I've never seen them look like coal. You looked . . .suspicious, or something."

Boyd had walked in. "Or something? Grace Marie, be precise."

Her shoulders sagged after two grammar corrections.

"I mean, your eyes looked like they were full of worry."

"You don't miss a thing, do you?" Rachel pulled the corners of her mouth up and angled some sunshine into her eyes, hoping to convince Grace. Rachel could handle things with Miss Willie at her house; she couldn't control this child forever, managing Grace's every move, whim and thought. Certainly, Rachel could not manage Mercy. *Mercy* could barely handle Mercy. Friendship is not a concrete block, a thing we can hold and touch and move around as necessary. It is soft, and bendable and sometimes more fragile than it appears.

Women know this. Entire worlds passed between Miss Willie and Rachel daily without so much as a murmur. Rachel studied the relationship and decided that women tell each other secrets with their eyes, by whether they look full in the face or carve an arc around the other's. Women call and collect others, sisters, with something no one can explain—they just know. They know that if we slam down the mug, we're angry. If we ring the shirts strenuously, stay away. If we dance around the edges of the room the other is in, we need to be asked to sit and talk and tell.

Mam had this way of pulling Rachel into her circle, and Rachel learned about friendship from that circle. Mam had her women over every week for tea. She touched every one of them in a different way. Some she patted on the hand, some she nearly swallowed in her vast arms when she hugged them tight. Still others, one arm around a shoulder, or slipped under an arm. Her closest friend, Beatrice, was awarded the spot next to Mam every week. The two leaned into each other when the others fell to various clumps of chatter. If Mam and Beatrice were busy talking with other women, one or the other reached out a finger, and the other would reach back with hers. Their fingers linked for a second, and then parted. In this way, they made sure the other was still there. Told her she was important. Special. When they walked to the door, arm in arm, they were two humans heaped full of the mess of life and the looseness of being unburdened. Beatrice made sure to be last to leave, and Mam made sure to walk her out to the main road, where they hugged again, kissed their papery cheeks and smiled.

Rachel recognized friendship in the girls, and it gave her a deep well of peace, like bringing all the air of the room into her chest cavity. Their friendship, their coded language of familiarity also pierced a tiny hole in that barrel of air inside Rachel, releasing her anxiety and letting it creep out into their space. They never noticed, but Rachel did.

Mam always said that life was bumpy. To watch her and Beatrice disagree about whether to start a house with the windows or the dusting, the temperature of wash water or what to do about the messes their children made was to know the truth of this. Still, that was just two women getting up to trouble. Grace and Mercy seemed, and were, an entirely different kind of thing.

Rachel was walking a whole tangle of invisible lines with her daughter, who was turning into a woman, a young woman Rachel didn't know yet. These systems outside her control, like color or puberty or trust, were hard enough to walk as a child, but to watch her own child nearly broke her.

If Rachel said, "Be careful, honey," and she did every day, Grace heard six other things besides.

"Mama!" She yelped. "It's fine." She spoke with the brazen confidence of youth, when the world makes as much sense as what we can see right under our faces. Rachel rued that confidence, and waited for the day it cracked and crumbled into dust, which would stick to her like a memory.

Mam was downright professional about letting Rachel make mistakes, and Rachel was determined to mimic that with her own children. Then again, Rachel's youthful mistakes were minor compared to the no-good danger Grace could get up to. Rachel borrowed her mother nature from Mam because she was a worthy model, and because Rachel's own mama was absent. Rachel never knew her; she died the day Rachel was born. Mam filled in as grandma and mama all in one. She wrapped Rachel into her arms and held on tight. She wondered, looking at this child of hers, if her mother would have done and thought similarly.

That's the other thing Rachel learned from Mam: loss. Mam's life was pocked with the wounds of grief. She had lost children, her husband, parents and friends. A person can't live through a war without losing someone. God knows that was a constant worry to Rachel when Boyd was in France. Mam also lost friends, and not to old age or war. Some were sold away from her. Some were killed. Some walked out on her over differences. Mam used to say, "You get your time to feel your feelings, and then you put your feet on the ground and you move. You don't have to feel like it, and you don't have to like it, but what other choice is there?"

Monday

Grace

"Fires Sweep Black Quarters, In Wake of All Night Riots"
Tulsa Tribune, June 1, 1921

16

Impossibly, the blue sky tilted toward Grace's window. Impossibly, the verdant, spiraling green of the oaks and elms wavered a wake up call, their branches bowing in the breeze, falling into a rhythm with the boys chanting for breakfast, giggling with Daddy.

Grace lay in bed, adjusting her eyes and her mind to the day ahead. They had not solved anything, Mercy and Grace. A storm had passed between them; they had survived. This was to have been their special day, the day they had looked forward to all spring. Grace had the temerity to remain friends with Mercy in the confines of Mercy's home, or in the yard, or down by the Arkansas. She was not sure she had the power to cord herself to Mercy downtown, to chain her brown skin to Mercy's whiteness in public.

"Getting a job today," Grace announced at the table.

Mama smiled wide, the smile of one with the inside story. Daddy paused from smacking and slurping his food down, racing the boys to finish first.

"Are you?" he asked. His face was two separate molds, pinched together just under his nose, like the sculptor had not finished the work yet, not being able to decide if his sculpture was proud, happy or concerned. Daddy's eyes spoke loudly the fear he had for Grace, for all of them. "Going downtown?"

Grace nodded. Is it possible to add a paragraph of thoughts into a gesture? She waited for Daddy to shush her noise, to brush away what she didn't say with her nod, to make her know she would be okay. That she was a big girl. That she could manage the city. That she was ready to work, that she understood how it was. Grace counted his breaths between her words and the expected lecture, or the warning, or the verbal shoulder punch. He paid her a compliment. "You look lovely. You'll find work in no time with a smile like that."

Grace reflected a confidence she did not possess, and her parents didn't know what had passed between Mercy and Grace in the past few days. She also had diminishing confidence in her acting skills, but the breakfast conversation gave her a chance to rehearse her swagger. To stir up her courage, to display her easygoing attitude, she jumped off the front porch stairs while the front door was still ajar, so everyone could see Grace, light and free, as she scooted off to get a job.

Then she swallowed hard, pretending not to feel the weight of each limb and sinew, fear pulling her back towards her house, her bedroom, her covers. She was afraid of seeing Mercy, not to mention the rest of the white population. As she walked, Grace had a keen sense of her smallness and her skin color. To quell the rising terror, she turned her thoughts to her father.

Daddy was smarter than Grace acknowledged, but all girls feel that way about their parents. She knew he was wise. She had watched him finesse the system that kept him in the same position for years while white boys, younger than him by decades, moved up and over him. The way he cut and recut those boards for Mr. Tucker, without opening his mouth was not the first or last time he had favored silence over reason. Just as many times as she had seen Daddy sidestep a confrontation Grace had seen him strike the soldier's spine, straight and solid, unmoving. On the trolley, waiting for an order at the deli, walking to church Daddy was like a polished shoe, a well-made bed, a picture of perfect order and pride.

He saved his complaints for home, for Mama only. Grace gathered any information like a spy, hidden behind doors, under windows, feigning sleep. The polished shoe gleamed less bright in his own home. There the burden of days, weeks, years of pinching closed his mouth, holding his anger and sense of injustice inside him burned like a furnace they saw only in the flare of his nostrils and a clenched hand.

Later, when the fighting had stopped, when the city had been strafed and they wandered vacantly through the rubble, Grace knew his fear. She knew what the other half of his face was saying on that Monday morning. When the car rolled up and she knew to worry, she felt the furnace of justice inside.

When she sprang from the porch, trying to convince herself that all was smooth, like the calm river at dusk, between Mercy and Grace, she had yet to discover that torrent. She thought, like the little girl she was, that they could prove something big to people who didn't care to have anything proved. She overheard Daddy tell Mama, "There's like to be nothing open today, being a holiday." She didn't hear Mama's answer. She had stuff to do.

Grace had chosen her clothes with care, and Mama had helped her get the pleats in the black skirt aligned, so many knives in the silver box, all pointing one way, each one separated by an inch of fine twill. The buttons on her blouse matched her earrings, pearly white domes, and were repeated in the elegant French cuffs at the wrists. Mama felt that long sleeves, despite the heat, would make a better impression. Grace had saved from her earnings, with her eye on the black pumps down at Driscoll's. Esther and Grace passed the shop after school sometimes, stopping to gaze in the window. Grace had held her fingertip to the glass, trying to make Esther laugh. She had said, "Hi, little shoes. You're gonna come live at my house, OK? I have plans for you."

Esther did laugh, but hers was not as light or convincing as Mercy's would have been, and telling Mercy about the shoes just wasn't the same thing. Grace had decided to surprise her, and to test her; to see if she noticed.

The shoes had taken up residence at the foot of Grace's bed, carefully crammed with tissue when she wasn't wearing them around, learning to walk in the modest heel, stretching the fine leather. She wore them out the door, not worried about the little jump from the house, like she was born to wear such lovely things. She listened to them clicking along the street, south on Greenwood toward Archer, then west toward Main, where she had promised to meet Mercy.

The day was as fine a late spring morning as any. The blue and the green that had woken her, pouring into her window, now formed a kind of tunnel through which she strolled. She was buoyed by promise; getting a job, having money, doing work that was not domestic and promised something different, more shiny shoes. The trolley clanged past, the voices of passengers like a chorus. Grace eyed the young women, rushing about on heels higher than hers, strutting faster than she could think. The faster they walked, the more important their tasks seemed. She could have spent more time tracking this gait-speed ratio. When Grace left her house, it was enough to return employed, but watching the trim women in silky skirts and tailored sweaters, the hosiery, the hats, the colored hair, sent her into a filmy daydream.

She gave herself an important job, like a secretary for a lawyer, filing very important papers. She decorated her desk, a solid, wooden number of feminine proportions and styling, with a framed photograph of her family and a crystal vase of flowers. The job she dreamed up for herself had her clacking manicured fingers along the rows of a typewriter that hummed with purpose at each carriage return; she was so imaginatively busy that eventually, she had to hire her own assistant. This assistant, naturally, had a smaller desk, and a smaller, less efficient typewriter. Her perfect little life scattered, the rose petals falling away when Grace heard someone calling her name.

"Grace. Yoo hoo!"

Grace had walked right past Mercy, and she was charging down the sidewalk trying to catch up.

"Thinking about Jack?" she asked, which broke the mood completely. She did not have a long memory. Grace colored. "Oh. Bad question. Forget I said it."

"Done."

"Besides, who needs Jack? We'll have much better prospects in the city." She looped her arm through Grace's and they took a few steps together, lost in what they had wanted, what they had planned. It took just one woman walking the other way, wearing the sourest face, for Grace to realize that what they had planned was gone, too. Grace disengaged herself from Mercy's arm. "It's so warm," she said, blaming the weather for her lack of courage.

The girls ignored the obviously wrong note in Grace's lie.

"It's okay," she said. "You're right."

"That you, Mercy? You feeling all right?" Grace attempted a laugh.

Mercy pushed her shoulder. "Yes, Grace Marie. I'm feeling just fine. Now let's get us some jobs."

The girls wandered into McCoy's on the corner, each striding up to their respective sections of the counter. They ordered coffee, black, and paid the same price. Neither had a particular love of coffee. The smell of it elicited dramatized gagging episodes which made their mothers cluck. As they had strategized their day, they had agreed that girls with jobs in the city drank coffee. They sat on a bench outside, choking back the acid and wondering how people ever got used to the taste. In the days that followed, Grace grew to admire the punishing bitterness. A cup of coffee thrust in her hand was a reminder that she was not dreaming, that she would not wake from the horror. The stinging heat and acrid smell washed her in a dull comfort, rescued her from the blandness of the living.

Mercy had asked around, and her sources suggested that the Drexel building was the place to be. A shoeshine service was stationed just outside, and a small clutch of people surged around the glass doors. Jules had explained to Grace that the fourth floor housed the washroom for coloreds. The boys who shined shoes had to use the elevator to reach it, wasting time and losing customers, but Grace thought the idea of using an elevator with an operator was glamorous.

"My breath tastes horrible!" Grace said. They swallowed to the bottom of their heavy mugs, and carried the empties back into the shop. They inched closer down the sidewalk, their steps shrinking and slowing. They ran out of words; a stream of sweat dribbled from Grace's neck down the length of her spine. Her brow, heated by the sun and the coffee, and her nerves, shone with perspiration. She worried her makeup would smear in the heat and that she would forget how to properly introduce herself.

Grace caught a blurry something in her periphery as Mercy laughed about coffee breath. By the time Grace turned to see, a young man crashed into the girls, separating them long enough for Grace to notice him, to take in the tiniest bits of detail, like that party game where you have to remember what's shown on a tray. Young, black, dressed in a uniform of some kind. Navy pants, white shirt, ironed but dingy. Trimmed hair, shiny shoes, clean hands. The scent of soap and sweat. And panic. His eyes rested on Grace's for a heartbeat. He mumbled, something like, "No. Wasn't me. Nothing happened."

The girls never made it into the building. They turned to continue walking when the whistle and siren blared. The boy rounded the corner, and an officer followed. Mercy was babbling about the man, and "wonder what he did," and nonstop prattle.

Grace tugged her close to the building, under a green and white canopy. "You need to hush, Mercy. Now. Keep your voice down."

When Mercy finally stopped talking and looked at her, a current of frustration coursed over Grace. Mercy looked so out of touch, so utterly clueless, so incapable of comprehending how invisible Grace wanted to become. Grace pressed against the cold brick building. She had just about made up her mind to stick to the plan when she noticed that while the police pursued the young man, a hive of women bustled around a white woman not much older than Grace. She caught crumbs of the girl's words dancing on the wind. "Nothing. It was nothing. I'm fine." She pushed against the women clucking around her, fussing, touching her hair. They deposited her in a black and white car, handed her a glass of water. Grace wondered ridiculously why a glass of water is the universal acknowledged technique for soothing every ache and agony. The young woman's hair had once been coaxed into a tight updo, but a stray wisp hung down across her left eye, a drooped and lifeless curl that stuck to her moist face.

Grace kept Mercy positioned against the building, watching as people from shops up and down Main poured out onto the walkway, piecing together the story like a badly played children's game with much higher stakes. Grace heard the things that made Daddy's spine soldier up. The words flew like missiles, and she shrank into the facade, praying the white girl could act as cover.

"Those people," a heavy woman in a tight skirt pinched the words out of her puckering face, squinting into the sun. A man sidled up next to her, agreeing, "Coloreds getting out of hand again." She bobbled her chins up and down. Mama had taught Grace that to judge another person was a vile habit for vile people, but the size of that woman struck Grace hard that day; as if she, in her mass, carried the thoughts of an entire people in her sausage link arms.

On every person along the street, one emotive consensus prevailed. They were disgusted.

"You can do what you want, Mercy, but I'm getting out of here."

She looked up and down the street, people hemmed each intersection, cars blockaded the streets. "How?"

Grace scanned the same street, clicking through the map of the city she had memorized. "I'll take the alleys to the tracks. I'll be safe down there."

Mercy didn't like her idea. She said, "Maybe it will blow over. It'll get sorted. No big deal."

The crowd had swelled, the force of their panic pushed the girls tighter against the bricks of the building. "Grace!" rising over the heads of the overflowing sidewalk, someone shouted. More clamoring bells in the distance sped closer

"Give me your hand," Grace ordered Mercy, taking her hand even while she fought to free herself. She pulled Mercy through the maze of anger, hearing nothing reasonable. Grace burned with confusion and hatred and frustration and fear. She had to get closer to the sidewalk. She had to find her dad calling her name.

Grace did not know how she found her father, parked at the corner of Fifth and Main, in a truck from the yard. She saw his face, sweaty and wide-eyed. Only later, days later, did she discover why he was down there. Having ascertained Grace's plans from her mother, Daddy wanted to check on his girl while delivering some lumber to a job site. That moment, though, Grace didn't care why he was there. She just wanted out.

It took the better part of an hour for Daddy to navigate the side streets of town, working his way through streets blocked by police cars and all manner of people, as if they were a moving and active part of an audience. They drove in fraught silence, except for mutterings from Daddy about street closings or people standing in the street or who knows what all.

They dropped Mercy at her front door. Daddy gave her clear instructions. "Go inside. Stay inside. Tell your mama to stay near the phone. Now, Mercy. Go."

For once, the girl did as she was told. Grace remembered every inch of that moment for the rest of her life. Her eyes captured a moving photograph of this young girl, going home.

A girl, running to the porch. Her hair, which had been calmed and pulled and tugged tight into a smooth ponytail, secured with a silver-colored band, wafted around her head, the ponytail bouncing as she ran. Her black pumps clip-clopped on the walkway. Pink crepe myrtles waved in the spring breeze, unaware of their garish audacity. A sweat stain, an amoebic puddle on the back of a once-perfect white blouse, socks dotted with mud kicked up her legs. The bright red door slammed closed behind Mercy.

Daddy drove home, and they spoke little on the way.

"What happened?" he demanded.

"I don't know, Daddy. It was the craziest thing." Grace told him about how the boy crashed out of the building, how the crowd was an instant frenzy, how the girl was being escorted to the police car.

His mouth took a grim set, the jaw bone worked up and down in his stony face, his fingers grasped the steering wheel making his veins pop. He screeched to a stop in front of their house, and repeated the instructions he had given Mercy. Adding, "Gracie. Help Mama with the boys. Be ready."

"Ready for what?" Grace's voice cracked a whisper. "Daddy. What's happening?"

"Nothing yet, baby girl. Just be ready to move." He stopped talking and peered through the rearview mirror. "Grace? Love you."

She reached for his hand, squeezed. "Love you, too, Daddy." Grace ran into the house, just like Mercy had done, sufficiently scared.

17

The remainder of Monday was lost to jangled nerves and false reports and tension. Grace worked her jaw mindlessly.

In the dark, while Mama waited on the sofa for Daddy to return. Grace tripped to bed, knowing sleep would not find her. The house was too quiet. Cars did not chug past. Voices did not call in the street. Even the usual settling of their home, with its groans against the clay earth, had somehow ceased to resonate.

There are different kinds of quiet. There's the quiet that fell when Mama and Miss Willie, Mercy and Grace were all working away in the kitchen on some project; each of them content in her own solitude, aware of the others as little more than vague figures in the same space. Rachel and Grace were acquainted, too, with the silence that settled on their house after the newborn twins had reluctantly found sleep, after the storm of their hungry tears, their mewling cries for dry bottoms, when their tiny ribs rose and fell with the deep breaths of sleep. The silent sound of a sleeping baby is the kind that lets mamas find their own comfort.

Plain quiet has its own flat texture; like a soft, clean cotton sheet or the smooth surface of a freshly washed cheek. Utilitarian and pleasant. Sleep slipped away from her as the silence unsettled her. She might have used the twins' sleep breathing to quiet her, or the ticking of the wall clock. Instead, she closed her eyes and made her muscles soft. She gave her full weight to the mattress and felt that the pounds of her sinews and worries grounded her to the bed frame, and to the floor, and to the earth. The earth spun, because she let her jaw become soft, and her brow, and her shoulders and her spine melted. When she released her screaming muscles, she sighed a breath that loosened something. A great chunk of knowledge had been rumbling around and only then in her deliberate and confounding silence could she jimmy it out. She had the parts of the equation, but no answer.

The knowledge began with the landmarks she knew so well. A looping map of the city scrawled against her closed lids. Routes she traveled frequently Grace traced pink, like the way to Mercy's; or yellow, her route to Dreamland; or grass green, her path to the river. A bold and black irregular square inked the perimeter of Greenwood. An explosion of purple marked the spot where she had seen Mr. Dub in the sick white hood. Grace marked all the relevant spots from the last few days. Booker T., the Drexel building, Fifth and Main, her own home. She calculated and recalculated, but the facts muddied. The facts, her known quantities, where the things had happened were only one part of the problem. Her answer was a tickle, a shadow, a specter that taunted her.

The answer was shrouded. She was piecing the information together like a crazy quilt. Grace sighed and let her body sink again. She added still another layer to her Tulsa grid. *Here*, she thought, *is where I'm happy, and here is where I hated her, and this is the place where I rescued her. And this is where I'm safe.* Then, *this is where I was scared, and this is where I ran and this is where I knew I didn't belong.* Now that her map was populated by places and people, she had a vague and dissatisfying sum.

Grace traced and retraced her imaginary map. What she missed was what she could not know. Grace's calculus included only her relationships and knowledge of these people and places. While she appreciated her parents' perspective, she was sure they didn't have the information she had. Still, Grace puzzled: Daddy and Mama trusted Mr. Dub and his wife. Mercy didn't trust anyone but she was harmless. *No, that's not right*, Grace thought. Mercy was far from harmless. Tucker occupied his space on the map, and every route Grace carved, every which way she followed the facts and her loves, she continued to wind up circling Tucker. She just didn't know why.

Tuesday

"Nab Negro for Attacking Girl in Elevator"
Lost archive Tulsa Tribune, May 21, 1921

18

Monday bled into Tuesday.

Grace kicked at her covers, restless and clueless about the immediate future. The night of hollow silence and figuring rewarded her with unbroken sleep. While her body reveled in the softness of rest, her heart twitched with suspicion and a dusting of fear.

Miss Willie had called to give Mama the day off, which did not auger well. Daddy had left for work, screwing his face into a semblance of the usual, but it rang false. Loudly. Mama handed Grace her breakfast. "Going to get dressed, honey."

"Enough, Mama."

"What's enough, honey?" Mama's smile stopped short and said more than her words.

Grace rolled her eyes. "You're just gonna go get dressed? Like nothing's happening?"

Mama leaned into the counter. "What's happening, Gracie?"

Grace exploded. "How should I know! No one's telling me anything, and the way you two are acting. What is going on?" Tears rolled and she slammed a trembling hand against the table. "Just tell me," Grace begged.

Children belong to their mamas. They curl inside a mother's body and live in there, forever, with every broken heart and every broken bone. A mother feels the treble of young love and the current of all their fears. Mamas clutch at every experience, and witness the lives of their children as if they were still little ones. Mamas always have babies, no matter how big they grow. As Mama watched her daughter demand to know, followed the slipping tears to her tender neck, she saw the two year old who lisped and the four year old who dug in the dirt. She saw the impossibly wide eyes of the child who read her first sentence. Rachel moved on her bare old soles and enveloped Grace. If she could have hugged the knowledge into her, Rachel would have. Her arms could do nothing more than just affirm her daughter, this young woman, and answer her questions.

When Grace's raging ended, and her shoulders no longer trembled, Mama filled a glass of cold water, her wordless cure, and took the seat across from Grace.

"They arrested that boy you saw running downtown yesterday."

Grace shook her head. "Okay. So?"

"You saw the boy, right?"

Grace opened the map in her mind and traced. She calculated. Black boy, white girl. Running. Officers. "I still don't get it. What's it mean?"

"Nothing. Yet."

***

Grace copied Mama's lead and pretended Tuesday was a day like any other, except with everyone home and knocking about. The biggest concern inside the walls of their home was how to manage a day cooped up with rowdy JacobandSam.

Mama cooked and cleaned and set the boys to chores and play. She handed Grace a basket of holey socks, and for once Grace was grateful to work her fingers, thankful for the resolute purpose of her body, concentrating on the small holes, the slim needle, the expert work she had been taught. Grace drifted along, deliberately blanking her mind.The boys varoomed their wooden train set, pretending to take a thousand head of cattle out west. Grace found her body in her home and rooted her senses there, focusing on the clink of spoons on pots in the kitchen, on the whir of the ice box.

The daylight hours crept like a predator. Grace pricked her fingers bloody as she mended, jumping each time she heard a door bang shut outside. Greenwood waited. She waited, brewing, and Grace didn't know the enemy or from which quarter he would rise. Daddy stopped home several times before supper while the neighbors came by. The boys grew restless and whiny. Each time a knock on the door interrupted them, Grace's frustration revved; there was no new information. Nobody knew anything.

"Mama?" Grace spoke low, her words stepped out like they were crossing low sand bars in the Arkansas River, reaching out for something she wasn't sure was there, or wasn't sure she wanted to find.

"What's happening?" Mama swiveled back to Grace, ready.

"I don't know yet, baby." Grace collapsed, unsatisfied with Mama's answer, again. "Maybe nothing."

The women read a thousand books to the boys, and made a chocolate cake, Mama said, "Just for fun," and swept the corners of the deepest parts of the house, and rearranged the pantry, and folded linens and put up some jars of strawberry jam. Finally, they sat in the living room and waited for Daddy. The neighborhood seethed outside, like a pot of sugar for candy making, just before the sugar burns beyond use.

They started awake when the door clicked open. Daddy's eyes were hooded, rimmed in the color of new bruises, his hat at a conspicuous angle. He looked tired standing in the doorway, looking down at them. He carried the odor of sweat and other men. Grace stretched and wandered to the kitchen.

"Cup of coffee, Daddy?"

He nodded and sat next to Mama, tossing the afternoon edition of the *Tulsa Tribune* on her lap. His breath gusted out of him; his exhale was long, like it could make him weightless. She opened her arms to him and he folded inside.

"It's nuts Rachel. Nuts."

Grace made tiny movements so she could spy. She slid a pan out of the cupboard, ran it full of water. She lit the gas stove and set the pan above the heat. She watched unfocused while the water rose slowly to temperature. Outside, darkness had fallen, but the neighborhood was far from the nestling down for the night kind of quiet.

Mama murmured something. Daddy answered. "Dub was called out. Tucker's got him patrolling the streets, trying to keep us where we belong."

Grace willed herself quiet, held her breath, strained her ears. Mama tsked. Grace frowned. Dub. Familiar acid flicked the back of Grace's mouth, residue of what she had spent the better part of Sunday trying to put to rest, trying to erase, like it was some silly misunderstanding.

No explanation for Mr. Dub fit with what Grace had seen. She could not make it compute. She was disgusted freshly. In her new anger, she had missed some of what her parents said. Grace pulled herself back to the task at hand, the people she needed to hear.

Too late. The rattle of newsprint filled the living room, and Grace's parents were silent as they read.

The water in the pan rolled to a boil. Grace added the bitter grounds and watched them sink under the bubbles. The water grew dark and a pungent steam lifted from the surface, the ground beans became heavy and gave their flavor to the water. Grace watched the clock on the wall, the long minute hand swept around the face three full times before she twisted the knob, turned off the gas, pulled the pan to a cold burner.

After pouring the coffee into two big mugs, Grace froze. She held the mugs in her hands, ignoring the scalding on her knuckles. The sound was as unmistakable as it was rare. Mama was crying.

Daddy shushed Mama. He did not sound convinced as he promised, "It is gonna be all right."

Nobody was sure of that, even Grace, who held, at best, a tenuous grasp on what was happening. Hearing Mama cry, and Daddy's unpersuasive speech only fortified Grace's fears. When they shifted in their seats and started talking again, she picked up the mugs and resolved to find answers.

"Mama? Daddy? You're scaring me."

Mama opened her arms to her daughter, and Daddy made room on the sofa. Grace read the headline.

"Nab Negro for Attacking Girl in Elevator"

Her parents shook their heads, a warning, but Grace grabbed the paper and read. "A Negro delivery boy . . ." the paper shouted. "Arrested on South Greenwood . . ." She swallowed. "Charged with attempting assault . . ." She had heard the boy, she had seen the girl. "Claimed he attacked her and scratched her hands and face, tearing her clothes." But. Grace shook her head.

The girl's clothes, she struggled to recall. They were intact. Weren't they? Grace tore through the pages looking for the rest of the story.

Her hope died when she found the editorial pages.

"To Lynch Negro Tonight"

"What is going on?" Grace refused to be calmed. The clucking and cooing of her parents did little. What she wanted was real, actual, truthful information.

"There's nothing to be afraid of, Grace," Daddy addressed his daughter. Then Mama said, "We'll tell you everything when we have to, when we can. Otherwise," she laid a hand on Grace's cheek, held her eyes, "you'll just be burdened with too much."

Oh, Grace hated that. Saying she wasn't old enough to understand, that she would know when she needed to know. Daddy saw the dissatisfaction spread over her face.

"Grace, we love you. We trust you. Believe me when I say you don't need to know anything now."

The silence in their words choked Grace.

19

Daddy called in again around eight. The sky brimmed at the edge of dusk, the constant hum of the cicadas' song made clear. In any other town on that night, summer had begun its perfect reign.

Mama pulled the boys from his legs and sent them running.

"We're ready."

"Good. Good girl."

They sent Grace to fetch the boys. "Grab coats. Yes. I know its summer, Grace. Do it. Pull the blanket off JacobandSams' bed, use the toilet. Take them to the toilet. Come on back."

Grace did not hem.

She caught her reflection in the hall mirror and it shocked her. She looked old, like Mama. Moons of swollen skin popped under her eyes, her lips were dry as a stone. Mama and Daddy had known this was coming, whatever *this* was, but Grace didn't. The questions slamming in her mind slowed her steps. She couldn't find the boys. She forgot what Mama had said to do. Dub. Again Dub rang through her mind. Daddy had been with him. Daddy had told her, "I trust him." Daddy and Mama had suitcases stashed all over the house and some kind of secret plan that had something to do with the boy they arrested.

Grace could not resist. She spurred herself, always obedient. She remembered the steps she was given and she followed them. She herded the boys into and out of the wash room, buckling their belts, tying their shoes, ignoring their questions.

Daddy strode to Mama and nearly hoisted her from the sofa, where she was making lists and organizing the contents of her pocketbook. She was a rag doll, weak-limbed and limp in his gruff arms. Her eyes, her eyes ignited in his strength. His embrace pushed her and pulled her into a human, capable of action and movement, with joints and purpose. Where she had moments ago looked like a housewife looking through her receipts, worrying about the price of milk, at his side, in his grasp she became animated, ready. The worry drained from her face.

He looked down on Mama, held her face in both arms. The boys turned to soldiers at attention, the quietest they'd been since they awoke. Grace lacked their will. She sank onto the floor by the suitcases. Daddy squatted down and lifted Grace to standing. Her arms twisted around him, her hands clutching each other, making a tight knot against his back, her head tilted up to peer into his face. He kissed her smooth brow while her eyes closed; their shoulders rose in unison, his calm exhales bringing hers into line. He murmured near her cheek, kissed her again. Daddy kissed both of Mama's cheeks, her chin, her nose, her mouth. Then she tucked her head into the hard crevice between his collar and his heart. She moved first, put her hands against his chest, pushed him back, making a small space.

"I love you, Boyd."

"I love you."

The boys turned their knobby knees toward Daddy and attached themselves to his legs. His hands rested on each head when he told them to mind their mama, to do as told and that he'd see them soon. His eyes were on Grace as he spoke, and she captured every word, knowing his words were for her, too.

To that moment, Grace had managed to keep fears sealed tight like a jam jar. Then, Daddy walked to the highest shelf in the kitchen, the one only he could reach. He pulled down a rusted coffee tin and riffled through it, bringing out a key. The key went with him to the room he shared with Mama. The clank of metal on metal, the turning of a tumbler, a lock coming loose. It sounded like his pockets were full of coins as he strode into to the kitchen, with a rifle slung over his shoulder.

Boyd had not touched a gun since he returned from Europe. He did not talk of his days spent abroad. To see the gun, in his hands, made a sober moment terrifying.

"Boyd." Mama's voice was like the crack of a leather strop, putting a short hitch in his gait. "Please," she said. "Be careful."

The door closed behind him. In the stillness that landed on the room like death, nobody moved. It shattered. JacobandSam ran to the window, pointing and shouting. A gang of men swaggered toward town, with similar rifles slung in similar style as Daddy.

Still they waited. News came like bursts of rain. Jules was the thundercloud; she called across the street that all the men, black and white, were rallying at the courthouse. Then she called over to say the whites were on the move. "They going to the armory," she added importantly. She said her biggest boy was passing the news. He said he heard Jim from down the street tell Eustace at the barber that the authorities were going to release the boy. No, the sheriff declined that idea. They heard that Tucker had a gang out patrolling the streets, and not in a helpful way. Daddy had his own group of men who ebbed and flowed into Greenwood all night long. Rumors gained momentum and edited themselves. Greenwood men offered to help, and were rebuffed. Tucker's mob expanded to include women and children, furious and thirsty, shouting at the courthouse.

Grace had no map for this.

When they heard the first shots, around midnight, Mama woke the boys and had them tying their shoes. Grace roused and hoisted what she could carry. Daddy rushed in again, surveyed their movements and bid Mama get moving.

"Stay low, avoid the South tracks, get to them as fast as you can, but don't run. Don't let them see you." He was off again. Grace searched for the key to decipher his code. "Get to them," he had said, but "don't let them see you." Grace did not know how to avoid them when she didn't know who "them" was.

Stepping off the back porch was like falling into a free summer night. The children had not been so much as in the backyard since the day before; JacobandSam took pains to control their sleepy muscles. Mama grabbed each one by the hand and marched her family, minus one, south and east, along the alleys behind the houses.

When they reached the corner, what looked like an impromptu party, caught Grace's attention. It was no party, Grace realized, noticing the menacing silhouettes of rifles, long, deadly arms angled surely at the sky. Swarms of men dashed through the streets shouting orders. Gaggles of women and children made the same circuitous route the Irons family had taken. Many of them ran unencumbered, no bags to slow them, no jackets or coats, just hands reaching for children, feet running, faces openly frightened.

If Grace had been able to stay at home, in Greenwood, that night, she might have seen the mob of white men lobbing torches into the Baptist church. She might have been present to see Doc, who lived up the street, surrender his home only to be executed on his front lawn. She might have seen the older boys running up Standpipe Hill, impotent observers of destruction. Some proprietors had had the forethought to board up the wide glass windows of their businesses. Nothing they did prevented the armed men from positioning themselves at key points on the edges of Greenwood, forming a barricade.

All Grace saw, though, was her mama's back as she crouched low, keeping her babies in tight formation. All Grace knew was that her vital responsibility was to keep the suitcases from dragging in the street, causing a ruckus and getting them all caught. Grace kept her eyes on the damask of Mama's coat as she forged the way through Greenwood, east, away from the river, and south. Grace did not know this route, but she followed blind. She gave up trying to keep mental track of where they were. It was enough to get farther away from the gun blasts. Each report echoed in the streets and raised incoherent wailing from the boys. They did not talk. They simply scrambled.

On her own, Grace could have made it to the eastern boundary of the tracks at a good clip. With her brothers and mother and bags of belongings, it took hours. They managed to make it to the other side of the tracks before the barricades trapped Greenwood's residents. They crept low and slow, sweat beading and breath flying until Mama found a ditch blanketed with soft grass and big enough for four of them. They tumbled in.

SamandJacob were stunned and empty of words. What passed between them, though, in tugs and winks and nudges, led Grace to believe that while they had been frightened, they were not immune to the thrill of a daring escape. Realizing this, a laugh floated out of her, and she clamped a hand over her lips.

20

No two mornings are the same. Grace built a timeline by linking up the color of every one of those mornings, from the bright and sunny blankness of Thursday's dreams to lead grey Wednesday. Some people make irrational connections between the weather and tragedy. They remember that it was raining the day someone died, or it was bright and beautiful when a baby was born. If Grace were to do that from her makeshift bed in the rural green of Tulsa, she would have said that the two matched each other like a cup and saucer, a grey day and death holding hands. She knew that was a lie and a bad one. People die. Weather and death are not in allegiance. Sun mocks grief and clouds deepen it. That's just people looking for reason or meaning or some kind of bigger truth. The only bigger truth working that day was hate. The sun doesn't care when you die.

Grace opened her eyes to stare straight into low plumes of smoke from burning buildings and flesh. If silence can be as calm as a baby's sleeping breath, it can also be disturbing and vacant, like a body in a coffin. A stone jabbed the soft flesh on her back. The shush of trees and grass dulled the crackling fires still burning in Greenwood. In one hazy breath between sleep and real life, she remembered what they were doing, jammed together in a grassy hole somewhere close enough to the tracks to hear the whistle in a distance.

Mama and Grace had coaxed the boys to calmness, and Grace remained tucked close around them. While they had not needed comfort, Grace had. The women had positioned themselves to absorb the shocks of gunfire and the screaming. Each shot glanced their ears, each scream landed a blow as they wrapped their bodies around the boys, hushing them needlessly with a repetitive fervor. They were springs or spark plugs or some kind of impervious blanket that took the brunt of the sound so the boys, at least the boys, would be safe, and calm. Calmer than the women had been.

The night had screamed on, the gunfire, the shouting, the flames rising from buildings to light the sky like unceasing lightning. They had held the boys in an urban foxhole. Mother and daughter curled around the boys, two parentheses hedging them. Grace had grasped Mama's hands and slept.

Grace blinked into the day and searched for Mama, who was drinking from Daddy's Army canteen. She heard Grace stir.

"Morning," she said.

Grace searched her mother's face, her tone, her one word for a clue. Grace wanted to ask if it was over. She wanted to know if they were okay. She did not ask, and Mama did not answer. Nothing. Just the fact, the time of day, no value added.

Mama stood, pushed the canteen into Grace's palm and scrambled to the edge of their crater, motioning with her hand for Grace to stay. As if Grace wanted to climb to the war and spectate. The boys slept on just as content as though they had been planning a night under the canopy of heaven. Pebbles slid down the face of the slope while Mama climbed. They landed without a sound. Mama stood tall and unafraid at the lip, hands on her hips as if she were preparing to deliver the mother of all lectures. Mama stood for a long time shaking her head in complete disapproval. Grace, the kid who had, just a day ago, laughed with her friend about coffee breath, chuckled to see her mother's stance; if it were a kid, Tulsa would be smart to fear this woman, this thoroughly disappointed person. The young woman who had run from a burning neighborhood did not find any humor in spending a burning night in a hole, unable to return home.

Home. It occurred to Grace that if the main drag in Greenwood had been aflame, chances were strong that their home had also been destroyed. No. Grace refused this idea. Not now. She could not do that now.

When Mama stumbled barefoot back down, tears marked dirty rivulets on her face, rain on dusty streets. She shook the boys awake. They chewed a little bit of crusty bread and drank the rest of the water. Mama said they had to move. They climbed the hill and marched.

Emerging from their curve in the earth, Grace wanted to locate them on her webwork of Tulsa. She did not recognize any landmarks. Hills rolled in every direction, as if the rising sun had some secret power to unfurl the sloping wilds. She saw, distantly and veiled in ash, the towering skyline of the city. She knew they were east, but she had known that before. Grace was lost.

They walked as the sun rose, angling up and over and down the hills. JacobandSam tumbled ahead, they said, "On the lookout." Mama played along, asking her sentries what they observed. She pointed to different trees, peeled bark from them to instruct the boys. *This is an elm. This is an oak. Here is a dogwood.* Grace ignored these ridiculous lessons. Her legs burned. Her throat was dry. Her home was gone. She didn't care what kind of tree was what. She could not live in a tree.

Grace tracked the sun to determine that they had turned northward. Cresting a hill, the winking slate blue of the Arkansas in full midday sun assured Grace. Finding herself within a hills' ramble to the river was hardly an adequate balm, but its presence secured her. She could locate herself at the river. She knew this city. She knew how to get anywhere if she knew where the river ran.

"Okay, Grace," Mama turned to her.

Grace had been what Daddy would have called the rear guard as they trudged onward. Her mother nudged her forward. Grace balked, uncertain.

"I don't know where I'm going, Mama." She spoke as if to a toddler, sure that her mother was delirious with hunger or exhaustion. "Drink some water, Mama," she offered. "You feeling unwell? Should we rest a while?"

Mama shook her head and let a slow grin overtake her face. "Take us to Mercy."

Grace would have been less surprised if Mama had instructed Grace to build an ark.

"Mama?" This was a bad idea.

"Trust me." Rachel had all these different ways of modulating her voice. Mercy was rather skilled at mimicking Rachel's angry tone, or her tired tone, or her do-it-right-now tone. Rachel brought her voice low, like a bear trap, and coated it with layers of the finest silk. Two words, a warning, a promise, a charge.

Still Grace hedged. "We can't go there."

"Yes, we can, Grace. You're going to lead us." Mama masterfully modified her tone again, brooking no debate, which Grace chose to ignore. She was unmoved by her mother's order.

"No, Mama. We can't. He's . . . Mr. Dub. He's . . . I saw him . . ."

Grace let loose. She spilled her map, her timeline, her routes, the landmarks of her weekend rushed out. Mama sat in the dirt across from her child, listening. She touched the tip of Grace's shoe with her own. Grace sobbed her way through the days, gasping and gagging and lisping and throwing words like the tantrum inside her. It felt so good. Lifting the gates alleviated the pressure she had not recognized until that moment. When the deluge slowed to a trickle, and she could breathe without a fit of hiccoughs, she faced Mama.

"We really can't go there, Mama."

Mama nodded. "Honey . . ."

"No! Mama, No! We can't go there. Listen to me. Friday, at the river. Wearing a hood." Grace chose words JacobandSam wouldn't understand. She bugged out her eyes, pushed her head forward, trying for any kind of charaded gesture to signal her; Grace was not kidding.

She hovered in the space of secrets between her and her mother.

Mama plucked a blade of grass and cupped the sliver between the edges of her thumbs. She brought the reed to her mouth and blew. The blade vibrated against her skin and the boys turned in awe to discover their mother's newly revealed talent.

The boys jumped into Mama's lap. She gave them a tutorial on grass whistling, then sent them off to practice.

She turned back to Grace. "I know what you think you saw. Grace, I need you to trust me."

Now Grace's eyes bugged in shock. Both of her parents had brushed off her concern, had downplayed her suspicions. "What?" It wasn't enough. "What?" Grace repeated. "You *know*? You know he's . . . like that? You know? Are you crazy?"

Rachel slapped Grace only once in her life. Once. Grace would later, much later, acknowledge that she had it coming. Mama's hand met Grace's cheek even while her eyes apologized. The slap was painful enough, but the sting of crumbling innocence took more to endure. The shiny veneer of naiveté does not rinse away with the gently passing years but with the crack of skin against skin, with the salt of ignorance pulsing in the open wound. Grace broke out of a childish shell and assumed the necessarily brittle crust of adulthood in that moment, in those seven days.

"Trust me."

Grace touched her cheek, forced the tears back, back, back. Grabbed a little hand, Jacob's or Sam's, and stomped away.

Grace led her family. They followed the northwestward bending of the river, and Grace scanned the banks for any sign of Mercy. If Grace had seen her, she wondered if she would run to her or away from her. She was surprised to feel the flare of anger in the pit of her stomach. When the family reached the swath of greenery near the cave home the girls had made, Grace stopped. She listened for the wild girl, hoping.

Rachel urged her to keep moving. They wound through an intricate system of back yards and garden borders, and arrived at Mr. Williams' garage. The shooting and burning started again with new force. The boys heard it first, the telltale hum of jets. They craned their necks toward the ash clouds until the planes emerged. They flew low and banked north, and Grace heard the unmistakable bleat of machine gun fire. She felt sick. As the jets strafed the city, Mama uttered prayers between her urgent cries to move.

Grace caught bits of words, segments of names Mama was thinking of, the men, their neighbors, their leaders. Grace was flummoxed by her Mama summoning the grace to lean on prayer as they fled for safety in the brightness of day, into dangers that were only beginning to become real.

At the door to the garage, Mama stooped and rummaged under a gravel path. When she stood, she opened the door with the key she had retrieved. Grace followed. The garage was dark and smelled of oil, gas, grass clippings and leather. They were like a row of ducklings, tucking as close to Mama as possible, being led to water or food. She found a lantern easily and lit it. She moved with certainty; not the fright and caution that consumed Grace. Mama moved like she expected everything she needed to be ready and within reach. Some kind of supply side miracle.

The family scooted around the car, and one of the boys knocked over an empty oil can. The clatter ran up Grace's spine and she squeezed his hand. Hard. He stifled a cry. Mama pulled a rope Grace had not noticed. A ladder descended, and wordlessly they scrabbled up into the space above the garage.

This was becoming a week of discoveries for Grace. The entire area was packed. Food, jugs of water, towels, blankets, a chamber pot, even clothes, candles, books. Mattresses, a large electric fan.

Mama pointed Grace toward a box of food while she busied herself brushing leaves and grass from the boys' pants and hair.

Grace opened cans and poured water into tin cups. The boys ate like wolves. Mama and Grace drank until their stomachs distended. Within minutes, the boys were two apostrophes clamped together on one of the mattresses, before they could lay a sheet down on it, sleeping. Again, Mama directed Grace to a box: sheets. Grace made up the rest of the mattresses with sheets she had laundered only days earlier. Mama sat with a heave on a bigger bed and beckoned Grace to her. Grace lay down next to her mother, each on her back, resisting the pull of gravity on their muscles and bones and hearts. Resisting the tears.

Grace did not ask her, as they peered at the beams above them, for an explanation. She did not beg understanding. She did not ask Mama what she wanted to know: how did these things get here? Grace did not ask her when, if, she'd see Daddy again. Mama did not offer. She said nothing. Grace listened to her breath, and tried to follow, keep following, her rhythm. If she matched it, Grace could unwind the knots that pained her shoulders, she could stop the twitching in her legs. Grace thought, then, of how much listening she had done in her life, and how much listening supported her. Listening, the casual, involuntary intake of sounds, vibrations on the air, information, was the foundation for everything she knew or thought about the world. Mama's breath in the Williams' kitchen was abrupt. She made precise puffs out of her mouth. Effort. In the secret attic though, her breath was a prayer. Deep, heavy, full. So many different ways to hear a person breathe.

Grace thought of Daddy's breath when he read to her, how the syllables of the words matched the rhythm of his hand stroking her forehead, each little glide of his finger drew out her frantic energy and replaced it with a calmness that closed her eyes, slowed her heartbeat. She thought of his voice like a deep chasm of hope.

21

Grace dreamt swirling dreams.

Mercy stood on the street in front of a skyscraper. She held an empty coffee cup in her hands that tilted as she craned her neck skyward, watching the arc of a beam sail through the domed atmosphere. Clouds in wonderful colors danced over her head. They were pink and green and fat like spools of spun sugar. Above them, red and black clouds bulged, banging into the softer, fluffier ones. Her eyes caught the swinging beam again and her neck followed. Her torso twisted while it landed where it had been aimed, into the skeleton of a new building that stretched like so many limbs into the same sky that had just beguiled her.

Grace did not appear in her own dream, on the sidewalk with Mercy. The girl was alone except for a faceless crane operator. A sound like rushing water flowed around Mercy. A lip stain kissed the edge of the mug in her hands. Grace saw her back, as if she were watching from behind. Mercy started to turn toward where Grace might have stood. In time with her movements, the sky turned dark, darker. It blotted her out. Grace called to her, and she returned the call, laughing.

Grace fought waking. Sleep was a precious gift she cupped in her hands, something cherished she was being asked to surrender. The sounds of late day drifted to her, the waking noises of SamandJacob, of her mother shifting on her mattress. When Grace slept that heavy sleep of sadness and fatigue, where the dreams popped like soap bubbles before they settled, when her body sweated as if she'd run for days and days, the waking was the hardest. After two days of exile, oppressive disorientation sunk down against Grace, a weighted blanket that whispered *stay asleep*.

When a body and a mind drift on the current between sleep and awakening, the colors blend and shift. The heat of a sleep-soaked body meets the coolness of an early summer morning. One turn—as the dreamer begs her body to stay rooted in the ether—and there's nothing the mind can do. The body is awake, and the dream is gone. If the dream does not dissolve the instant eyes open, then it will dissipate throughout the day, bobbing in and out of mind's view. Grace groped for the sound of Mercy's laugh. She fought to keep the mirth in her ear, but the sound retreated. The dream crashed away from Grace, Mercy's laughter carried away by transient night currents. Before too long, Mercy's jeweled giggle was replaced with a deep roar of loss.

The attic space impressed Grace, both in its existence and in the waves of heat swamping the space. What she had failed to take in when she had first slung herself over the lip of the ceiling hatch into the bright room she inventoried. What in another time she would call food and water seemed now like rations and fluid, pure sustenance without the luxury of taste. Tins, cans, jars, boxes. Dried goods, canned goods. She recognized sheets that had once decorated Miss Willie's room, a rug that had covered a spot on the floor by the commode. Toys that had known better days before their conscription as refugee castoffs.

Grace had lost track of every untangled end. She could not piece together the history of this place. She knew the physical location, that it was the garage attic of the house that belonged to Mr. Williams. She knew the landmarks and signposts and the botany of this house, this plot, this space on this street, in this town. But she did not know why she was there.

Curiosity mingled with sour anxiety, and Grace called to Mama. Mama lay on her mattress, still, watching the boys sleep, their small chests rising and falling, their eyelashes just glancing the apples of their cheeks, beads of sweat haloing their brown foreheads.

"Sh."

Grace rolled to her back and stared at the knots in the beams above her. Her Daddy had shown her the grain in a newly planed beam once, and Grace had run her thumb the length of the dark striping. She had held the lumber close to her face and inhaled. She had said, "It smells like green, Daddy." And he had laughed.

In the attic, Grace followed the grain in the attic beam, tracing the crazy path with her eyes. When she reached a knot, she stared until a fistful of wood became the silhouette of a president, or an elephant or a letter, like some people do with clouds. Grace occupied herself tracing each beam, identifying the simulacrum in each knot while she waited. Waited.

She tried to find the question she had wanted to ask Mama, but whatever it had been, she knew the silence in the space did not deserve to be tainted. Whatever she had wanted to know corrupted this room. She knew that her family, like this room, was a secret, and that Miss Willie was the keeper.

Grace followed her thoughts as she followed the grains. If Miss Willie was the keeper, then Grace ought to have found some slice of comfort, surrounded as she was by shards of her. In a gabled recess Grace watched a spider web drift with the breeze, absent its maker. Lemon meringue sun shone on the tight spiral in the center. She remembered that day in the kitchen, when Miss Willie had begged her assistance. She thought of how Mercy had cowed to her mother, had left the house in all appearances a fine young lady. The web puffed out like a parachute on the wind, and a smile floated across Grace's mouth to remember the different young lady who had met her at the river later on the same day. Outside the window, beyond the gauzy web, the rioting sounds had nearly ceased, but Grace clenched her fists, expecting more at any moment. Her mind continued its path through the funnel of the last days, and she flinched to recall how Friday had begun with a tempest from Mercy and ended with a shock. Grace now remembered her question for her mother. She knew the reason for the ache in her gut.

The day grew hotter, and the air in the attic was stultifying. Eventually, Mama could no longer simply watch the boys sleep. She rose and ducked behind the wash closet curtain, at which point Grace ascertained the purpose of the curtain and the nook behind it. The boys roused soon after Mama. Grace did not want to listen to their voices. She did not want them to wake and spoil the blandness in the room. As they sat on their mattress, SamandJacob rubbed sleep out of the corners of their eyes and stretched their soft limbs. They blinked into the light, their heads swiveling like fans. They did not speak. They curled against each other, wakefulness having not reached maximum strength. Grace sank with relief.

One of the boys stood and wobbled over to Grace, who opened her arms to him. He climbed inside her embrace and stared out as she rocked him. A fly thunked against the wall. A bee buzzed near the window, but refrained from entering a wide hole in the screen. Car doors clicked and thudded out on the street. Birds tweeted in oblivion. The day crawled.

Grace heard a grumble from her brother's belly. "You hungry?"

He nodded. His twin, across the room, nodded, too.

Mama gestured toward the boxes. "Something small, Grace. Don't know how long we'll be here."

Grace released her hold on the boy and stood. Her shoulders ached. The muscles in her shins and thighs screamed from walking all those hills, those circuitous, relentless miles. Stretching hurt in the same way her heart surged toward Mercy. It hurt in a good way.

They heard the door below them creak open, and they froze. The listened to the footfalls on the ladder that approached their little attic space. Then, Miss Willie poked her head up through the hole in the floor, or the ceiling. She tossed her head, asking Mama without words to approach her.

Grace stood while they whispered, washed her face with cool water. Her knuckles knocked against the ceramic and the water sloshed. Her dust covered body left a dingy ring in the wash basin, but clean hands and a clean face refreshed her. She ruffled the boys who pinged about the room, dubious and careful but with renewed interest in their adventure. Grace found a loaf of bread and a jar of jam. She set out a plate for the boys and then poured water for them. She wandered closer to the women. Routine movements, so much flutter. She angled for news, any news.

Grace was rewarded with a whole lot of nothing until Miss Willie cleared her throat, rushed ahead, asked Mama, "You see Mercy?" Her voice sounded thick like custard stuck in her throat. Mama put her hand to her heart, shook her head. Miss Willie hung her head. She started back down the ladder when Grace interrupted.

"When's the last time you saw her?"

Mama threw a glance at Grace, but Grace did not preface her question with the prettiness of manners. She did not excuse herself or ask leave to speak. Grace did not refer to Miss Willie by name. Grace didn't care. She shook Mama off.

"When did you see her last?" Grace asked, urgency propelling her.

Miss Willie's shoulders shook, her chin rested on her white chest, a simple gold chain hung around her neck, glanced against the pale pink blouse she had been wearing on Thursday. A stain, a dribble of gravy or sauce marred the placket near a pearly button on her blouse. She wore no makeup except a gloss on her lips and the day old smudge of mascara under her eyes.

"Tell me," Grace demanded.

"Last night." She rushed on to explain as Grace glared at her. "She, I put her to bed. We talked. I told her. We had a plan, we knew what we were doing. I told her you'd be here." She sobbed. "When I didn't see her this morning, I assumed she was sleeping in. I checked her bed at noon. Oh. God."

Grace pushed past her, forcing herself down the ladder.

All three heads turned in unison, a feminine jerk of attention toward the sound of doors slamming and a voice yelling into the day. Mr. Tucker. Mama shrank back and Miss Willie shooed Grace back up the into the attic room.

From there, Grace could neither see nor hear the front of the house. She threw open the window, hoping to catch any part of any phrase, to gauge by the tones what was happening. Mama pinched her brow together, two angry grooves clouded her face. Grace bit her lip. Earlier in the day, Mama had told her, Jules had been forced from the House Next Door, two gun toting men loudly explained it was for her own safety. They carted all the domestics off the street. To where Grace did not know. No more news reached the attic, but later, they learned the truth. Everyone who did not manage to escape was taken under guard to the ball park and the fairgrounds. Their families could not gain their release without piles of paperwork. Those who had been processed received a tag to be worn, which was supposed to mark them for liberty. Imprisoned, tagged and released. Like animals.

Mama begged the boys with soothing hands to be still and quiet. They thought they were safe, if they could just keep quiet.

Quiet broke. One moment, they were statues, afraid to breathe, even at a distance from the street. Afraid any movement would arouse his suspicion. Then, like a rushing wind, the torrent of oceans, the still quiet calm ripped opened into a riot. Miss Willie screamed.

22

Grace acted.

She wrapped her fingers around ladder rungs, touching each lightly, skipping down, sprinting toward the scream. She registered the bang of the car against her thigh as she slipped past it, heard her mother calling, noises she couldn't decipher, from behind her. Grace saw a dress in her peripheral vision as Mama overtook her. Rachel caught Miss Willie as she crumpled like wet paper, falling to the grass.

Grace stopped dead in front of Mr. Tucker whose face was a white mask, a tortured mask. He looked almost like a man she could know. Mr. Dub was there, suddenly, appearing like a wish. He walked to and stood in front of Tucker, blocking Grace's view of both men's faces. Their heads shook, their lips lisped and sizzled like snakes. Tucker's hand encircled Mr. Dub's arm, offering himself as a crutch. Dub brushed him off. He ran a hand through his hair as he turned to Grace, to see his wife leaning back in Mama's arms.

Grace heard them. She heard the words. They didn't sound like words Grace would speak, or have to hear; they were foreign and harsh, guttural and urgent. He walked, Mr. Tucker. He walked in short, hard steps, popped open the car door, too loud the lever worked, too loud the door swung wide. Grace saw his pants rise around his showy white calves, the curly hairs skipping ring-around-the-rosy at the edge of his black socks that circle his bony ankles. He bent, pulled and grunted and straightened.

Mercy dangled in his arms.

Wednesday

"Clear Streets by Martial Law
Troops in Command; 9 Whites, 68 Negroes Dead"
Tulsa Tribune, June 1921

23

When JacobandSam were small, they shared a rag doll. They used to tug o'war with the poor thing, each of them holding fast to a limb and yanking. Eventually, the thing gave out, but for so long, when the battle for ownership was won, the victor held the limp figure in his arms, the spoils of war. Mercy limp in the arms of her and Grace's enemy reminded Grace of that poor rag doll. Miss Willie sobbed on the front walk. Mr. Dub shifted his girl to his arms and brought her into their house.

She was Grace's first loss. The first loss is a necessary agony, wedging itself against ribs, stretching sinews and marrow. Edging out light like an eclipse, swallowing easiness in a gulp. Leaving a cold emptiness. The first loss does not make subsequent losses easier but it leaves its own kind of wound.

Grace stood outside the Williams' house, lost again.

Eventually, she became aware of a presence beside her. In the distance, smoke rose in dusty plumes, and the sound of sirens was noticeably absent. She had survived actual tornadoes, and the spooky quietness unnerved Grace, as if the storm had centered in on her, on them all, in this quarter of an acre of browning hell. Grace felt she had tromped outside too early, thinking the worst had passed, not realizing the backend was about to thunder through her.

She filled the vacant space, vacant herself until she noticed the steady inhale and exhale that was not her own. Then, a hand on her shoulder, warm and large and heavy. An arm around her, pulling her into a stained cotton shirt. She leaned against the body and it steered her inside. The car that had brought her, Mr. Tucker's, started up and idled away. The engine and the rubber connecting solidly with the sticky hot asphalt like a dirge.

Days later. Years later. Forever later. There was a dryness in Grace that remained. Soft murmurs, cold cups of water pressed to her lips. The rip of a cry escaping from the dining room. Subdued anguish, smothered against the firmness of another, bigger, body. The delicate touch of fingers between the blades of her shoulders. The hunching over and away from those fingers. Grace rejected the comforting touch so many wanted to give her. The table, the kitchen table, where they had folded napkins and wiggled their eyebrows. Fingertips spread wide on the steady surface of the plane, her cheek smoothed against the everyday waxed tablecloth. Eyes closed, lashes flicking against her hard pillow. Grace slept.

She slept the sleep of drool and darkness. Grace examined, when she woke, the color and the taste of mornings. She figured Daddy or Mr. Dub had carried her to bed. She liked to picture this; both of them wide shouldered, barrel chested men of work and industry and obligation. Sweeping her deadweight into arms too big for the job. Tucking a chin onto Grace's head and cuddling. Maybe it was Mr. Dub who carried her to the bed his daughter had not ruffled in the night. Maybe he held Grace because he could not hold Mercy. Maybe it was Daddy. Maybe he drew Grace close because he could. Maybe none of it. Maybe she walked, sleeping and oblivious.

When she woke, she woke the way Mercy would have; in her bed, the singsong of birds beckoning. Her mama's voice in Grace's ear, a tear splashed onto her face finally did the work. Grace opened her eyes when she'd have rather succumbed to the blank sleep of unknowing. Where she could forget all of it, even her. Not wanting to move, she shifted her eyes to find Miss Willie, who smiled at Grace; it was a real smile though her lips remained closed and her face did not grow sparkly with joy. It was a tired smile.

Grace pushed her face into her pillow. Mercy's mama, Miss Willie lay next to Grace, her hand twined around Grace's, a climbing weed of grief. They lay like that while the sun circled up and over. While the morning birds flew off in search of lunch. They were sponges; silent, inert, absorbing Mercy.

"I always pictured a day when you two would get your sleepover."

Grace rolled over and wiggled closer, rolled her head to look at Miss Willie again.

Miss Willie's tears pooled, dammed up, overflowed. "I don't want you to go, Grace. Not you, too. Not yet."

24

The whispers started when Grace entered the kitchen, holding Miss Willie' hand. She sat Grace down and fixed her a cup of tea. Mama toasted two thick slices of bread, smeared them with butter and drizzled them with honey. Grace sipped the tea. She bit the toast. She tasted nothing. She did not chew.

Miss Willie nodded at Grace. They sat, as they had lain on her bed. Mama busied herself in the kitchen, sweeping up and wiping down and pressing herself into the wallpaper, out of sight. Miss Willie reached across the table, touched Grace's fingertips. Grace pulled them away but Miss Willie reached fast, for her, caught Grace's hands. She held the tips as if they were made of fine crystal. She examined them, lifting each finger, touching the padding at their tips, pressing the mooned cuticles. Tears dropped, a sort of symphony of sadness and they plopped against the cloth.

Her eyes were full of questions.

Grace realized that these mothers knew the language of friendship; if she could bat her eyelashes a certain way, and Grace knew what she meant, well, that just proved . . . something. It was like catching the right thread amongst a sea of them; finding this connection she did not know she had, could not have been bothered to see.

Miss Willie pushed back her chair and stood in a motion so fluid Grace was startled to find her next to Grace, urging her to her feet, walking her, unsure and quite afraid into the front room. They stopped at the doorway. After a while, Miss Willie was gone; Grace did not hear her leave, neither did Miss Willie announce her exit. Grace did not want to go in the room. She did not want to see her any more clearly than from the doorway, a still body, prone on a long sofa, cast in shadows.

That was enough, wasn't it? To make note of this thing, this shape that was neither her friend nor any kind of representation of her?

Grace thought of her fingers in the diamond of the fence. She thought of Mercy hip checking her as they walked to the river. Grace thought of the blonde baby hairs flying every which way. She was at Mercy's side, sitting next to her on the floor in three strides. She held her hand; cold and hard.

Grace heard the women in the kitchen. They made their lips small, shrinking their words. As if they could contain the syllables of grief, as if making them unintelligible also made them weak. As if whispers were not their own kind of agony. Grace had not cried. She had not opened her mouth except to let a wave of tea slip over her tongue, down her throat, into her empty belly. Grace worried, too. She knew her persistent silence was an alarm, and she knew they had enough on their minds.

A fly knocked against the window behind the sofa on which her body lay. Grace followed the flight as it lit about the room, stopping for seconds near her face, near her hand planted on the soft green plush of the rug beneath her, then off again. It flew toward Mercy, toward her. Mercy did not raise a hand to bat it away.

Grace did. She sent the fly away on a gust from her palm, standing to keep Mercy safe from another swoop. She followed the fly for a heartbeat, two, three. Feeling free from its menace, Grace looked at Mercy. Really looked at her.

The linen napkin highlighted the landscape of Mercy's face, the short nose, the wide brow, a strong chin and full lips. Grace tugged at one corner and watched the napkin fall to the floor. Dirt caked at the corners of her mouth, on that clear forehead. A drop of blood settled into the curve at the edge of where her smile would have been. Sweat had dried on her throat, leaving dirty tendrils sweeping along her veins.

Mr. Williams stood in the doorway.

"It's not her," Grace said.

He lifted his hand, let if fall back to his side, as if he no longer had the circuitry for mobility. As if maintaining an upright stance was the last and only faculty he had. He said, "I know."

Boyd

25

It was hot in that kitchen. It was hot everywhere. They couldn't escape. Not the heat, not the sirens, not the girl in the living room, crushed into the carpet like a forgotten stain. Not the dead body lying next to her.

Boyd worried about the heat, and the body. They couldn't let her stay in there much longer. He held his breath against the knowledge.

Dammit. The job would fall to Boyd. He'd make the arrangements for the coroner or whoever you call for that kind of thing. He'd also have to steel himself to go in there and tell his child, this is how her friend died.

Rachel had got Miss Willie to drink some tea, chew on a cold sandwich. Her throat, this long white gash of skin, thumped as she struggled to choke down the dryness. Rachel coaxed Miss Willie like a child, laying her hands on her back as a prayer, stroking her arm to calm the ocean ripping through her, this vastness in her eyes that scared Boyd by its hollowness.

None of them thought it would come to this.

When Mr. Dub first approached Boyd, when they had first laid the plans, it was just a contingency, a storm shelter kind of thing. He had surprised Boyd, in many ways, with the notion.

"Getting more pressure from Tucker." He had sidled up to Boyd, not unusual, nothing to raise his suspicions. He was in the habit of sidling; when Boyd caught a phantom in the corner of his eye, next he knew, Dub's talking in the white tones of the confessional. He could approach people in a way that dictated what they'd do with their own bodies.

If Dub walked up straight and tall, Boyd met him the same, eye to eye, man to man. If he put a palm to Boyd's shoulder, Boyd nodded, heard the words behind the touch and then moved to the action Dub's touch indicated. Cut this plank, see this customer, fetch the finishing nails for so and so. Shorthand of the working man. The nod, the grunt, the eye slice to the left, to the right. Boyd figured this out fast.

Tucker was harder to read. That was the difference between those Tucker and Dub. One stood straight and tall like a man because he was a man. The other made his spine into a column of strength built on fear and danger. There's only one of those kinds Boyd respected easily, fully.

Straight and tall. It can hide a multitude, or nothing at all but the plainness, the steady nature, of a good man.

Pressure from Tucker was all they ever got, some more than others. The sidle told Boyd keep working and listen, don't slide your eyes around, don't so much as wipe your nose. This is important.

Dub had sidled, and Boyd made a noise to tell him he had heard what Dub didn't say, to tell him go on.

"I don't want to do it," Dub had said.

Boyd measured the timber, a long blonde plane. Ran his palm along its grain, felt the warm density in its story. There was a beauty to a well-cut plank. The smell of sawdust intoxicates, almost as much as the scent of new baby skin or of Rachel, covered in pie crust. Boyd imagined the best parts of the world smell like that; clean, angled, chiseled and drenched with the honey and heat of soil.

"I don't want to do it," he had repeated. Boyd had never been so close to the heart of a white man. Had never wanted to be; never cared to see the aching chunk pried loose from a chest, beating rawness and anger, humanity and the devil. Did not care to see the cavity from which it was wrought, the ribs as planks, the veins running lengths, dispersing the story through cells, coursing with the dank heat and earth of his innards.

Damn that man. Boyd had resisted him like a schoolgirl shy about her skirt hem for as long as he could. Dub had prized him loose, made Boyd see him, the goodness, then he threw down that beating heart and made him see more.

"What you gonna do?" asked Boyd.

Dub penciled slashes along the board, quarter inch, three inch, foot long slices, nicks to keep track, nicks to show this is where to cut, this line, right here, be precise.

"Thinking about a charade."

Boyd lifted the plank onto his shoulder, heaved it around Dub and carried it to the sawhorse. Dub made notes in a book while Boyd made the cut. He ran a thumb along the incision, where he had cleaved one into two. The sharpness of splinters, dull daggers pricking calloused fingertips. Boyd smiled, satisfied, tossed the board into a pile growing at his feet.

Another plank, parceled out first by someone's wishes, then Boyd's ruler and pencil, then the slick teeth of a saw, eating a perfect line. Boyd stood by Dub, marking out the lines.

"What if I join up, follow through, act the part?"

Couldn't be helped. Boyd looked up at him, doubt spilling out of his large face. Could Boyd say out loud, to his boss, who in his pap's time would have been his master, could he say, "You crazy?" Could Boyd take Dub's shoulders and shake the nonsense out of his mouth, jarring it loose from his head? He could no more do that than use the same water fountain. His face would have to say enough, and more.

Dub yelled across the yard, hustling workers about, a pummeling swarm of lifting and throwing, cutting and hauling, slamming and shouting. He surveyed his domain until Boyd got himself back to quarter inches and yards.

"What else you got?"

Boyd shrugged, lumbered off, cut more wood. Slammed another plank down on the table, lay the ruler along the spine of another beam. "Nothing. I got nothing."

Decision made, Boyd ambled off. The women were notified, plans made, contingencies upon contingencies. Layers of deception like one of Rachel's fancy cakes. Not nearly as enticing.

Grace didn't know. She couldn't know. Because none of them thought it would ever get this far. They thought it was a just in case, a for instance, something to smooth the tide for Dub, for all of them.

Now, in the kitchen, Rachel coaxed the dead girl's mama to sip, just a bit more, honey, come on. You need to drink something, to eat something. Her words had always been ministrations, her food the sacrament, her touch the benediction. Into what, though, now? Benediction into a new kind of hell.

Hell is having to pull back all the layers of that rotten cake for your child, your baby. Hell is showing her the way a coffin is made and walking her down the blood soaked road that made that coffin, those hundreds of coffins, necessary. It wasn't just telling her Mercy was gone. It wasn't just saying, A led to B and the gut kick sum at the end is a dead child, your best friend. It was the false mask Dub wore, the stockpile Grace'd already seen and not comprehended in the attic. It was using a fire hose to blast away the innocence, to reveal the blood slick hood dropping from Tucker before the world, exposing the ugly sinews under his Sunday School clothes and his smarmy, toothy smile.

If a man can do that to his child and not feel some reluctance, that man has no soul, no smidge of masculinity, no desire to push his child into more than he himself had.

Boyd cast his head about, hoping to catch Dub's eye without raising Miss Willie into another fit. The tears of a mourning woman are a force Boyd avoided when possible. Couldn't take it.

Finally, he saw, he worked his way toward Boyd, as he worked his way toward the span between the hallway and the kitchen, a sort of neutral territory between two caverns of agony.

"We got to get her out of there."

He was lost. "Who? Which . . ." He bit his words, slicing into the next one, as if keeping it in his mouth, in his throat, would be the prayer of resurrection, the silence that did the work, " . . . her?"

Boyd swallowed. "Well. Dub. Both of them, I guess I mean." If he could make the sentence longer, then the nonsense at the end could sure take the sting, could sing away the need.

Dub nodded. "We have to tell her. All of it."

"Yup."

The men stood there, all long limbs and swallows, sweat and fury, staring each at his own patch of floor. Boyd picked out the mauves and greens that blended with the sturdy lug sole on Dub's boots, the skinny laces tied so tightly, pinched at the ends to near whiteness, the aglets hanging loose down the sides of his torpedo feet. Those were feet cemented to their spot. Boyd gathered in the length of him; his feet firmly planted, his ankles, one crossed over the other, his back pressing into the door jamb, his head tipped forward. His purpose was to hold up the house. He could not possibly be asked to move.

Boyd wanted to know, "All of it, all of it? Does she have to know about the hood?"

Dub blanched. "Mercy," her name flew from his lips, she was alive in that moment, he had forgotten. For just that glimmering moment. Then he remembered, and a fat tear filled his left eye. "Mercy told me they saw me." He folded against a rising current forming in his lanky abdomen; the man was not big enough after all, to hold this mess like a bucket. "Oh, God. They saw me."

Boyd did not need to know more than that. Not then. He left Mercy's father where he was, walked the longest short walk in fewer steps than he would have preferred.

Four—three now—women in the house and each of them with haunting, deeply empty eyes. Each of them like a cracked saucer, shaken loose from its cupboard, separated from its pair, useless without its matched cup. His daughter, his child, this strange creature he struggled to recognize, sat on the floor, holding the cold hand of Mercy.

If Boyd had bothered in the five steps from kitchen to hallway to door to contrive some sort of speech or routine of gestures, they abandoned him when he drew near. Nothing but a father's will to protect drove Boyd closer. He enfolded her in arms that suddenly seemed too small and too weak to make a difference. Where Boyd could neither stomach the gasping moans of Miss Willie nor rest his eyes on the heaving waste of Dub, shrunken by loss, Boyd had ears only for this one, pressed like a preserved leaf between the pages of his chest and arms. He wanted it to be enough.

There are these moments, Boyd thought, when we have a chance to be exactly what we need to be. They are not often enough. There are too many demands and too many impossible ways for things to go just wrong enough to leave a scar. Like an errant nick of the timber pencil, we can speak exactly the wrong word at the most inconvenient time. All future measurements will be off. Maybe you can't see them, but train your eye on the wainscoting long enough, or walk a tipsy porch too many years, and see. The single mistaken tick mark makes an unmistakable blemish. Life is, for most of us, so long we make more bad cuts than good. Boyd held Gracie, and after she had been kicked around like a spoiled cabbage those seven days in May, this was the worst and the best Boyd had ever been. Boyd was content that it was one time he measured precisely. God bless.

When she stopped crying, when the reserves had been depleted, when wave after wave had ebbed, she lifted her face to her father.

"What happened, Daddy?"

Boyd treated her like a fresh coat of paint, nimbly, testing, pulling her to her feet and walking her to a pair of chairs. He wanted to make space between their bodies. She submitted like a doll; he positioned her far into the deep back, into the wide arms, twisted her legs so that if she wanted to look around, the first thing she would see was her daddy. He pulled his chair closer, so that his knees touched hers, so she could feel the warm suppleness of the living.

Between Dub, Tucker, Miss Willie and Boyd, they assembled an idea of what had happened, each adding what little they knew.

Boyd told her blunt like a hammer.

Mercy had snuck out and was at the courthouse when the riot broke out. Tucker had seen her, tried to reach her. The crowd, it just opened like a gaping maw and swallowed her. Tucker had spent the better part of the day trying to get through, to get her back to her family.

"Tucker?" For once, the flash in her eye, the seething spit of his name, gave Boyd sureness that Grace was inside Tucker's bent bones and slack skin, the distant eyes.

"What would Tucker be doing bringing her back to us? To us? That man is nothing but a hateful bastard! I hate him. He didn't see her fall. He made her fall. And you!" She was frothing; accusations flew from her like punches landing on Boyd's gut, one, two, three. She said, "You worked for him! So did Mr. Williams. Mr. Williams, he hates us, Daddy. Hates us!"

Hysteria won out; her words hurt, but they hurt less for the lack of sense she made. She railed and vented and poured molten venom. Boyd let the blows fall, flinching but yielding. He almost missed it; her hand flew out so fast, so unexpectedly, she nearly landed a slap on his cheek. He caught her by the wrist and in a moment when she drew another breath, he told her the truth.

"Mr. Williams was pretending, Grace."

Any will she had remaining left her. This poor girl. You wonder how much you can heap on a child. How much they can understand. They think they know; they think they get it. They don't know. You don't want them to know. It's too ugly; it's too early to kill the innocence. Maybe it is watching that innocence die that leaves such a tremendous gap, such a knotted mess of scar tissue, the kind that aches at rain, hobbles on sky weepy mornings.

"What?" She could not believe. She could not understand. Boyd tried to help her reconcile the two images, but that kind of piecing together, the scraping away of layers, wiggling and forcing the pieces to understanding, it takes time. The picture unfolds slowly, like watching an artist daub the colors into the sketch.

A knock at the door, a distant thunder of chairs being pushed back, feet on the floor, a lock sliding open, a small crowd of quiet men enter the room. Boyd pulled her again to her feet, she leaned into him, reminding him of how she use to fall asleep while he read to her, her tough little body slackening, her breath deepening, her eyes drooping. She let Boyd navigate her from the room.

Once he had deposited her back in the kitchen, with the other women in similar states, Boyd returned to the men. No one spoke. They lifted the broken body onto a board, shifted her weight, exchanged the linen cloth for a crisp white sheet. Then she was gone.

Grace

26

There was no time for funerals.

Some bodies were buried properly, with caskets and markers and grief. Lots more filled hastily dug chasms, covered with earth and wiped away. It overwhelmed Grace how in one minute, life bustled through streets and in the next minute, everything was waste. How quickly we breathe past the dead, how fast we move beyond life so savagely stopped. Grace knew why. She knew the secret. If she stopped, if she hovered over the sore spot inside her, it threatened to rip open, a roaring yawn. So she let Mercy's eyes be filled with dirt and she pretended she couldn't still see her, as if alive and suffering under so much rock.

Grace still saw her. For a long time, she could see her. She wasn't hallucinating. She wasn't conjuring her up to fill a void; nothing could fill a hole the size of Mercy. Grace simply could not stop seeing her on her mother's sofa, dead. For the next days or weeks, Grace didn't know how long, the tableau in the living room replayed itself in her mind. Even later Grace recalled Mercy, and herself, and their fathers, positioned by bullets and fire and color into a sort of terribly inaccurate masque of loss.

Grace got all the information, about the riots, and the destruction of Greenwood, and the deaths, and the loss, and the savagery to come as she held her friend's dead grasp. That couldn't be true. She understood that Jules had been carted off with the rest of the domestics from that side of town. Under guard, they said, for their protection, all the blacks rolled like cattle to the fairgrounds. Mrs. Whitehurst could have secured her freedom, but Mrs. Whitehurst was not the generous sort.

Grace understood that her daddy had been released by Mr. Dub. She knew the green tag hanging from Daddy's jacket meant that he was under Mr. Dub's care. She pretended she didn't care that his safety was only ensured thanks to a white person.

Grace didn't get angry about that aspect, among many aspects, until later, when she had learned the college words for what she had felt. Daddy, tagged and marked, why, it smacked of branding, of ownership and submission and lack of agency. When the entire town crawled under its blanket of ashes and smoke and shame, all Grace saw, all she thought of, was her Mercy. Their Mercy. Stupid, stupid girl.

People love to ask questions without answers. They wondered what would be if Mercy had stayed where she was told, for once. If the first shot had never been fired. The hollow answers at the end of these questions comforted no one. They only reinforced Mercy's absence again, vinegar in the open wound.

Grace's family stayed in the garage for the next few weeks. Their Greenwood neighbors scattered. They never did see Jules again. They never saw many folks again. Those who stayed erected a tent city and hunkered down with a fierce resolve. They didn't know in May that soon they would endure a frozen winter in homes of fabric and wood. They didn't know lots.

Miss Willie and Grace lurched around each other. Miss Willie looked like someone had pinched her between their fingers, sizzle and pop and she was gone, leaving just a wisp. Her eyes sank into her face, which had turned a greying yellow color. Her hair hung in disarray, and she refused to change out of the pink shirt and skirt she wore when Tucker had brought Mercy.

Mama and Grace cooked food she didn't eat. They brewed coffee that grew cold. Mr. Dub skirted the edges of the house afraid to make a noise. He made a line between the bedroom and the chair near the sofa on which Mercy's body had rested. Daddy, Grace's own fearless daddy, refused to enter their house. He waited every morning at the base of the back stoop until Mr. Dub gave him instructions. The tasks were small and stupid. Raking and weeding, checking on a worksite, as if anything was happening.

When the fires had extinguished by Wednesday afternoon, Daddy seemed relieved to have a job that was somewhere, anywhere, else. Grace was stuck, though, with SamandJacob crawling the walls for something to do. She carried yet another cup of tea into Miss Willie. When she put the tea cup down, Miss Willie reached for her, wrapping her hand around Grace's wrist.

Grace waited, half bent over the table, one foot turned toward the door, making sure to move away from the empty sofa. Miss Willie held her arm. When Grace looked at Miss Willie, Grace buckled to the floor, and in the same motion, Miss Willie was out of her chair, on the floor with her, arms wrapped around Grace, tight and tighter.

Her blouse was soft and it carried the smell of sleep and sweat and day old food. Grace curled her fists around it and pounded into her back. She felt so small, like she could be crushed to dust inside her arms. She felt too small for the bigness rushing through her. She didn't feel she could do much to contain it, and that made her angry. Miss Willie didn't try to contain it, to reduce Grace, to minimize her, and that made her grow. Just a fraction, but enough.

There was nothing left when they slumped together on the floor, leaning against a wall.

They sat until their ragged breath calmed, until the salt dried on their cheeks. Until the sniffles stopped. Then, Miss Willie turned to Grace.

"She loved you," she said.

"She loved you, too."

"I know."

"But, she was so . . . " Grace trailed off. She had not lost her words. She worried it was too early to bring up her faults. Miss Willie jumped in to save Grace, though.

"She *was* so . . . " she smiled. "And still I know she loved me." She choked on the past tense like a bone, but she got past it with a smile.

Mercy

27

Really, it can't be helped. Mama and I circle each other. I want to go talk to neighbors, to get the story, but she has her girdle in a pinch. I ask her what's happening, she tells me get my work clothes on. I say I want to go back to town. She turns toward me like God has stopped a spinning top right where he wants; in front of me, hands on her hips, eyes boring into my skull, her body tense and coiled.

She tells me I am not going anywhere and what was I thinking, trying to get back to that place. She starts strong, determined; believe me, I get the point. Her voice unravels; she is an unfinished sweater, spooling wildly off a needle. I can't make sense as phrases fly at me, looping one around another: *you think you understand. You think you can go anywhere. You have no idea how dangerous. Suppose they'll just cut a path for you, Miss Mercy on high, so you can see what's going on.*

When I skip in the house, I think we will knock about in the afternoon and then have dinner. Same as every night. It is obvious that my illusions are just that. She is mad. She is mad at me. I can play that game.

I wish I can say I'm ashamed of myself. I wish I can say I would have done it differently. Give me a break. I am a kid. I haven't lived long enough to learn how to control the temperature of my words. I am proud about my smart mouth. If she is going to be mad at me, I will make it worth her while.

"What's going to happen, Mama?" I throw it in her face like hot water. "If I go downtown? Nothing. All everybody every does is talk. Talk talk talk. We hate them; they hate us. Nothing ever changes. Big deal. All those people at the courthouse, just hollering about justice, as if they know what that is."

She shakes her head, that way she does, tells me I don't know what I'm talking about. Seems plain to me. Bunch of cranky old men fighting about stupid stuff again. Their gun wagging doesn't frighten me. Everybody carries guns, same as they carry their coins. I understand. They are mad at that boy we saw running out of the store. They think he hurt the girl who was smeared with tears. They want him to pay. I understand, alright.

"You're not going out there, Mercy. Done. Final. Now get in there and set the table." I am not dumb. I know when to quit. The veins on her neck throb, her right eyebrow arches perilously high. She gives me the look; the one I think parents have to learn before they're allowed to take their babies home from the hospital. They have to be able to tell you they're disappointed, proud, you're in their way, or they love you with different flicks of their facial muscles, different angles of lips set inside the puffy cheeks of the 40-year-old. We're supposed to be able to decipher the code.

There is this to-do happening downtown—I can read the papers just as well as she can—and she wants to set the table with our every day dishes. Just because she means it doesn't mean I have to like it. I slam the cupboards, fling open the silver drawers, huffing and puffing and generally making myself a nuisance. Just to be clear. Plunking plates down, clinking glasses together. I mumble, "It's not fair. She tells *me* what to do." Until I remember what Mr. Boyd said. The way he said the words, like a command, when he said to run into the house, he'd never spoken to me like that before. When I hear the words echoing in my mind, I admit; I am a little afraid.

Still more curious.

The command calms me. In the china cabinet, Mom kept an old housekeeping bible. On cold or rainy days, if we could get out from under Miss Rachel's thumb, or we ran out of ways to entertain ourselves, Grace and I practiced folding napkins. The housekeeping bible had pages of napkin folding instructions. We took turns choosing a design and we pretended we were the Ladies' Auxiliary. We spoke in the pinched tones of, say, Mrs. Tucker who disapproved of napkin flowers on the basis that they were too showy. Really it's because she could never quite master the art of folding. She had people for that. Grace and I pretended to pour hot tea from the silver service, splashing imaginary sugar cubes into a dainty cup. Holding our pinkies aloft, we sipped our invisible tea and laughed.

Remembering our games, I sit, making napkin flowers; they are lovely. They are untouched on Tuesday night. Mom finds me in the dining room.

"Great work, honey." Her tongue is plaintive and thick, hiding reconciliation in the sugared tenor. "Daddy will be home soon. He can tell us the news."

The phone rings through the day. I let Mom get it. No one ever calls me anyway. I don't want to move from my seat at the table, pressing the napkins into curls and swirls. I don't know any details but I know something was roiling. I never, ever think it will come to anything.

I snort. "Daddy. Pfft."

She could have done thousands of things. Mom could have broached the space between us in three easy strides and slapped me. She could have whipped a reprimand into my ears. She could have turned on a prim toe and left me stewing. I wish I had seen my mom as a person sooner; that is the first glimpse of the woman behind the mother.

Instead of doing any of that, she pulls out the chair next to me, smooths her skirt, tucking it under her legs. She crosses her ankles and rests her head on her arms, twists up with her elbows on the table. So much of this startles me, chiefly the elbows on the table. I mean, what a faux pas.

"What's that all about?" Mom asked.

"What? What's what about?"

Mom's eyes get dewy and soft, she pinches her lips together, the dam against the tears. I think *well snot, now I feel bad.* See? She could have negotiated the end of the war with that look.

"Why are you so mad at Daddy?" She tucks a strand of hair behind her ear, then does the same to me. I shrug.

Since Friday, I had avoided Daddy. He was gone when I woke up on Saturday. I didn't talk to him on Sunday, or on Monday at breakfast. I ate and left the table to meet Grace. Things were smooth with her.

Nobody teaches you how to ask your father if he's racist. I think if I avoid eye contact, something will mend it. Some invisible—and imaginary—force like some kind of cosmic happy glue will make it all right. Will change what I had seen, what I had realized. It will just be like it never happened.

Damn her. She is a wizard. The look, the tone and the words are her spell, and with them she conjures the boiling cauldron until it steams. Tears spring to my eyes despite myself. Boy howdy, I cry. First just the sort of tiny streams you see on the faces of actresses at the end of love stories; the kind that make some people love them even more, or make me roll my eyes. The tears erode my fury until I am a bawling mess, a tomcat in the alley frustrated with the empty garbage cans and starving. My chest burns as my ribs expand in sobs, cracking bone against muscle, fear against a need to know.

That woman. She always surprises me. If I think she will explode, she shows the serenity of the moon, and vice versa. I can't figure her out. We are like two sides of a ball, rolling though the world, each touching the same people and places but never at the same time, and never each other. In the dining room, she sits, arms linked around each other, eyes roving over me. Waiting.

Meanwhile, I drop my arms onto the table, and hide my head in there, until it is too hot to breathe, paying no mind to the tears falling all over me, the snot dripping from my nose onto my lap.

When I start the gasping, lip sucking, child-in-a-tantrum thing, I feel her hand flat against my back, arcing circles like careful finger painting. With her other hand she holds my wrist as if the union of both hands on me, skin on my skin has the power to coax the truth out of me without any hurt. As though her touch could calm the waters and set the ship right again. It does. Sort of. Her touch gives me a way to look at her.

"I know about Daddy."

Now she really confuses me. I expect her to lose it. To remonstrate. To deny. Instead? She sighs this giant sigh and confuses me. Again. Then, she laughs.

"Mom!" I push her away and throw a fabric flower at her.

"Mercy." She smiles and clutches for me; I continue to evade. "Mercy. Please. Come here."

She stops laughing, and I keep my distance. "Are you crazy, Mom?"

"Oh, honey. No. Listen."

She tells me. Everything. Maybe not everything, but so much that I feel as much relief and joy as she had shown when I whispered my horrible confession, my knowledge about my ugly racist father.

She and Daddy had employed Grace's parents for over a year. When that man got beat last year across the river—not even a black man—Daddy got worried. Talked to Boyd. That idiot Mr. Tucker, Daddy's boss, had to be managed. He had to give in, to make appearances. Misguided for sure. Daddy, it makes my stomach hurt to think of it, Daddy joined that awful group. Boyd knew, Rachel knew. Everyone knew except me and Grace.

As relieved as I feel, I am also irritated. I can't imagine why she didn't think to tell me. She knew Grace and I hung out near where those brutes did their beatings and marchings. It escapes me how these smart people could not have assumed there was a possibility of us seeing *something*.

***

None of us has much of an appetite; my gorgeous flowers go to waste. When Daddy gets home, late, Mom has already sent me off to sleep. Her news settles me; I am confident this whole whatever it is downtown will be a ripple by the morning, and we will all move on to the next big scandal.

As I wash my face for bed, I hear my parents in the kitchen. The tone is not easy and confident. They drop their words quietly, like crumbs. From my position at the top of the steps, I am too far away to scoop up the crumbs; I cannot stick them to my finger to examine. I cannot follow the meager portions to an explanation. I creep lower and lower on their stairs until I get the whole cake.

Riot. Guns. Shots. Sheriff won't release the boy. Girl isn't talking. Tuck's getting a group together, rounding up the blacks. Rachel. Boyd. Court house.

My plan is as stupid as it is brilliant. Stupid-risky and brilliant, shining with plain old charm and goodness. What can go wrong? I lay in bed until the voices in the kitchen stop. I wait, growing anxious with that kind of jittery you get when playing hide and seek. When they finally shuffle off to the front porch, I move.

First, I check the garage; I am desperately curious about this little storehouse my mom and Miss Rachel had put together. They had thought of everything; impressive but not surprising. Even toys for the brothers. More canned food than at the grocery.

Purple haze hangs over the horizon, orange flecks of sun rinsing away into night. Tall oaks throw gentle shadows, their silhouettes like a dull patterning on an unfurled bolt of fabric. I take the route Grace would have followed toward the river, but then I cut back east and into town. The alleys had been the perfect camouflage on Sunday. I expect the same tonight. The shouts and cries are like a siren. I had planned to head to Grace's, to tell her the whole story, to get her to my place with her family, before anything happened, even though I know those loud mouths are just making noise. Hearing them piques my curiosity.

I am never afraid. Not even when I see the barrels of the guns, slung high over broad shoulders. Not when the separate crowds pulse toward each other. I don't feel afraid; I know these people. All of them, I think.

Approaching the courthouse from the west, I make out two throbbing masses, organized by skin color. The pale moon-colored group is far larger. They are far louder. They carry ropes, guns, cans of gasoline. They yell for the boy, for the rope, for justice. Trucks are parked sideways in the street, men rest rifles on their hips, hoist them in the air. Men gambol up and down the courthouse steps. Tongues throttle, uvulas exposed, wide mouths gaping open in protest, not one man using his ears instead of his voice.

Near the confluence of the groups, a quietness, a stab at listening, then a shot blurts, expected and surprising at once. Surging white bodies sweep on a crest, spittle on my neck, a tug at my sleeve, then a fiercer tug. I think I hear my name; I hope I hear my name; my daddy calling out, rescuing me like Grace's daddy did the other day. Wheel my eyes, whip my head, searching for a hope that can't be found. He ins't there. No one is calling for me.

The crowd shares my skin color, they look like me. But they don't sound like me. They call for blood. They call for weapons. They spit words that make me blush. A crunch on my foot sends me sprawling.with my knees landing in gravelly holes in the poor street. Hands bloody and scrambling. Grasping a grey leg, a boot flies back, connects with my nose. Screaming, begging, my throat stings and fills with dirt, blood hardens on my lips.

I feel every crack and blow and each foot that blasts the bones in my hands. Each kick to the ribs as they march. No sound but the blood pulsing to each new wound in a race to heal itself. I am not up to that task. A rib, two or three, snapped. Buttons pop and scatter. So many boots dragging my head by its ponytail. So many feet. I taste the blood. I am an afterthought, a necessary injury. I am simply in the way.

Grace. I think Grace. Learning embroidery. Her mama, Miss Rachel, teaches me embroidery. The slender strands pull taut through the glossy weave of linen, shiny pink threads make rose after rose, greens for the leaves, blue for trim. She pricks her finger, flips the dot of blood away without a glance. I prick my finger and want to go see Dr. Bledsoe. My panic tosses my hand, dribbles blood onto my work. No matter; Grace will bleach out the stain, pull out the threads, make mine as good as hers.

Eyes crust and swell, thick with blood and dirt, vision blurs. Tucker. That hateful man. He stands over me, his mouth puckers open and closing like a fish desperate to return to his bowl. I try to kick him away, *don't touch me. Get away.* His fat arms grow closer, he lifts me. His mouth keeps smacking, lips slapping together. I hear him. "Amelia."

Amelia. I am Amelia. I am Mercy. Don't call me Mercy. His ugly face cannot whisper my true name, my real self. More from his breathing mouth. My head hurts. It hurts so much. I blink, and Tucker is Daddy. Oh, Daddy. I'm sorry. I'm sorry. Daddy. My head on his shoulder. "Daddy."

Each of his steps jars me, I can't make the words into the order I want. I can't make him hear me. I can't say the thing I need to say. "Please. Daddy."

He wants to get me to my daddy and I want that, but I'm with my daddy. It hurts to think about. The sounds of my thoughts ping against my skull. I feel like I'm chasing the letters I need to make the sounds, but my lips and my ears and my tongue and my head are broken and I can't put it together. I can't tell him that I want Grace. That I want to see Mama. That I need Grace. Get her to my house. My house. Where Mama is. Rachel. Boyd. Tucker.

It's Tucker. He is far away from me. I see him through an opening, the thing holding my body is cushy but sticky, like skin. It smells like cigars. I vomit, tearing open from pelvis to collar bone. "Goddammit," Tucker says. I think, *God don't want a thing to do with you.* I make my words come from me, I push them out like they each weigh a thousand pounds. He doesn't hear me. He's grumbling and honking. He's turning over the engine and, what's this, a prayer? Maybe his god will hear it. Maybe the god of this chaos will care.

He's talking to me. "I know, honey. I know. I'm gonna get you to your daddy. I promise."

My heart slows down. There is no room for breath. It is okay. I don't mind. It is dark and it doesn't hurt when I don't breathe. I listen. His voice is like nighttime or a sermon. I like it; it is like the bottom of a clear pond. I want to swim into it and peer at the moon from the shallows. It must be nice, down there, where it's quiet. Where I can't feel my veins pulsing. I tell myself to swim down. To follow the current. He leads me down with the sermon voice, dripping with heaven. Then his hand is on my shoulder. He yanks me back to the surface, shaking and shaking, I want to push him off. It's too settled down here. Don't unsettle the sandy bottom. Don't scare away the fish who gape at me.

My body slams forward, then backward. Doors yanking open, screaming closed. His breath in my face, his dirty fish mouth on mine, he's pushing into my face, his breath. I don't feel it right away, but then my chest rises and it hurts and I vomit. I think I did this already, felt the sickness in my mouth mixed with the stench of my sweat. If he didn't push his air into me, it will stop hurting, but it feels a little good. Like a gift I thought I wanted and then forgot about.

He does this twice more and I think *just stop*. I want to stop. Lights splash across my eyelids. Shocking reports glint into my ears. My brain is aflame; I see torches in my face but why can I only smell it. It is lightning. And thunder. No rain. I open my eyes, there is no rain on the glass behind me. His nighttime words are the rhythm in my lungs, in the veins that run in the downy hair on my temples. *Oh, please slow it down.* He does. His voice is underwater and distant.

Grace swims behind my eyelids. I'm swaying, like in a cradle but sticky and it hurts still and I'm hot but cold. My feet are cold. Grace stays there; she's on guard. Her eyes dart around and then she finds me. She's smiling. She's running ahead. She stops and looks back at me. Comes back, holds my hand. She's beside me but I can still see her. I want to tell her, *I tried to come get you. They wouldn't . . . I couldn't get through.* Her mouth doesn't move, but she tells me to hush, and that she knows. I understand her face, I feel her flick me on the arm, teasing me to smile.

I tell her, *Grace, it hurts.* She knows. Her fingers are on my eyelids, but I can still see her on my eyelids. I don't mind. Again. I don't mind. *I just wanted to get you.*

Hush.

I don't understand.

Hush.

Grace?

Grace?

She's still there when my veins stop throbbing. She's still there when the last air I save up in my lungs blows away, like a gust into the northern sky, carrying the smoke clouds and the stories far west.

Acknowledgments

Thank you to Kurt, Abby, Bronwyn and Elliot for dinner time stories, after-school snuggles, and the general goofiness that marks our days. My parents, Helen and Charlie, taught me to listen and look and use good words. Ellen Martucci, Andi Cumbo-Floyd, Shawn Smucker, and Kristin Tennant are true friends who held my figurative hand. No writer writes alone, and I'm thankful my life is peopled with tales from inspired, interesting, fun, and thoughtful individuals. Special gratitude to Chad Johnston for his stellar cover design work. Finally, thanks to Billy and Johanna for making me laugh.

Jennifer Luitwieler is the author of *Run With Me: An Accidental Runner and the Power of Poo* and is a contributor to local and online magazines. Her essays have appeared in several collections. She lives with her husband and three children in Tulsa, OK. Find her at jenniferluitwieler.com

CPSIA information can be obtained
at www.ICGtesting.com
Printed in the USA
FSOW02n1251050516
20108FS